T0208854

RATS WITH BADGES

RATS WITH BADGES

LOU MARTIN

RATS WITH BADGES

iUniverse books may be ordered through booksellers or by contacting:

iUniverse
1663 Liberty Drive
Bloomington, IN 47403
www.iuniverse.com
1-800-Authors (1-800-288-4677)

ISBN: 978-1-4917-7717-6 (sc)
ISBN: 978-1-4917-7716-9 (e)

Library of Congress Control Number: 2015916541

Print information available on the last page.

iUniverse rev. date: 10/27/2015

CHAPTER ONE

It wasn't going to be a good day for the Detective—all the telltale signs were in place. He'd received a call from his captain who had ordered him to report to his office immediately. It was a crummy, mid-winter day in Washington, D.C., cold and dark outside, with rain coming down in buckets. He was irritated that he had to leave his girlfriend Lina in their warm, comfortable bed and go out into the mess. Throw in the usual Capitol Hill traffic, with a million government workers all with different driving habits, headed towards the same spot he was, and you get the idea. Being summoned to his captain's office without being told why, usually meant that he had screwed up, or was going to get screwed. Knowing all this beforehand should have reminded him to pay close attention to what his boss had to say or bad things could happen. That proved to be the case. Anthony "Tony" Spinella, is a thirty-five-year-old, slightly out of shape twelve-year veteran of the Metropolitan Police Department. A Detective Sergeant currently assigned to the Robbery Squad as a supervisor of six seasoned Detectives, he was told earlier in the week by his Captain that he was going to be assigned a case that originated in the Internal Affairs Division, allegedly involving police officers. The captain's office was a perfect reflection of the type of efficient, no-nonsense guy he was. The office was arrayed in a typical mid-nineties government style, with a gray metal desk and chair, and a beat-up metal filing cabinet with a combination lock set into the top drawer face. In front of his desk sat another gray metal chair that those Detectives assigned to the Robbery Squad dubbed "the hot seat." It was named for those people who'd screwed up, and were forced to occupy it while getting chewed out by the captain. The only picture on the dull gray office walls was of him shaking hands with our Chief of Police. When he walked into his office, the captain stood up and handed him a case file.

"Sergeant, I want you to understand that what you see in that case file and what I'm about to tell you goes no further than this office, and that's a direct order! I want you to investigate this case and report directly back to me, and only me, as the case develops. You and I will have to be on the same page on this investigation, and you'll need to completely understand what I'm ordering you to do."

"Yes sir. I understand what you are saying, Boss, but why me? How come the Rat Squad needs us to do their work? We're Robbery Squad, not Internal Affairs."

To know Captain Frank McCathran was to appreciate him. He stood approximately five eight, and carried about two hundred and thirty pounds of mostly solid muscle. The term "mostly," fit, because in the last couple of years his waist line had expanded in direct proportion to his desire to retire from this pressure cooker. He was not what most people would call handsome, having been born with bushy hair and eyebrows that seemed to reach out to all points on the compass. His rugged complexion, along with a permanent frown, gave one the message that this guy was not into trivial social conversation. Whoever walked into his office had better get to the point fast. Despite all that, those who worked for him knew that beneath that tough exterior was a soft streak a mile wide. That particular morning though, he just looked like a worn-out civil servant overwhelmed by the office he occupied.

Curious, Spinella stepped back and closed his office door and sat down on the hard, gray metal chair that everyone in the squad believed was specially designed to make sure no one got too comfortable, and began to listen to a story that pushed his bullshit meter into overdrive. At first he didn't believe what he was hearing, and started to get a little pissed off. He continued to listen until he couldn't control his anger any longer.

"Come on, Captain! This is bullshit! You and I both know that my team is loaded with cases right now, and we sure don't need to be adding to our work load by doing IAD's shit."

His boss held up his hand.

"Let me finish, Sergeant. I don't like this any more than you do, but we have to investigate it, and you're the only one I can trust to do the right thing with this case, so sit back down, shut the hell up, and let me finish! Besides, I mentioned this case to you earlier this week so it shouldn't come as a surprise."

He could see the captain felt badly that he couldn't tell this tough ex-marine the whole story right at that moment, but he knew he would eventually be brought up to speed as the investigation developed.

"Sergeant, some of the senior police officials in our department think our squad's infected with cops who are actively involved with the bad guys."

Spinella's pucker factor upped about ten points when he realized from his Captain's expression that he was deadly serious.

"What senior officials we talking about, Captain?"

"The Chief, for one, and right now all you got to do is listen to what I want you to do. They didn't exactly pinpoint all the people they thought were involved with the local thugs, but they did give me the name of one person in our squad that Internal Affairs believes is positively linked to the criminal organization in question." Spinella had already skimmed the case file and hadn't noticed any names of suspects listed.

"What name did they give you?"

"Sergeant, the name wasn't in the case file for security reasons. It was given to me verbally because of those same security reasons. I think you can understand why."

He wasn't gonna be stonewalled.

"What's the *name*, Captain?" He looked across the desk at me, and in a somber voice said,

"Your partner, Maurice White."

Maurice White had been Tony's partner for almost three years, and they had become good friends during that time. Spending a minimum of forty hours a week together in a police cruiser and depending on one another during several life-threatening situations had resulted in their becoming very close.

Incredulous, Tony looked at his boss.

"I can't do this. Captain, why can't you give this to someone else? There are other good investigators in the squad you can give it to. He's my *friend* for God sakes!"

He pointed his finger at Tony.

"You *will* do it, and you'll do the right thing because you know Maurice better than anybody in the squad, and if he's innocent, you're the perfect person to prove it. But remember this, if he's guilty, he won't allow you to take him down without a fight! You should also know that there are some folks who are not very happy with me giving you this case because they think you're dirty too. I know better, but my ass is on the line right along with yours. I need you to do this, and I'll be available to you twenty-four seven if you ever need to contact me."

He then handed him a slip of paper, adding,

"These numbers are only to be used if absolutely necessary."

Spinella glanced at the slip of paper and then stuck it in his pants pocket. He rose from the chair and stood there with the case file in his hand, wondering where he was going to start.

"Take some time to review the file," the captain said. "And then bring it back to me personally with an idea on how you're going to work it. Don't let anyone see it, and for God's sake don't discuss this case with anyone but me, especially Internal Affairs. We really don't know who we can trust right now, and you know what can happen if this gets out prematurely. Now get the hell out of here and get started."

Tony looked at him, gave a half-hearted wave, and started to leave when the captain abruptly motioned for him to come back in. He stepped back into his office and shut the door.

"I've already assigned Sergeant Elliott to cover your team until this is over. You'll tell your partner that I have specifically assigned you both to investigate the recent series of liquor store robberies over in southeast. The investigative notes and PD 251s from all of the robberies are on your desk. I think that should cover any questions that might pop up as to where you've been or what you're doing. You and White are working four to twelve this week, right?"

Tony nodded.

"I want you to pay attention to everything he does, and also try to eavesdrop on any phone conversations he receives."

Yeah, right! Tony thought. After three years as partners, all of a sudden he was supposed to be interested in his partner's phone conversations.

"Oh, and Anthony, try and show your face around the squad room whenever you can; it might save some questions being asked."

He gave the captain a long look, turned and left his office feeling like dog shit. *No,* he thought further. It wasn't a good enough metaphor for his dilemma because dog shit could be cleaned up easily with a scooper and in the end he might still smell like dog shit.

When Tony left Frank's office he was in such turmoil from the news about Maurice that he barely noticed the usual hum of activity in the squad room. He walked right past Anita, the squad office manager, and the one person who actually made the office work, without offering his usual greeting. Anita knew all the dirty secrets that percolated around the office, especially who was doing what, and to whom they were doing it. She had been working at the Robbery Squad for more than twenty years, starting out as a typist, preparing and documenting the cases investigated by Robbery Squad detectives. Since most of the ham-fisted detectives working in the squad could barely type, she became an instant hit with everyone, and they had all gone out of their way to keep her happy. As a result, Anita's desk would often have small boxes placed in her inbox that contained perfume, and occasionally, bouquets of flowers left for her by grateful detectives whose fat she'd pulled out of the fryer because of the late reports she took care of for them. Over the years, because she knew how to keep a secret, she became the most trusted person in the squad; no one is more secretive than a bunch of cops.

"Sarge, what's up?" she asked, as Tony passed by her desk.

"Nothing, just busy," Tony said with a quick look over his shoulder. He kept on walking down the hallway towards the elevators. Rehashing all of the information he had just received, he wasn't even aware of the other people who shared the dingy elevator with him. He arrived at the lower garage level where he got off and made his way to his equally dingy car. He got in and drove out of the underground garage of the headquarters building.

What am I gonna do now? Tony knew enough that he had just landed in a no-win situation. *This can't turn out good for me, or my career.* He had seen this same thing happen before, and the good guys always ended up not just losing their careers and pensions, but in a couple of cases, their wives and families, too.

He needed a quiet place to think, and his first inclination was to head over to Barney's, a local cop hangout, get a cold one. As he headed towards Barney's, he realized that that was the worst place he could pick to study the case file. The place was full of cops! He didn't want any interruptions or be forced to engage in small talk. Instead, he decided to go to his place, where he would have the privacy he needed, and no interruptions.

CHAPTER TWO

It was a dreary, windy afternoon with a heavy rain still beating down, when Tony arrived at the hundred-year-old red brick row house that he had inherited from his parents. It was located in the trendy, and very expensive, Capitol Hill area of southeast Washington D.C. When he first got it, it was pretty run down, with a small, fenced front yard that hadn't seen grass in years, and a brick walkway with most of the bricks missing which led to an old wooden front door that had seen too many coats of paint. The interior was badly in need of work, with walls that needed plastering and paint, floors that had to be sanded and finished, and a coal heating system that had been installed when the house was first built. Because he was pretty good with his hands—and stubborn— over a period of about two years he was able to make the place look pretty decent. Since it was situated in a safe and very desirable location on Capitol Hill, close to his work place and worth a lot of money, he had kept it.

The wind picked up and was driving the cold rain almost parallel when he parked in the assigned space near the front of his house. He flipped the visor down to display his special neighborhood homeowner parking pass, supposedly designed to keep his car from getting a ticket, or being towed away. He exited the car and ran through the driving rain towards his house. He ascended the four iron steps leading to his front door—and noticed that the door was slightly ajar. His cop's sixth sense immediately kicked in, because he knew that no one, not even Lina, had a key to his place. He pulled his service weapon from its holster, held it down by his leg, and slowly approached the front door.

Pushing the front door fully open, he stuck his head inside the door.

"Police officer, come out!" he shouted.

No response. Tony did the smart thing: he backed out onto the front stoop, pulled out his cell phone, and called for back-up. He was standing by the curb in front of his house when the scout car arrived about five minutes later. He identified himself and explained the situation to the uniformed officers.

"The front door was open when I arrived home, and I'm sure I double- locked it when I left to go to headquarters early this morning. Nobody has a key but me, and there shouldn't be anyone in the house. I want one of you to go in the front door with me, and the other one to cover the back and wait for us to clear the house. Is that clear?"

"Yeah, Sarg, but we need to know if there are any dogs in the house," said the older cop. "The last time I went into a situation like this I almost got my johnson bitten off, and was out on sick leave for two weeks, so I don't need any more of that shit to happen."

"Officer, there are absolutely no animals in the house, so let's go," Tony replied, heading towards the front of the house with the uniformed officers close behind.

The old row house had a simple floor plan which helped to make searching easy. The first floor, completely renovated by Tony, contained a small, neat living room filled with what could only be described as "bachelor furniture," with a nice-sized dining room and a large country kitchen filled with modern appliances. The upstairs contained a bathroom, two small empty bedrooms and a larger bedroom that Tony used. The first thing they did was to search and clear each room in the house before letting the officer covering the back door inside the house. They didn't find anything.

A quick check of the few valuables that Tony possessed showed nothing missing, and the officers finished their report and started to leave. Tony stopped them.

"Before you guys go back in service, I want a forensic team to come out and check for prints."

"Sarg, there's no evidence of forced entry or any property missing, and you know they'll probably shit-can the request unless you personally ask for it," said the older cop.

"Note my request in your report, officer, and I'll follow it up with a call to the crime scene office. Thanks for your help."

After they had gone, Tony still wasn't satisfied. Something didn't seem right. He began to thoroughly check out the house for anything out of place. It didn't take long to find what he was looking for. He kept a lock box for his service weapon in the master bedroom closet. When off duty, he usually carried an old snub-nosed .38 caliber revolver that had belonged to his grandfather when he was a police officer back in the forties.

The lock box was sitting in exactly the same spot where it always sat, but the sweaters usually piled on top of it were now sitting over to the left side of the lock box. Before he touched the box, Tony went to his dresser, pulled out a pair of socks, and slipped them over his hands. When he lifted the box, he knew right away that something wasn't right—it felt light. He opened the lock box and saw that his grandfather's gun was missing. He also noticed that the box was unlocked when he opened it, which wasn't normal. Checking further, he saw that the box showed no signs of being forced open.

In the bottom of the box there were some very rare five dollar gold pieces he had also inherited from his grandfather, along with the Silver Star and Purple Heart medals awarded him during his time as a Marine—all untouched. Breathing a sigh of relief, he spotted a piece of folded paper in the bottom of the lock box, underneath the gold coins, that shouldn't have been there. Tony went to the bathroom and got the tweezers he used to pluck the hair out of his ears, and extracted the piece of paper. Carefully unfolding it, a short computer printed note read, "Do yourself a favor and stay off the case. This is your first and last warning. We can get to you anytime."

Tony felt the hairs on the back of his neck stand up. *Who could this be?* He had only known about the case for less than an hour! He began to get that old familiar feeling he hadn't felt since his time as a grunt in Vietnam, a gut feeling that he had better watch his ass!

Tony called the dispatcher and requested the original responding officers to return to his house for some additional information. Later that day, the officers returned, and he showed them the lock box where the gun was kept, and also gave them the serial number for the snub-nosed revolver to include in their original PD 251 report. He didn't mention the note.

After they left, instead of allowing his anger to take over, he picked up the lock box and went to the closet to return it to its original place on the shelf so the forensic people, when they arrived, could get to it for fingerprinting. He also left the sweaters where the burglars had moved them, so the lab guys could check them for any clues that might have been left by the intruders. As he turned to walk away from the closet, he noticed a slight movement under the pile of sweaters on the closet shelf.

Thinking he might have mice, Tony went to the kitchen to find something he could use to pry under the sweaters and whack the mice with. He took an opportunity and opened the fridge and grabbed the cold beer he had been thinking about, and took a couple of hefty swallows. He found a long-handled wooden salad spoon—part of a salad set that had been a wedding gift years ago to him and his ex, Debbie—and returned to the bedroom closet. He had kept his socks on over his hands for protection. Laughing to himself, he thought about how much good these socks would do if one of the little bastards decided to latch onto one of his fingers. He pushed the wooden spoon under the sweaters and lifted them up about three or four inches, when something black shot out from under the pile of sweaters and struck the handle of the spoon, causing it to fly from his grasp.

He was so startled that he fell back and tripped, falling and hitting his head on the small bench at the end of the bed. After hitting the floor, he scrambled away from whatever it was that lunged at him from under the sweaters. Quickly pushing himself up off the floor, he noticed that he was bleeding and couldn't see out of his right eye. Backing away, he wiped his eye with the sleeve of his shirt, enabling himself to see a bit more clearly. He desperately looked around for the wooden spoon and spotted it lying on the floor directly in front of the closet door. As he bent down to pick it up, he noticed something long and black on the floor, slowly moving along the bedroom wall, away from the closet.

Tony was no naturalist, but he remembered reading about snakes while in school, and what little he remembered led him to believe that this was not a friendly snake. He was scared shitless, and his first thought was to use his gun, but he swiftly discarded that idea because he might damage his property, and still not hit it. He ran to the bedroom door, and even though he didn't want to, closed the door to keep the snake trapped in the bedroom. Terrified, and shaking all over, he went over and picked up the small bench that had tripped him up. He was barely able to hold onto it because of his shaking. Holding the bench out in front of him as a shield, he went looking for the snake. It was easy enough to find, coiled up in the corner by the dresser, just waiting.

As he slowly approached the snake, it rose up and began to strike out at him. The snake struck three times, actually hitting the bench he held in his hands, twice. Still scared, but also pissed off; he wanted to put a hurting on this fucker. He waited for the snake's next strike, and when it came, he followed it up with a swing that contained every ounce of strength he had. The bench connected with the snakes head, and seemed to stun it, because Tony had enough time to wind up and hit it two or three more times before it could strike again. The snake became still except for some quivering and curling of its long body.

Tony felt like he was going to throw up, but the adrenalin was still pumping through his body, and even though he was still scared, he walked very carefully over to where the snake lay motionless, and poked at it with the bench that he still held in his hands, nothing, no movement, so he hit it again, hard! It was dead! All of a sudden his body was shaking so bad he knew he'd better sit down right away, or he'd be sick to his stomach. He found a chair, sat down, took some deep breaths, and slowly began to calm down. Sitting there trying not to be sick, he realized that someone was trying to kill him. The big question was "Why?"

Still sitting there ten minutes later, he remembered the slip of paper in his pocket containing the numbers the Captain had given him. He pulled out his cell phone and punched in the number. When his boss answered, he blurted out, "Captain, this is Spinella. Something happened; I need you to come to my place. Now!"

He barely moved an inch between the time he called his boss and when he heard the pounding on his front door. He went downstairs to the door, opened it and Captain McCathran pushed his way past him into the living room.

"Show me!" he growled. He took him upstairs to the bedroom and pointed to the corner of the room where the snake lay curled up dead.

He took a long look and turned to Tony.

"Anthony, do you know what kind of snake that is?"

"Hell no, I don't do snakes."

"Well, you better bone up on your research because as a teenager, I used to collect snakes, and I'm pretty sure that's a black mamba. If it had bitten you, we wouldn't be having this conversation because you'd be dead."

"Captain, you want to tell me what's really going on?"

His boss paused for a moment.

"Anthony, since we're in this mess together, you can call me Frank when we're alone. In answer to your question, I don't exactly know what's going on except to say that some very powerful people are involved in the drug business here in town, and I believe some of them work in our Internal Affairs office."

"Frank, how does this connect to Maurice?"

He looked Tony straight in the eye, took a few steps toward him so that his face was inches from his, and lowered his voice to a whisper.

"Since my wife died, I sometimes treat myself to a nice dinner at restaurants that ordinarily I wouldn't go to because of the expense involved. But in the last six months I've had dinner a couple of times at Angelina's—you know that fancy Italian restaurant on K. Street, near Fourteenth Street? Well anyway, both times I was there, I spotted your partner and Lieutenant Kirby from IAD sitting in the back booth together having an animated conversation. That immediately caused me to ask myself why one of my men was meeting with IAD without me knowing about it. I didn't finish my dinner, left some money on the table, and I think I got out of there both times without being seen."

Tony started to ask a question when Frank stopped him and said, "That's not all of it; I'm being followed."

"You're being followed? Who's following you?"

Frank held a finger up to his lips.

"I'll explain all that later; right now, let's get out of here."
As they were leaving, Frank asked him if he had any kind of
security system for the house.

"No I don't. I was gonna put one in, but money was
tight and my neighborhood, being on Capitol Hill, is pretty
safe, so I decided for now to save the money and get one
installed later. Looks like I guessed wrong." As we got into
his unmarked, department-issued sedan, Frank said,

"I've got a couple of people that I think you'll want to
meet—and they can put in a security system that I guarantee
none of these assholes we're dealing with will be able to
overcome."

CHAPTER THREE

After riding in complete silence for almost thirty minutes, Tony noticed that Frank was headed up Wisconsin Avenue towards Bethesda. He glanced at Frank, whose eyes were fixed on the road ahead except for the times he checked his rear view mirror, every couple of minutes or so.

"What are you looking for, boss? Is there some reason you think we're being tailed? Can you at least tell me where we are going?

"It's clear for now. Anthony, I told you earlier that I have a couple of people that I want you to meet. These guys will be the only ones you'll be able to trust completely while this investigation plays itself out. So just sit tight. We'll be there in a few minutes and I'll explain everything."

They drove north for another thirty minutes, with Frank making numerous turns and running at least two red lights before they left the city behind and were surrounded by undulating hills and freshly tilled farmland. They passed a few isolated houses with bright lights glowing from their windows in the early evening darkness. Finally he made a hard right onto an old, bumpy, single-lane gravel road that was so overgrown with tall bushes and scraggly weeds that no one would have been able to see it unless they were right on top of it. After bouncing around for another ten minutes, we finally pulled into a large clearing and stopped right next to two battered old pickup trucks.

Both trucks looked like they hadn't been driven for many years, and although it was dark, Tony could see that the truck beds were loaded with old car tires. They were sitting in front of an old abandoned farmhouse.

"What is this place?" Tony asked.

"This is where I grew up, Tony. My parents built this place when they were first married. I used to hunt rabbits all around here when I was a kid."

Pointing out the cruiser window he said, "Over there by that group of trees is a pond where I used to catch blue gills and swim during the summer." Tony exited the car and waited while Frank came around to his side of the cruiser. Frank turned on a flashlight.

"Follow me!" he said.

They slowly picked their way around the overgrown yard towards the back of the house. Frank walked straight over to what was an entrance to an old storm cellar, lifted the door up and stepped down. Other than the light from the flashlight, it was pitch black. Tony smelled damp earth.

"Close the door behind you," Frank said over his shoulder.

Tony stepped down several steep concrete steps and almost tripped before he was able to turn around and lower the heavy metal door. He turned around and saw Frank shine his light on another metal door. It looked like he was rubbing the side of the door when Tony heard a soft buzz. After a minute or so of standing in the dark, the door opened.

At first, all Tony could see was bright light.

"It's all right, come on in," Frank assured him.

Tony followed him into a big brightly lit room that could only be described as techno-geek heaven. The room was filled with computers, routers, printers and other machines that he couldn't begin to identify.

"What the hell is this place?"

"It's just a place that a couple of friends of mine helped me fix up so we could have a place to play with our gadgets. I'll explain all that later; right now there are some people that I want you to meet. Follow me."

They walked into another smaller room that contained more electronics, along with two men who were on the other side of the room, looking down at a machine and talking.

"Hey guys, there's someone I want you to meet." Both men turned and walked over to Frank and gave the burly police captain a big hug.

Frank pointed to Tony.

"This is Anthony, but you can call him Tony. He works for me, and we might be in some serious shit and need your help." He pointed to a tall, thin white guy with long, gray hair that reached down to his shoulders.

"Anthony, this is Scopes, and he knows more about electronics and computers than those shitheads at NSA will ever know. This other character is Lamont, my first confidential informant, and if you need to know what's going down on the street, or how to overcome any locking device, he's your man."

Tony was struck by just how small Lamont was. He couldn't have been more than five feet six, and weighed maybe a hundred twenty pounds, with a smile on his face that could light up a stadium.

"Just so you know, Anthony, Lamont saved my life when I was a rookie undercover officer working narcotics in northeast. He pulled my fat ass out of the fryer when I was just about done for, and he's my friend."

Lamont shook his head, and started to say something when Frank cut him off.

"Don't say anything Lamont, you saved my ass, and that's it! By the way, I'm godfather to Lamont's son, and speaking of junior, how's he doing since he got those braces?" Tony reached out and shook hands with Lamont as he brought Frank up to date about how much his son's new braces had cost him. Scopes then stuck his hand out and shook his hand without saying anything.

"Nice to meet you, but I still want to know what this place is. Frank, can you just tell me what the hell's going on, please?"

"Tony, I'm gonna explain all of this in due time, but right now we need to bring these guys up to speed on what's happening. Scopes, you remember when I called you last week and asked you to sweep my house for bugs?" The tall, reed-thin Scopes nodded.

"Yeah, I scanned your joint and found two devices. One was in the phone in the living room, and another in the bedroom. I was gonna take them out, but decided to modify them a little bit so that you can disable them anytime you want to. All anyone will be able to hear when you do that is a lot of static. I also modified a tracking device I found on your personal car and fixed it so when you don't want to be followed, you can turn it off and confuse the shit out of whoever might be following you. I'll show you how to use them, but Frank, I need to know what's going on, too. Just who the hell are these people who have the balls to bug a police captain?"

Frank walked over to an old metal chair, sat down and began to tell a story that, if it hadn't been coming from his boss, Tony would not have believed. He said that he knew months ago about an ongoing investigation into corruption within his department, and was personally told in a private meeting with the Police Chief that he would be investigating the case.

"I tried to argue the point that I was in charge of the Robbery Squad and this should be handled by the Internal Affairs Division, but the Chief told me they already had it, and he needed a separate parallel investigation to be handled by me. I asked why he picked me, and he told me that it was because he knew I was an honest cop, and that we had both gone through the Police Academy together, and he knew I was the kind of man that would do the right thing.

"He told me to take the investigation wherever it goes, and do whatever's necessary to clean out the trash from our department. He also told me that I better watch my ass because he thought there were a lot of cops involved in this mess, and he didn't know who most of them were."

Tony started to ask him if the Chief had speculated on any names of those involved, but Frank waved him to silence and went on.

"Other than your partner, whom we already know about, the Chief believes almost half of the Rat Squad is involved. If you think about it, they're perfectly situated because nobody questions them about anything, and everybody's scared of them. They come and go at will, and they have access to all police department personnel files, technical equipment, and even the police armory."

Lamont had become somewhat agitated while Frank was talking, and started to walk back and forth ranting about how much he hated four-legged rats, and now he had to worry about the two-legged kind.

"At least we know who some of the rats are, and can plan for them before they bite us on the ass," Scopes said.

"The Chief told me that information he had received indicated that one of the kingpins might be a Lieutenant James Kirby, from Internal Affairs. I personally think it goes even higher. Somehow, they've known about my involvement from the very beginning, and even though my meeting with the chief was supposed to be private, they could have bugged his office. Speaking of bugs—" Frank addressed Tony— "I had been hearing some funny noises whenever I used my home phone, and that's why I contacted Scopes to check it out. As for you Tony, there is no doubt that they are behind what happened in your home today, and they'll kill you if they think you pose any kind of threat to their organization. Shit, they've already tried once."

"What happened today?" Lamont asked, looking puzzled. After Tony related the day's events, Lamont shook his head. "I hate slimy-assed snakes."

It was Scopes' turn to react.

"What do you expect us to do against your whole Internal Affairs Division? There are only four of us, and I don't want my ass shot off by some crooked cop—and by the way, you know I don't do guns!"

Frank smirked, letting everyone in the room know that he wasn't depending on Scopes for his fighting skills.

"Scopes, how long you known me? Have I ever put your skinny ass in danger? I'm the guy who got you out of jail when nobody else would. All I need from you and Lamont is your technical wizardry, to help get us the information we need."

"Sorry, pal," Scopes said apologetically. "I'm with you, but this shit still scares the hell out of me. Just tell us what you need us to do."

"Yeah, Frank, we're with you. Do I need to get a piece?" Lamont said.

Frank shook his head.

"Not right now, but there might come a time when you'll need something. For now, we just don't know exactly what's going on or who all the players are. Scopes, I want you to make up a couple of tracking devices, and Lamont, I want you to locate the department parking lot where the unmarked cruiser used by Lt. Kirby is usually parked. It should be parked on the detective division lot at night, because he doesn't get to take it home after his shift. But that could have changed, so check it out. I also want Kirby's boss, Inspector Billings' cruiser to have one, too. He'll probably drive his cruiser to his home because he's a division head, and department regulations allow him to drive it home when off-duty. I don't know that he's dirty, but I'm taking no chances at this point. Be very careful when you attach the trackers because these guys, if they're doing what we think they're doing, will probably be alert to anything unusual. Tony and I will be in touch every day, either by phone or in person. If one of us doesn't contact you by three o'clock every afternoon, get away from here as fast as you can, keep your phones close to you, and one of us will contact you as soon as possible."

Scopes nodded.

"Do you want the trackers to record all of their vehicles' movements, because I can run a program that will make it clear as day where they went and the amount of time they spent at any location? Oh, and while we're at it, why don't we bug their vehicles so we can hear what they're saying."

"You can do all that?" Tony asked.

Scopes smiled and pointed to his head.

"That's the easy part. I can put together just about anything you can come up with—just don't ask me to shoot anybody." They laughed at Scopes' remark and it seemed to ease the tension in the room for a moment or two.

Tony studied the trio in front of him. *One cop, one street smart ex-confidential informant, and one paranoid ex-con- ex-CIA tech wizard is all we've got right now to put a stop to this. I guess it's gonna have to do.* He stood up and motioned to Scopes.

"I need you to go to my house and install a security system that will keep the bastards out, or at least alert the local precinct to any intrusion."

"No problem, do you want me to put in some surprises while I'm at it?"

"Not right now, but I might need you to do that later on, and while we're all here, let's exchange cell numbers so that we can be in touch at all times."

CHAPTER FOUR

Lieutenant Jim Kirby, a veteran police detective, could have posed for a department recruiting poster: with his lean, six-foot-two frame, full head of blonde hair, clear complexion, and blue eyes. He sat in his department cruiser in a run-down area of older homes, situated across the street from a neighborhood coffee shop a couple of blocks west of headquarters. As he waited for Maurice White, he sipped his latte and thought back to when his life turned to shit.

Two years earlier, his beautiful wife of twenty-two years was diagnosed with stage four pancreatic cancer. She had been the love of his life, and he vowed to use every resource he had to get her the best treatment available. After seeing most of the top cancer specialists on the east coast, along with one in Mexico and another in Brazil, nothing worked, and she died. After her death, he jumped into the bottle with a vengeance, until he came out of the alcohol haze to find that he was out of annual leave, broke and in debt. He had also been notified by the bank that he was going to lose his house because of missed mortgage payments. It wasn't much longer before he bumped into an old childhood friend, Timmy Coglin, at a local bar where he spent a considerable amount of time attempting to free his mind of the previous two years. Over several drinks, they discussed his wife's death and his financial problems.

Timmy had listened, and then told him that he might have a solution to his problem. He said that he had a friend who owed him a favor, and even though this friend might occasionally do a little something outside the law, he was a pretty decent guy and might be able to help him. A meeting was arranged, and when they finally met, it only took a moment or two to figure out who Timmy's friend was, and what he did for a living. The meeting had gone very well, with Timmy's friend, Lorenzo Staples, a local book maker and loan shark, coming off as both personable, and easy to talk to.

"I'll help you! Tell me what you need, and it's yours," Lorenzo had said.

"You know that because of my job, the first thing I'll need is complete secrecy, and a reasonable repayment schedule."

Lorenzo nodded.

"You need twenty grand right?" He told Kirby that he could pay him back a grand a month without interest. When Kirby remarked that not charging an interest rate wasn't normal, Lorenzo had laughed.

"You cops don't trust anybody! Here's what I would like for us to do. Occasionally one of my people gets into a little difficulty, and I would like to have a friend in the right place to help them out. This is something that you can easily do, and it would probably require little or almost no effort on your part. If it works out that you can help, I would feel inclined to reduce the amount of your loan significantly."

There was only a moment of hesitation on Kirby's part.

"Fuck it! Why not?" He stuck out his hand to the fat little shit and told him to count him in.

The twenty grand in cash helped Kirby catch up on his bills, including his past due mortgage payments. He went back to work and began to put his life back in order while making payments to Lorenzo on schedule. About six months after receiving the money, he got a phone call from his friend Timmy telling him that Lorenzo needed him to do him a favor. Right then it dawned on him that he had made a deal with a criminal, and now he'd have to pay the price.

He met Timmy at their usual watering hole. They sat down in a booth in the rear of the joint, ordered a couple of beers, and Tim told Kirby what Lorenzo wanted him to do. One of Lorenzo's number runners had been picked up with money and betting slips in his possession. Kirby remembered thinking that after checking and making sure the guy had no prior arrests, it would be an easy fix. Later, the arresting officer was conveniently unable to produce the money or betting slips in court. Somehow the evidence had gone missing from the evidence room at police headquarters. His new-found friend had shown his gratitude by taking five grand off his loan. He now owed the bum around nine grand, and he was feeling pretty good about his arrangement. With a little overtime money he should be able to get clear of his debt.

Six months later his debt was paid to Lorenzo and they had parted on good terms. It was almost a year later that Kirby received a call from Timmy asking if he would meet with Lorenzo to discuss something that could prove to be beneficial to them both. After thinking about it for a few days, he got curious as to what Lorenzo wanted, called Timmy and told him to set up the meeting.

They met the following day at a local coffee shop. Kirby was a little late, and when he approached the table he saw someone had already ordered coffee for him. He sat down, and after the usual handshakes and hellos, took a sip of coffee and asked Lorenzo what was on his mind.

"What's the hurry? Enjoy your coffee. We can talk like civilized businessmen in a few minutes," Lorenzo replied and shot a patronizing look at Timmy.

Kirby had thought to tell him to stick his coffee up his ass, but then reconsidered. After all, Lorenzo had pulled his fat out of the fryer once before.

After a few minutes of general conversation, Lorenzo leaned over the table and in a low voice told him what he needed. He went on to outline a bold plan to gain access to the property room where all the evidence related to ongoing cases was kept. He seemed to know an awful lot about the evidence room—most specifically the procedures used by the department to transport narcotics no longer needed as evidence to the Drug Enforcement Administration for destruction. Kirby was fascinated by the sheer audacity of Lorenzo's plan, and quickly started to poke holes in it. Lorenzo clapped his hands together.

"*That's* it, that's what I wanted!"

Of course. He needed a troubleshooter. Kirby had held up his hand to stop him from saying anything else, and told him he wanted nothing to do with his plan. Once again, Lorenzo leaned across the table and quietly spoke the words that changed his life forever.

"Twenty percent of the street value of anything you can get out of that room is yours."

Kirby couldn't believe the offer. The amount of confiscated drugs in the evidence room at any one time would exceed a million dollars in street value. He didn't have to be a mathematician to understand the amount of money he could expect to make.

Lorenzo then began to outline his plan to replace the actual drugs with other materials that looked and felt the same as the real stuff. Kirby's first question to him was how he was going to gain access to the evidence when it was always under lock and key, and everyone had to sign in with the officer on duty. Lorenzo had grinned broadly and proceeded to brag about all three officers currently assigned to the evidence room being very amenable to doing a few favors for an old friend.

Kirby began to think that this plan of his, with a few minor adjustments, just might work. His greed kicked in and he rationalized that if he were smart and careful, he could end up a rich man. He also realized that he was now in a full blown conspiracy to violate the oath he had taken when he was sworn in. Well, it was too late for that. They talked for another hour while eating an assortment of pastries and drinking lots of bad coffee. Kirby had noticed that sometime during their conversation Timmy had separated himself and was now sitting about two tables over.

Kirby glanced at his watch and realized that he had been sitting there for almost two hours. It wasn't a good idea to stay any longer and maybe draw attention to themselves. After they decided to meet the following day at the home of one of Lorenzo's friends, Kirby had an afterthought.

"By the way, how'd you get the information about the amount of drugs kept in the evidence room?"

For a brief moment, Lorenzo had looked like a deer caught in car headlights.

"You don't need to know that," he muttered and motioned for Timmy to follow, leaving Kirby with the unpaid bill sitting on the table. The first time they put the plan into action occurred three weeks later on a late Friday afternoon, when the evidence room wasn't too busy. The switch went flawlessly, and even though Kirby had carried an attaché case, no one questioned it, or his presence. He had even hesitated over the sign-in sheet, but the uniformed officer just waved him through. He knew then the plan was going to work. It nonetheless had been a scary, nerve racking experience the whole time he was in the evidence room. It wasn't until he had made the switch and started to leave the room with his attaché case filled with two kilos of uncut heroin that he noticed his hands were shaking. He approached the front desk and had a horrible feeling that he was going to get caught. He envisioned himself in handcuffs, being walked out of the squad room while everyone there looked at him in disgust. But when he reached the sign- out desk, the same officer who had let him in gave a slight nod, waved his hand for him to pass, and then he heard the buzzer unlocking the evidence room door. He was out!

Kirby couldn't believe it. His shirt was soaked with sweat, his hands still shaking, and he walked on air as he exited the front door of headquarters. He figured out that he had just made around twenty thousand dollars for a few minutes of terror-filled work. That had been the beginning of many profitable trips over the past several months by his reluctant accomplice Maurice and himself. Nobody had gotten wise. Kirby had squirrelled away more money than he ever imagined he could in his entire lifetime.

Kirby knew that Lorenzo couldn't be the one running the entire show. He just wasn't smart enough to run an operation like this one. That was made obvious when he sent his nutty snake guy to break into that detective's house and leave a wake-up call. He completely fucked that up. Kirby started to think that if he could figure out who the real brain was behind the scam, he might be able to work a better deal for himself. He'd also be better insulated if the whole operation went tits up. It was time to get serious and follow the money.

His reverie was interrupted by some idiot in a van honking his horn for someone inside the coffee shop. Common sense told him that, while waiting for Maurice to arrive, he'd better stop thinking about the past and develop a plan to handle the problem that had just dropped into his lap. Kirby, a sixteen- year veteran of the department, three of those with Internal Affairs, knew exactly how the department's internal investigations were handled. He also knew from the bug they had planted in the Chief's office that he would have to make a decision about how to neutralize both Sergeant Spinella *and* his boss, Captain McCathran, without raising a lot of red flags.

It's my own fault, I've known about this mess for a while now, and I left it to a bunch of assholes to fix, and they fucked it up. Now I've got a real problem on my hands. I should never have involved myself with that damn Lorenzo in the first place. Who in their right mind collects dozens of deadly snakes for pets? Lorenzo has been sitting back and raking in the money without any risk. I'm the one who has everything to lose, and I'm not gonna let that happen. Let him put his ass on the line for a change. In a way, the best move I could make would be to add some distance between him and me. I've got almost two million stashed, and I'm not going to lose that because of some stupid thugs and a nosey cop. I'm smarter than them, and all I need to do is put together a plan to put the blame on either that bumbling asshole Spinella, or my so-called partner.

All of a sudden, he got an idea. He knew that Lorenzo had told his snake guy to wear gloves when he broke into Spinella's house, and since the only prints on the stolen gun belong to Detective Sergeant Spinella, two of his three immediate problems would be solved at one time: Spinella taken off the case and maybe put in jail, and the snake man removed.

Kirby failed to see Maurice approach his car. He opened the passenger door and slipped into the seat next to him. Kirby was so startled that he spilled his latte down the front of his shirt.

"What the hell is wrong with you? You scared the shit outta me. Never sneak up on people like that!" he yelled while dabbing the front of his shirt with a napkin from the coffee shop. Maurice, a slightly built black man with a receding hairline, was dressed like he was going to a men's fashion show, wearing a cream colored silk sharkskin double breasted suit with a bright blue shirt and matching tie. He looked at Kirby in disgust.

"What am I supposed to do? Do you want me to quietly walk up, politely knock on your window and ask permission to get into your car? This shit is bad enough without taking a bunch of shit from you." Kirby turned in his seat, still dabbing at the coffee stain on the front of his shirt, and gave Maurice a superior look.

"Do you know who you're talking to, Detective?"

"Yeah, I know exactly who I'm talking to mothafucka," snarled Maurice. The veins in his temples stood out like a road maps. "I wouldn't be here if you hadn't threatened my family. So, Lieutenant, *sir*, cut the bullshit and just tell me what I need to do to finish this so I can get my life back."

"Settle down Maurice. I promise you that this will all end soon. I only want you to do one more thing for me, and then you can forget this ever happened."

"I want out!" said Maurice. "I ain't gonna do no more of this shit, and whatever you need done, get someone else to do it. Why don't you get some of your buddy Lorenzo's boys to do it?"

"Pipe down! Somebody might hear you, and then we'll both be in the shit. I told you, this will be over soon, and I'll even slip you enough money so you'll never have to worry when you leave the job."

"Easy for you to tell me to calm down! I ain't never done nothing dishonest in my life until your nasty ass came along. So I made one mistake! You've been holding it over my head all this time, and I want out! I don't care if I go to prison— I'm through!"

"You sure about that?" said Kirby. "Because that shit you pulled off with your punk assed friend won't go away. Murder is forever pal, and don't forget it."

"I was just a fifteen year old kid trying to get some money to help my mother pay our rent," Maurice pleaded, "and nobody was supposed to get hurt. We didn't have no guns. I've never done nothing like that before. All I wanted was to keep my family from being put on the street. It wouldn't have happened if that guy hadn't started fighting with Tookie.

He was the one with the gun, not us! It was self-defense! He would've shot us! Besides, Tookie was the one who took the gun from him and shot him, not me."

"You know the law! You're a cop for Christ sake!" Kirby said with a smirk. "You're just as guilty as your junkie friend, so shut up and listen to what I need you to do!"

"Fuck You! I'm not doing nothing else for you, not taking no drugs from no evidence room, not destroying no files, not nothing!" Kirby, seeing that the situation was getting out of control, softened his approach.

"Listen to me! I promise on my mother's grave that this is the last thing I'll ever ask you to do." Maurice turned to get out of the car. "I'm done! Do what you gotta do, and leave me the fuck alone!"

As Maurice strutted off, Kirby leaned his head out of the car.

"You're gonna be sorry, Maurice! Whatever happens is on you!"

The two men, wearing dark blue, rumpled track suits, sat quietly in a nondescript, three-year-old SUV, smoking and watching the neighborhood kids play kick ball halfway down the block from where they were parked. The heavyset one sitting behind the steering wheel looked over at his slightly smaller companion.

"When is this mope supposed to be getting home?"

"I don't know," said the smaller man, "but my ass is getting tired, and I need to take a leak. Oh and by the way, it better happen soon, because it won't take too long for the neighborhood busy bodies to figure out that two white guys sitting in a car in a black neighborhood ain't right, and when that happens, all bets are off."

"Thanks for your enlightened assessment of the situation. Now shut the fuck up and pay attention because—" At that moment, the big guy stopped talking and grabbed the rear view mirror.

"Here he comes. He's coming from behind us carrying a bag, so keep your head down so he can't I.D. you. Make it quick, and let's get outta here."

The slightly built white man exited the SUV and began walking directly towards a middle-aged black man carrying a large paper bag. Keeping his head down, the man removed a knife from his jacket pocket, flicked it open and held it down by his side as he closed the distance between them. His target showed no evidence of suspecting anything unusual, and when they were about to pass each other on the sidewalk, the man bumped into him, hard, knocking the bag out of his hands spilling groceries onto the sidewalk as he struck the black man several times in the stomach with his knife. After the attack, the man turned and casually walked back to the SUV. The car slowly drove away without anyone seeming to have noticed what had just happened.

As the two men drove the car away from the scene, making sure not to violate any traffic laws, the big guy heard his cell phone make a chirping sound and, reaching down to the front seat brought it to his ear. After the short conversation, the driver kept his eyes on the road as he spoke to his partner.

"That was Kirby. We have another mess to clean up and it needs to be done right away."

After a short drive, they pulled into a dilapidated scrap metal yard filled with old junk cars piled three or four high. The men got out of their vehicle, leaving the keys in the ignition, and after a quick look around to make sure nobody noticed them, quickly got into a black four-door sedan that was parked inside the scrap yard fence and drove away.

CHAPTER FIVE

Tony had just finished showing Scopes where his electrical panel was located in his basement when his cell phone rang.

"This is Tony."

"Maurice! Hey man, what's happening?"

Tony tried to maintain his usual tone with his partner, so as not to arouse suspicion.

"I'm kinda busy right now, Mo. I'm with somebody. How about us hooking up a little later at Barney's for a cold one? .... Okay, man, if it's that important I'll wait here for you, but give me a couple of minutes to get rid of my company... Right, fifteen minutes."

Tony put his phone down and looked at Scopes.

"Trouble?" Scopes asked.

"That was Maurice. Something's up. He's on his way over here right now. I'll need you to stay outta sight while he's here, and if it's possible, I want you to tape our conversation."

"No problem! Where in the house are you gonna be talking?"

"Probably in the kitchen, because that's where we usually go to have a couple of beers whenever he comes by." Scopes scratched his head.

"I've got some old-school, voice-activated stuff in my bag that should work. Let me get it and get started. How much time do I have?"

"About ten minutes," said Tony. As he headed for the kitchen, he heard Scopes mutter something about Rome not being built in a day.

A few minutes later there was a knock on the front door; Tony went into the front room, looked out the window which had a clear view of the front porch of his house, and saw his partner Maurice standing at the front door. Tony made his way to the door, opened it, and Maurice, without saying a word, rushed into the house and went straight to the front window and peered out.

"What's up Mo?" Tony asked. "You expecting somebody?" Maurice said nothing for a minute, then turned away from the window. "Let's go into the kitchen and I'll explain."

They made their way to the kitchen and Tony turned to Maurice.

"What the hell is going on? Why all the cloak and dagger shit?"

"Can I get a beer? I could really use one right now."

"No problem," said Tony, "but I still need to know why you're acting like this."

Tony grabbed two beers from his fridge and they took a seat at the kitchen table. Maurice looked across the table at Tony as he took a long pull from his bottle.

"I crossed the line, Tony. I'm in over my head with some people who are gonna ruin my life!" Tony studied his long-time partner and friend. *Shit! What do I do now? How the hell am I going to handle this situation?*

"Okay, Mo, just start at the beginning and tell me what's going on," Tony replied, trying to calm his partner. He listened to Maurice tell a story that seemed about as believable as the training manual they gave him in rookie school.

Mo told him that James Kirby, an IAD Lieutenant, had coerced him into working for him by threatening to expose a mistake he had made as a teenager.

"What mistake was that?" Tony asked. Maurice started to reply when they suddenly heard the Temptations' song "My Girl." Maurice motioned for Tony to wait and he answered his phone.

"Natalie, what's up?" Tony saw Mo's complexion instantly change, and he could hear screaming.

"When did this happen?" Maurice replied urgently. "Where did they take him? O.K., I'll be right there." A distraught Maurice stood up, looked at Tony and blurted out, "It's my fucking fault! He warned me! I caused this to happen!"

Tony grabbed Maurice by the arm. "What just happened?"

"Bernard's been stabbed! I gotta go. He's at St.Vincent's, and it don't look good. I'll come back later and tell you everything, okay?"

"If you need me you've got my cell number; give me a call and let me know how he's doing. Call me soon as you can because we need to get this shit straightened out."

Maurice nodded and bolted from the kitchen and out the front door. Tony called Frank as soon as he heard the door slam. As he waited for his Captain to answer, he heard what sounded like gunshots coming from the street. He ran to the window, and saw a dark-colored vehicle pull away. He threw the phone down, pulled the nine millimeter from his shoulder holster, and slowly stepped out his front door to investigate.

It had already been a shitty day with Frank's revelations and snakes in his closet, so Tony was on his guard. He was careful to look around the dark street before he ventured past the front porch. As he carefully descended the front steps, he could just make out the silhouette of a man sitting up against the big oak tree in the box space in front of his house. Keeping his gun ready, he called out.

"Police! Don't move!" He continued to slowly move towards the man.

"Are you okay? Do you need some help?" He had taken two more steps before he realized it was Maurice, his face covered in blood. He ran to his partner and knelt down by his side, attempting to wipe the blood from his eyes. As he slid his hand across his friend's face, he felt a warm mushiness around a large hole where Maurice's left eye should have been. Checking for more injuries, he moved his hand behind Maurice's head and felt something that he knew could only be brain matter. His friend was gone. Tony desperately tried to find a pulse. It was no use. Maurice was dead.

Tony cried as he held Maurice in his arms, oblivious to the arrival of his nextdoor neighbor, Dave Watts, who was asking if he should call for help. Somewhere in the midst of his grief he found his voice.

"Somebody call 911! Get an ambulance!" He sat there holding his friend in his arms for what seemed like hours until one of the first arriving officers gently pried him away and led him inside his house.

CHAPTER SIX

Tony collected himself enough to locate his cell phone where he'd dropped it and called his Captain to tell him what had just happened. Frank told Tony that he was on his way over there—that Scopes had already phoned him. "Don't mention the investigation to anyone," Frank told him.

Twenty minutes later Captain McCathran pulled up in front of Tony's house, exited his double-parked, unmarked cruiser and headed for Toy's door. He observed several police officers doing a routine neighborhood canvass in an attempt to gather information or witnesses to the shooting.

Tony was giving his statement to the homicide detectives when Frank walked in. He waved to his boss, who gave him a nod as he stepped into the kitchen and sat down at the table to wait for Tony to finish his statement. After a few minutes had passed, one of the detectives walked into the kitchen.

"Hey, Captain. What brings you here?"

"Do I know you, Detective?" asked Frank, surveying the man's appearance. He wore an ill-fitting, rumpled gray plaid suit, a green shirt in a similar state, and black tie. He was also badly in need of a shave.

"Yes sir. I'm Ray Fitzpatrick. I worked a couple of months in Robbery Squad before I transferred over to Homicide," replied the overweight detective.

"Yeah, I think I remember you. In answer to your question, both Sergeant Spinella and the victim, Detective White, work for me. Sergeant Spinella called and gave me a heads-up about what happened, and I stopped by to see if there was anything I needed to know. Spinella's a good cop, and I don't want any shit to stick to him about what just went down."

"Well Captain, so far it looks like a robbery gone bad, but we're still in the early stages of the investigation. You never know what might come up later, but rest assured, me and my partner will do everything we can to catch the bastard that did this. The guy they killed was one of us, and we're not gonna rest until the shooter's ass is in jail."

"I feel the same way too, Detective!" said Frank, "Remember, he worked for me, and since you think this might've been a robbery, I want you to keep me informed of any progress you make in the investigation."

"Will do, Captain. I'll let my lieutenant know that you want to be kept informed," the detective replied and left the kitchen.

As Frank watched the two detectives leave, he thought to himself Detective Fitzpatrick must have been a piss-poor investigator, because he really didn't remember him being assigned to Robbery Squad at all.

He had just entered the kitchen when Scopes walked in, sat down across from Frank and started talking so fast they had to make him stop and take a couple of deep breaths. He was clearly scared shitless. He shot a frantic look at Tony.

"Is there any chance that I'm gonna get shot like Maurice?"

"Scopes," said Tony, addressing him as if he were talking to a young child, "you're not going to get hurt; you're strictly behind the scenes in this. Nobody knows who you are or what you're doing, so tell us what you got." Scopes took another deep breath.

"Tony told me Maurice was on the way over here and asked if there was any way I could record their conversation. I told him I might be able to use some old equipment I had with me to get their conversation on tape. But, it's not the best equipment and I can't promise good quality." Frank asked Scopes to get his equipment and play the recorded conversation for him.

When Scopes left the room, Tony vented. "I'm gonna find the bastard that did this and I'm gonna kill him!"

"I don't want to hear that shit right now," said Frank. "You're no good to me, or yourself, if you go off half-cocked. All you'll accomplish is to fuck up what we're trying to do, and maybe get yourself killed in the process! We're going to get them—all of them—and now we know for sure who one of the ringleaders is."

"So what's our next move?" asked Tony. "They've killed Maurice, and he was the only one who could've given us the scoop on their operation." Just then Scopes came back into the kitchen with his equipment and placed it on the table.

"The quality is pretty good, but you guys know this recording was taken illegally, and we can't officially use it."

"Yeah," said Frank. "Just play the damn thing!" After hearing the tape, Frank looked at the two men. "Now we're going to put some pressure on those assholes, and I know exactly how we're going to do it."

After leaving Tony's house, Homicide detectives, Fitzpatrick and Sipe got into their cruiser and drove away. As soon as they turned the first corner, Sipes, the smaller of the two, began bragging to his partner about how well he thought the whole thing had gone down, and how smooth he thought he'd handled it. "I'm better than any of those CIA clowns any day. They could take lessons from me on how to handle tough situations like this." Fitzpatrick looked over at the smaller man and said,

"So Dave, you think because you stabbed some unarmed punk carrying groceries and then ambushed a cop, that it makes you some kind of a hit man? You keep that attitude little man and we're gonna be in the shit. You little fuck! Do you have any idea what we've got ourselves into? We killed a cop!" yelled Fitzpatrick as spittle flew from his mouth. "You better stop patting yourself on the back and start paying attention, or we'll find ourselves on the wrong side of the bars, and you know what happens to cops in the joint. That ain't gonna happen to me, and if you don't get your miserable ass straight, you might be the one who don't make it to the finish line."

At that very moment, Dave Sipe realized that his partner would just as soon kill him as anyone else who got in his way. Even though he was no genius, he began to understand that he was into some serious shit, and he'd better let his partner know right away that he would get it together.

"Sorry about that Fitz. Whatever you say. I'm with you one hundred percent!"

"You'd better be," snarled Fitzpatrick as he picked up his cell phone and punched in a number.

Jim Kirby was sitting in his car eating a hamburger from a nearby fast food joint when his cell phone started buzzing on the seat next to him.

"Yeah," he said, talking through a mouthful. He hesitated for a moment before replying to the voice on the line.

"Meet me at Fort DuPont Park, by the ball fields in thirty minutes, and make sure you aren't followed." Kirby threw the rest of his unfinished hamburger out the car window onto the street and pulled out of the parking lot, nearly hitting an elderly man walking his dog.

Stupid ass, he should be more careful. He looked in his rear view mirror and saw the man holding his little dog and shaking his fist at him. Kirby was in northwest Washington and it would take him at least thirty minutes to get to the meeting place. Maybe it wouldn't be a bad idea to start taking his own advice and make sure he wasn't being followed.

CHAPTER SEVEN

After telling Scopes to pack his equipment and activate Tony's alarm system, Frank called Lamont and told him to meet them back at the "spot." The Captain put his cell away and looked at Tony.

"Pack some clothes, enough for a few days, because you won't be coming back here until we have a better idea who all the players are in this mess, and how far it goes into the department."

Tony went into his bedroom, got out his old duffle bag, and began to throw in enough clothes to last him a few days. His mind was in turmoil. Somebody was going to pay for killing his friend.

Frank and Scopes were waiting for him in the kitchen when he came downstairs with his bag. Scopes had already packed up his electronic gear and appeared to be in a hurry to leave, while Frank was walking around the kitchen talking on his cell phone. When he saw Tony re-enter, he finished his call.

"Tony, check outside and make sure it's clear. Scopes, you ride with me, and Tony, you take your car and follow us. Make sure we're not followed!"

"Okay, but where are we going?" Tony asked.

"You'll know," said Frank. "Just follow me."

Tony knew within minutes where they were going when Frank's car turned to go north on Wisconsin Avenue N.W. He spent most of his time checking his rear view mirror and kicking himself in the ass for not knowing that his partner had been in serious trouble. He needed to start connecting the dots in this investigation if he ever hoped to find Maurice's killer. Frank's car abruptly turned onto the same gravel road they had used before, and a few minutes later both cars pulled into the cleared space in front of Frank's parents' old farmhouse.

They silently made their way to the back of the house, down the basement steps and into the main room in the basement. They found Lamont sitting in front of a computer screen busily clicking away.

"Where the hell have you guys been? I've been worried sick since you called."

"It's okay, Lamont. We're all good, but we need to bring you up to speed on what's happened and find out how you did placing the tracking devices," replied Frank.

A grin appeared on Lamont's face. "It's all good! As a matter of fact, one of them is moving right now, and the one on the inspector's cruiser hasn't moved since he drove it home after he got off work. So, tell me what's going on."

Just then Scopes, who had gone directly into an adjoining room, came in carrying cold beers and handed them out.

"May Maurice rest in peace," he said.

Tony almost lost it, but then gathered himself long enough to raise his beer and bow his head for a moment before taking a sip from his bottle.

"What the hell was that all about?" asked a stunned Lamont, his eyes scanning the other three men. "What did you mean 'Rest in peace?' Did something happen to Maurice?"

Frank glanced at Tony and then back at Lamont.

"Everybody grab a chair and I'll bring Lamont up to date, and then we start planning how we're going to put a hurting on these bastards."

Over the next twenty minutes Frank explained what had been going on since they were last together, and then opened the floor for suggestions on what their next step should be. First to speak was the frail looking Scopes, who again offered his previous idea to bug Kirby's cruiser as well as his home, followed by

Tony, who felt they should pick up Kirby and beat the shit out of him until he talked. Frank, who had said nothing while both men talked, stood up.

"I know how we'll get them, and it's gonna be pretty simple."

Everyone was listening to Frank, who had a big shit-eating grin plastered across his face.

"Okay, how we gonna do it?" the men replied more or less in unison.

"Follow the money!" Frank responded. When no one said anything, he continued, "We know he's raking in some big bucks, so where's he putting it? Lamont, I want you to get into Kirby's house and check for any stashes he might have. If we can find out for sure that he doesn't keep the money at home, than we go on the reasonable assumption that he keeps it somewhere else where it can be safe. Like maybe the bank.

Scopes, if that turns out to be the case, we'll need you to turn your electronic genius loose and find out all the information about his account and how much money he has hidden."

Tony had said very little during the exchange of ideas about Kirby's money. Finally, he interrupted.

"Lamont, if you can't find the money at his pad, then I'll have to start surveillance on Kirby before Scopes can perform his magic. Once I locate where he banks, we can start applying some pressure."

Frank pumped his fist in the air. "Now we're cooking!"

Scopes raised his hands for everyone to be quiet.

"Not only will we find out where he keeps his money, but when we do, I'll transfer every penny out of his account into one offshore that I'll set up." That way, we'll have a big bargaining chip to play."

"Now why didn't I think of that" said Tony.

Frank pointed at Lamont. "Get started on his house, and Scopes, you keep Lamont aware of Kirby's location at all times. I don't want him coming home and catching Lamont inside his house."

"Gotcha boss," said Scopes with a big grin. With that, everyone began to pick out the equipment they would need to do what was required of them and then said their goodbyes.

Outside by their cars, Tony stopped Frank.

"Frank, before I do anything else I've got to go see Mo's sister, Natalie. She's Maurice's only family member, other than his brother-in-law, Bernard. Maybe Maurice mentioned something to her that might shed some light on our investigation."

"It's worth a try," said Frank. "Let me know if you find out anything worthwhile."

CHAPTER EIGHT

The cruiser was parked in the early summer darkness near the baseball field at Fort Dupont Park, just off the road under a big oak tree surrounded by large bushes. It was well out of sight of anyone who might be driving by. Fitz and Dave sat quietly waiting for Kirby to arrive. Fitzpatrick, who was still slightly ticked off at his partner, got out of the cruiser to have a smoke. He had only been out of the car a few minutes when Dave got out opening a pack of cigarettes.

Walking around to the other side of the car, Dave offered him one of his cigarettes.

"You wanna try one of these?"

Fitz, leaning against the fender, looked at his partner, smirked and shook his head. After a lengthy silence, Fitz turned and looked at Dave.

"You and me got to start planning how we're gonna protect ourselves if this shit turns out bad. We need to figure a way to get some leverage on Kirby in case he decides to bale and leave us holding the bag."

"How we gonna do that?" Dave asked.

"Just leave that to me, and be ready to do exactly what I tell you to do. I'll let you know when," said Fitz. "Until then keep your mouth shut and watch what's going on."

A car approached suddenly and they returned to their car. A dark-colored, plain- clothes cruiser pulled alongside their parked vehicle and shut off its engine. The driver's side window came down to reveal their boss, Lieutenant James Kirby. He motioned for them to come over and join him in his vehicle. Fitz took the front passenger seat while Dave sat in the rear.

"Bring me up to speed," said Kirby. Fitzpatrick explained exactly what he and his partner Dave had done in the last twenty-four hours. He also expressed his concerns over the necessity for the hit on Maurice White.

"After all" said Fitz, "that's going to bring a lot of heat down on us and we don't need any departmental investigations right now."

"Shut the fuck up!" said Kirby. "I do the planning for you, and all you have to do is just follow orders. Don't you think I've thought this through? Who's running the investigation into White's shooting?"

Fitz looked back at Sipes. "We are!"

Kirby grinned and said, "Correct! And we can make it go any way we want it to go. You guys continue working the theory of a robbery gone bad, and because there's no evidence to refute your theory, stay busy and continue to go through the motions until your boss tells you to start working your other pending cases. After a while, there won't be as much pressure on you and you can just occasionally progress the case to show you're still actively investigating."

"Yeah, that'll work, but we need to talk about our arrangement," Fitz replied. Kirby frowned and lowered his voice.

"What's wrong about our arrangement? You're not happy with it? You want I should give you a paid cruise to Tahiti?"

"No, not anything like that boss," Fitz reassured him. "We just think that we're the ones taking most of the risk here, and if the shit hits the fan, we're the ones who will get the needle, not you." Kirby sat there saying nothing, so Fitz decided to go for it.

"We just thought that you might see your way clear to slip us a little bigger piece of the pie. We're with you one hundred percent, and you can count on us to get the job done. We're just asking to be treated fairly."

Kirby's mind raced with thoughts that somewhere down the line he would have to do something about these two idiots' before they caused him serious trouble. For now, he needed both of them for the immediate future. After Fitz stopped talking, Kirby smiled.

"Of course! I was thinking the same thing on the way over here," he said with feigned enthusiasm. "You've both done a good job and deserve a better shake in our deal. From this point on, you'll be getting significantly more money for every transfer we make from the property room."

"How much more?" blurted Dave from the back seat. Kirby, seething with anger at both these clowns for putting him on the spot, forced another smile and told them they would get an additional grand apiece for each transfer of drugs out of the property room.

"How does that sound to you?"

The two detectives gave their mutual assent.Kirby sensed that he had regained control of the situation.

"Here's what I want both of you to do. Keep your daily routine the same, and continue with your investigation into the unfortunate killing of a police officer. Fitz, you know how to go through the motions without anyone getting wise, and while you're at it, I want you both to keep tabs on White's partner, Spinella. From what I've been able to dig up about him, he's a very capable investigator, and a pretty damn good cop. Make sure he doesn't get too close to your investigation or start asking too many questions. If he does, you can block him administratively without raising any suspicions, by complaining to your supervisor about him impeding your investigation. If he doesn't back off, call me right away, understood? In the meantime," he went on, "I have a plan to take Spinella outta the picture and maybe off the job completely."

"How you gonna do that?" asked Dave.

"Simple," said Kirby, and he began to outline his plan.

"Damn Boss!" laughed Fitz. "You da man!" Not to be outdone, Dave, from his seat in the back, chimed in.

"Brilliant, Boss! That's fantastic."

Kirby knew then that he had them. What with their getting more money, and his plan to get rid of Spinella in play, he knew he shouldn't have any more problems with these two meatheads in the near future. After giving them further instructions and reminding them to stay in close touch, he drove away. Fitz and Dave gave Kirby a minute or two to clear the area then followed him out of the park, passing the dugout behind which Scopes' beat-up, gray Toyota sat hidden in the darkness.

CHAPTER NINE

Tony's mind was in turmoil as he drove through the dark towards Maurice's sister's house. He dreaded seeing her so soon after Maurice's death because he had nothing to tell her about the case. He also knew she wouldn't understand why he wasn't a lead investigator and, in her grief, might hold that against him. Nonetheless, he had to talk to her.

The cell phone in his pocket began to vibrate. Tony pulled over to the curb and saw that the call was from his girlfriend, Lina. He hadn't been in contact with her for over twenty four hours, and she was probably a little pissed with him. In the brief moment before he answered her call, it dawned on him that he was becoming more attached to her with each passing day.

Tony had met Acqualina almost a year ago, while having lunch at the local Fraternal Order of Police lodge, and it wasn't long before he was calling her "Lina." She and two of her girlfriends, who worked nearby, had a standing lunch date at the lodge every Tuesday and Friday. As she later told Tony, the food was good, the beer cold, and the prices were friendly for working folks. After several weeks of flirting, Tony got the nerve to ask her out on a date. After a couple of dates, he learned that she was thirty-one years old, with a political science degree from American University, and worked as the Administrative Assistant to a Congressman from California. She was tall, slim and beautiful, with short brown hair and a fantastic personality. He was hooked!

Tony punched the talk button and immediately heard Lina's voice.

"Where have you been, sailor?"

"Working," he replied, trying to match Lina's playful tone, but failing.

"Well, I've been feeling a little neglected lately and I was just wondering what you're going to do about it?" she teased.

Tony sighed, and decided to tell her what had been going on since they last spoke. He knew that Lina was sharp and wouldn't go for any of his sugarcoating bullshit, so he told Lina exactly what had happened to Maurice, leaving out the part about the attempt on his own life. Lina began to cry, asking if there was anything she could do.

"Don't worry about me. I won't be coming over tonight because I don't know how long I'll be at Natalie's. I wouldn't be good company anyway. I'll see you as soon as I can, ok?"

After some final words of reassurance, he hung up and drove on to Natalie's.

Tony had met Natalie several times over the last couple of years, at times when he and Maurice were on duty and also at their family gatherings. Tony liked Natalie and her husband Bernard, and he really didn't want to question her about her brother so soon after he'd been killed, let alone after her husband was stabbed. He had little choice, however, due to the critical nature of the investigation.

Tony parked his car across the street from a group of well-kept red brick row houses that dated back to the fifties. Natalie's house was easy to spot because of the bright red color of the window shutters her husband had recently painted against her wishes, and the small iron porch jutting out from the front of the house. He had just stepped out of his vehicle when someone shouted,

"What you want, Whitey?"

He looked over to the front of Natalie's row house and saw several young black teenagers standing around the steps to her door. When he approached, the group blocked his path. Tony stopped and eyed the five young men.

"I'm a friend of Natalie's and Bernard's, and I'm here to pay my respects. Anybody got a problem with that?"

One of the young men looked closely at Tony, then turned to the others.

"I know this dude. He be a friend of Maurice and Nat. Get out de way and let him through."

Tony nodded, and continued up the stairs. Before he could knock, Natalie opened the door and fell sobbing into his arms. After a few minutes of clumsy attempts to console her, she stopped crying long enough to invite him into the living room where she began to pepper him with a barrage of questions about Maurice. He told her about what had happened at his house, and went on to explain why he had come to see her.

Natalie answered all of Tony's questions about what she knew about the attack on her husband. Tony asked her if there had been any witnesses to the attack..

"Three of the local teenagers told me they saw a dark-colored SUV with two white guys inside drive away right after Bernard was stabbed."

"Did they see anything else?"

"No. And I asked them."

Tony figured that the suspects must have totally surprised Bernard, and continued to ask more questions about the attack on her husband.

"How's he doing?" he finally asked.

"His wounds were bad; the doctor said it was touch and go for a while, but he's going to be all right."

Tony was glad to hear that Bernard would survive, and that the prognosis was very good for his complete recovery.

After asking all of the questions he could think of concerning the attack of her husband, he asked the one question he had put off for as long as he could.

"Natalie, have you been in contact with Maurice lately, and if so, did he say, or do anything that you thought was unusual for him?"

"Yes. He started acting funny about six months ago, and I asked him if there was anything he wanted to tell me. He said 'Nat, I'm into some serious shit, and I need you to hold something for me until I ask for it back.' I got scared because I know my brother, and I could tell he was afraid of something. He made me promise that if anything happened to him, I was to give it to you."

"Natalie, tell me exactly what he said to you."

"He told me that he wanted me to give the package to you and nobody else. That he was in serious trouble, and you would know what to do with it if anything happened to him."

Tony felt a surge of excitement. He stood up.

"Natalie, what did he give you?"

"He gave me a package with a notebook inside!"

"Did you read it?"

"No, I didn't. Wait here, and I'll go get it for you."

Tony's mind was racing with the possibilities this new evidence might bring to the case. He sat down after Natalie left the room, but jumped back up when she re-entered. She handed the plain, brown paper package over to him.

"Tony, all I want out of this is for you to get the bastards who shot my brother. You either kill them or arrest them, but make them pay. I would prefer the former, but I know you have a sworn duty to uphold and I hope this helps."

Tony took the package, and after reassuring Natalie that he was going to find the people who did it, quickly left the house, making his way once again past the wary group of teens who were still congregating on the steps.

CHAPTER TEN

Scopes, wanting to contribute more to the investigation, elected to tail Kirby's car. After following him to southeast Washington's Fort DuPont Park, where the tracking bug showed it had stopped, he entered the park from a smaller, less observable side road instead of the main road, which ran straight through the park. After winding his way around the deserted park, he slowly approached the location where his equipment showed the target vehicle had stopped. In the early evening darkness, he could barely make out the two cars parked under some large oak trees just across from the ball field. He needed to figure out a way to get closer if he was going to get anything worthwhile to tell the guys.

Scopes spotted the dugout structure, which was situated several feet back from the ball field's third base line; if he could get behind it unseen, it would give him a great view of the area where the two cars were parked. He looked closely at the area around the dugout and noticed there was a deep depression in the ground directly behind it that could keep his car out of the line of sight.

Both hands shaking with fear, Scopes slowly eased his old car into the area behind the dugout and cut the engine. If he had to make a quick getaway, it would be impossible because of the large trees directly in front of his car. He was so nervous that he almost laughed out loud at the thought of pushing the gas peddle to the floor while trying to get away with his old car in reverse. He refocused his thoughts on getting his specially customized camera gear ready to take some pictures.

He had to be careful getting out of his car so as not to alert attention, so he removed the key from the ignition to prevent the pinging sound that would occur if the key were left there. Being extra careful not to make a sound, he grabbed his camera and got out of the car. He crept to the back wall of the dugout, leaned around the corner of the building and took a quick peek across the field. From his vantage point, he couldn't get a good look at the people in the car closest to him, but with the special lens on his camera, he knew he would be able to get a clear shot of the driver. His only problem—other than almost pissing his pants— was being able to take the shot with some assurance that he wouldn't get himself killed in the process.

Scopes knelt down and the silence was suddenly shattered by a surprisingly loud popping noise coming from his knee joints. Smiling at the irony of being discovered and killed because of arthritic knees, he waited another minute before he again eased around the corner of the building. He snapped several pictures. At the very least, he had gotten one good picture of one of the drivers.

After getting the pictures, Scopes, sweating and close to panic, carefully got back into his car and sat quietly behind the wheel. Roughly ten minutes later he heard one of the cars start up and begin to drive away. As fate would have it, the first car to leave passed almost directly in front of Scopes. Sitting behind the wheel of his little car, Scopes had a clear profile view of the car's lone occupant. After the car drove out of sight, Scopes, feeling the coast was clear, breathed a sigh of relief, and then almost made the biggest mistake of his life.

Just before he turned the key in the ignition, he heard the distinct sound of another car being started. In his nervous state, he had forgotten the other car parked under the trees; his hand froze on the ignition key. He quickly slid down in the seat and listened to the second car drive away. He was overcome with relief when he peered over his dashboard and saw the car turn into the opposite direction from the dugout. Despite his good fortune, he still waited a couple of extra minutes before starting his car. As he drove away, he felt an exhilaration unlike any he had felt in the last twenty years. Maybe he was a lot better at this detective stuff than he had originally thought. He had better call Frank right away and let him know what had just occurred, and make arrangements to meet and go over the pictures. His first call had to be to Lamont, however, to let him know that Kirby had just left Fort DuPont Park.

CHAPTER ELEVEN

It was just after seven on a crisp, cold evening when Frank pulled out of the police garage underneath headquarters and into the last of the evening rush hour traffic. He had just crossed the nearby intersection of Third Street N.W., when his cell started to beep. He pulled the phone from his jacket pocket.

"McCathran! …What's going on, Scopes? …You did *what*? What the hell were you thinking? Do you want to get yourself killed? …Wait, I'm on my way, and don't do anything until I get there!"

Frank pressed the 'end call' button on the phone, and immediately dialed Tony. After a moment or two, Tony answered, only to hear his seriously pissed off boss holler in his ear that Scopes had damned near ended up getting his ticket punched while doing something very stupid.

"Frank, calm down and tell me what happened. Is Scopes okay?"

"Yeah, the idiot's ok!" Frank groused.

"Thank God," Tony replied. "I'll meet you at our spot. I've got some stuff you gotta see."

Tony hung up abruptly and Frank hit the gas, headed for the farm.

Thirty minutes later, after making sure he wasn't followed, Tony made the turn onto the old gravel road to Frank's hideaway. He pulled into the clearing in front of the old farmhouse and was glad to see both Scopes' and Frank's cars already there. When he first opened the door to their underground room, he could hear Frank's voice yelling loudly at Scopes, who said nothing as he took Frank's verbal assault.

"What's up guys?" Tony said in a congenial tone, trying to lighten the mood.

"This asshole is trying to get himself killed, and at the same time, fuck up this whole operation," hollered Frank. Tony could see that his boss was on the verge of having a major meltdown.

"Listen you guys, we won't beat these bums if we can't work together. Frank, you know that Scopes was only trying to do something to help, so let's just sit down and exchange whatever information we have. That's the only way we can catch these bastards."

Both men shook their heads in agreement, pulled up chairs and sat down across from each other. Tony stood between them. "Scopes, what have you got for us?" he asked.

Scopes began to relate his spying adventure while handing out copies of the pictures he had taken of Kirby and the two men in the park. Right away, Frank pointed at one picture and snarled.

"See that fucker in the other car? I know him! He was the detective who took your statement when Maurice was shot." Tony moved around Frank to get a closer look at the photos. He could clearly see Lt. Kirby's face just past the front windshield of the other car. Looking closer, Tony recognized a face in the front seat of the car parked next to Kirby's.

Frank caught the rush of anger in Tony's face.

"Tony, you mentioned that you had something that you wanted to show me."

"You bet I do! But before I do that, you should all know that when I catch the bastard that shot my friend, it might be a good idea for all of you to be someplace else. You can't be forced to testify about what you don't know." A short silence fell upon the room before Tony resumed.

"Remember I told you that I was going over to see Maurice's sister, Natalie, to see if I could get any leads or information Maurice might have passed on to her?"

"Yeah, I remember. So what did you get?" Frank asked impatiently.

"Well, it seems that Maurice must have known that at some point the people he was involved with wouldn't need him anymore, and might take steps to insure he would never pose a threat. Guys, Maurice had a journal, and he gave it to Natalie to keep in case something happen to him. The best part is, Maurice, like a lot of cops, was pretty good at writing reports, and this journal is filled with really good shit: dates, times, locations, and best of all, names." At this point, Tony held up the package containing the journal that Natalie had given him earlier.

"He must have started this from the very beginning of his contact with Kirby because it goes back almost a year, and it has dates of when drugs were stolen from the property room, along with meetings Kirby had with others involved in the scheme, and names of other cops involved," Tony went on.

"No shit!" said Scopes, who was sitting on the edge of his chair squirming with excitement. "Frank, I think I better start carrying a gun!"

"In your dreams," snapped Frank, "You'll end up shooting yourself and maybe one of us. So forget about it for now, okay?"

"Yeah," said Scopes, "you're right. I just got a little excited and didn't think it through."

Tony pulled up a chair and had just begun to read portions of Maurice's journal, when Frank's cell phone beeped and he motioned for Tony to stop. He had a brief conversation and hung up.

"That was Lamont. He's on his way. He was able to gain access to Kirby's place and he'll fill us in when he gets here. Let's wait until he arrives and we can all hear what's in the journal together."

"Sounds good to us," Tony replied, looking at Scopes.

Thinking this would be a good time to call Lina, he got up and wandered over to the corner of the room for some privacy. She answered on the second ring.

"Yeah honey, I'm fine…I'm with my boss and a couple of other people going over the case file… Honey, listen, I'll tell you all about it as soon as we can hook up, okay? …Yeah, but I'm kinda tied up right now, how about meeting for lunch at the club tomorrow? …Yeah, eleven thirty like always. If I'm a couple minutes late, order me the cheeseburger special…Alright baby, no cheeseburger, I'll see you tomorrow, bye sweetheart."

He returned to the other side of the room where his comrades were quietly talking.

"Anybody home?" Tony and his friends looked up. It was Lamont coming through the door, a broad grin on his face.

"All right everybody," said Frank, "grab a chair and sit down, so Tony can read the journal Maurice left."

"Maurice left a journal?" asked a surprised Lamont.

"Yeah," said Frank, "just learned about it a little while ago, and Tony was just about to read it when you called. For right now, let's all listen to what Maurice left us, and then I want to hear what you've found out."

"Okay boss, I'm all ears," said Lamont.

CHAPTER TWELVE

Reading and discussing Maurice's journal took almost two hours before they called for a break to get something to drink and visit the bathroom. No one had much to say during the break; Maurice's last testament had overwhelmed them.

"Before we go any further with the journal," Frank said when they reconvened, "let's hear what Lamont found out about Kirby's stash, if he has one, and then we'll get down to planning some misery for these sonofabitches."

Tony knew he would be one of the people making sure some dirty cops were very unhappy, and he eagerly embraced the prospect. *Finally, we can hit back.*

"It was a piece of cake getting into Kirby's house," Lamont related. "As a matter of fact, I thought that with him being a cop, he would have had better locks on his door. Anyway, getting in was easy, but I had to wait for his neighbor to get through fucking around with her roses, and go back inside her house before I could make my move. The man is a neat freak, and I mean neat freaky. Nothing was out of place. I checked all the usual places people hide their good shit, but found nothing. The last place I looked before I beat feet outta there was the garage. It took me almost a half an hour before I was able to find his hidey hole, but I found it."

"Where was it?" asked Scopes, squirming with excitement.

"Inside a five gallon gas can," replied Lamont.

"Who the fuck would hide anything inside a gas can?" interrupted Tony.

"If you guys would just let me finish my story, I'll tell you," said Lamont. "Kirby is a pretty slick dude; he'd cut the back off of a plastic five gallon gas container, and then placed it on a shelf in the garage with only the front part showing. The back piece was held on by duct tape, and all he had to do was pull the tape off, put whatever he wanted inside the container and then seal it up again."

"Come on Lamont! Quit teasing and just tell us what the hell you found," said Scopes.

"All right man, keep your pants on. None of you mugs are going to believe this, but I hit the jackpot. I found money, *lots* of money. I also found papers detailing his meetings with a guy named Lorenzo, and best of all, five different safety deposit box keys."

"Did you take them?" asked Scopes.

"Hell no! That would've let him know that somebody had been in his crib and found his stash, but I can go back in anytime and get the keys and the cash if you want me to."

"Good job, Lamont!" Frank said, nodding. "Did you happen to notice anything else while you were looking around his place?"

"Now that you mention it," said Lamont, "I did see a couple of passports, and a nice little thirty-eight revolver sitting on top of the cash."

"What did it look like?" Tony's ears pricked up.

"Like any other thirty-eight revolver," said Lamont.

"No, I mean can you give me a better description of the gun than that. It's important," pleaded Tony.

"How about a picture of it?" Lamont pulled his cell phone from his pocket and brandished it proudly. The picture of the snub nose thirty eight revolver that popped up was especially clear and detailed.

"That's my grandpa's gun," Tony said, pointing to the phone. "I'd know it anywhere. That picture ties Kirby to the break-in at my house!"

"Don't forget, it also ties him to the attempt on your life with that snake," added Frank.

"I'm not gonna forget *nothing*," Tony replied ominously. He caught Frank studying him closely. Looking away, he turned to Lamont.

"Lamont, did you notice anything that might tell us where those safety deposit boxes are located?"

"Will this do?" Lamont located another photo on his cell. Tony grabbed the phone and held it so the others could see.

"My man Lamont has kicked ass again! He has all the bank info we need right here in this photo. Scopes, this should be all that you and Lamont will need when we get ready to hit back at these pieces of shit." The picture showed five small envelopes with the names of five different banks plainly showing, along with box numbers.

"It's a start," Tony continued thoughtfully. "But it won't be easy. We'll have to access the boxes to get the cash, and hope no one remembers Kirby's face when we go in. Oh, and by the way, we don't really know what's in those five boxes either. But common sense tells me that those boxes are crammed with cash—lots of it."

"Hey man," said Lamont, looking at Scopes. "Don't worry about it, these banks don't give a shit who asks to look at a safety deposit box as long as you got the key, and the box number. Besides, they're so busy that the same bank personnel don't always work where the safety deposit boxes are located."

"Alright guys," interjected Tony, "let's get back to reading the journal, and then we can get down to planning our next move."

Tony read for ten more minutes and then he paused. He could read the faces of his friends.

"This is some bad shit! They have a bug in the Chief's office, and probably know almost everything we know. Frank, have you been keeping the Chief up to date on what we've been doing?"

Frank shook his head. "Yeah, I've been in almost constant contact with him about our investigation."

"Shit!" said Tony. "On top of that, we now know that there are two more cops in IAD working with Kirby: Harris and Ortiz, along with the three uniforms in the evidence property room. That's eight dirty cops that we know of, and there might be even more. At least we now know that Kirby's boss, Inspector Billings, ain't dirty. Frank, do you think we might be able to bring him in on our investigation?"

"First of all," said Frank, "I'm sorry! I should've been more careful when I was talking with the Chief. I should've known better."

"Bullshit!" interrupted Tony. "You don't owe us any apology, and I speak for everybody in this room. No one could've known they would be sophisticated enough to bug the Chief's office, and besides, now we know and can act accordingly."

"Thanks guys. I'll make sure any further contact I have with the Chief will be away from his office, and as far as Inspector Billings goes, I have an idea of how we might be able to use him. Let me finish figuring out my approach, and I'll let you all know before I make that move."

"Before we leave," said Tony, "we've got to figure out how to get some solid evidence against these assholes. What we've got so far, and I'm not bitching, is Maurice's journal, some pictures, a list of the players, and where some of their money is stashed. That's great, but now we've got to turn somebody so that we can find out who the real boss of their operation is. We know from reading Maurice's journal that it's not Kirby, or that rat Lorenzo. We need to find the head man and shut him down."

"Lamont," said Frank, "I'll need you to start watching Lorenzo. He's the one who'll lead us to the head man—and make sure you're careful. Lorenzo is a piece of shit, but he ain't stupid."

CHAPTER THIRTEEN

After leaving the park, Kirby decided he had waited long enough to get rid of Spinella and made a call to Lorenzo. When he answered, Kirby was abrupt. "Meet me in twenty minutes. Our usual place." He hung up.

Kirby parked his car a block away from the coffee shop, making sure he hadn't been followed. A glance through the window showed Lorenzo and Timmy seated in the rear, drinking coffee. When Lorenzo spotted him he signaled to Timmy to move to another table. Kirby gave Timmy a nod and sat down across from Lorenzo.

"Ok, Kirby, why are we here? What's the big emergency?"

"You gotta understand something Lorenzo, that snake guy you got working for you knows too much. He can cause us some serious problems if somewhere down the road he decides to switch sides and throw us to the wolves. If you think about it, he's the only one who can tie you into the attempted murder of a police officer. Not only that, but I've checked out this cop Spinella, and if he finds out any information about who put that snake in his house, he's the

kind of cop who can really cause us some serious problems."
He then outlined his plan to get rid of the snake guy, and take
Spinella out of the picture at the same time.

"Here's the way I see it happening," said Kirby. "Your guy
messed up when his snake thing didn't pan out at Spinella's
house, and he messed up again when he stole a thirty-eight
he found there. If I remember correctly, you told me that this
guy was a professional and always wore gloves, right? Well
if that's the case, then the only fingerprints on the gun he
stole would have to belong to Spinella. So, if this snake guy
is taken out with the thirty-eight from Spinella's house, and
it's left at the scene, the prints on the gun will lead right back
to Spinella, and he'll be out of our hair for the foreseeable
future."

Lorenzo offered up a cryptic smile. "Ok, I'll get the piece
to you right away, but *don't get caught!*"

Kirby felt like he had just been punched in the stomach.
He took a moment to recover.

"No fucking way! I'll get the gun back to you! Remember,
you gave it to me. Anyway, it's your man, your mess. You
clean it up!"

Lorenzo eyeballed him keenly for a moment or two, and
then casually threw up his hands. "Ok, I'll take care of it."

Kirby wasted no time making his exit. He drove home
hoping to relax and finish his plan of escape.

It was almost midnight and Vince Kelly was in the basement
of his small bungalow, located in the southeast section of
Anacostia, getting the small rodents and other food together

for tomorrow's feeding. Vince took great pride in his unique collection, doting on the fact that collectors of exotic snakes from all over the country came to him for advice and direction. He himself had never been much of a physical specimen; while attending high school some of his classmates called him "Stick" because he was so thin. As a result of having so few friends while growing up, he became passionate about collecting snakes, and over the years began to acquire many rare specimens.

To look at him, one would never know that he was also one of the top professional burglars on the east coast. Because he was so very good at what he did, those persons who did business with him understood in advance that they would have to pay heavily for his services. As a result, his reputation for both success and discretion grew, and there was always a list of clients waiting to engage his services. This success enabled him to acquire and expand his collection of exotic snakes, to the extent that he was considering a move to larger quarters.

Vince had just finished closing the lid on a box containing several small rodents when he heard his front doorbell ring. Looking at his watch, he saw that it almost midnight. He went to one of the cages that contained a recently fed carpet viper that he had worked with over several years and knew to be relatively docile, especially after eating, and gingerly removed it from its cage. He knew he was taking a calculated risk by taking the deadly snake with him, but lately he had begun to have a bad feeling about some of his clients. Anyway, he'd been bitten before, several times in fact, and he knew his system had built up anti-bodies against most of the neurotoxic venomous snake bites he might encounter, even the carpet viper. At the very least, he felt that he would be able to get to a hospital in enough time to counteract the viper's bite if it even happened.

Approaching the front door, Vince saw a silhouette through the door's small glass inset. He turned on his front porch light to see who was there. It was Timmy, one of Lorenzo's guys.

"Hey man, what are you doing here this late at night?" Vince said after he opened the door.

"Can I come in?" Timmy replied. "Lorenzo needs you to do something for him right away."

"Yeah, come on in." Vince stepped back from the door, and after Timmy entered, closed and locked the front door behind him.

"Hey, man, any chance of getting a beer? I'm dying of thirst," said Timmy as he moved further into the living room.

"Come on in the kitchen and I'll get us a beer," said Vince.

"Vince," said Timmy as the snake man walked towards the kitchen doorway, "stop for a minute. I need to tell you something."

The sound of the gun being cocked caused Vince to turn towards Timmy just as a shot rang out. The bullet caught Vince in the throat and knocked him to the floor. He lay in the doorway between the living room and kitchen.

Timmy quickly walked over to where he lay, unmoving. Standing over the fallen man, he could see the blood squirting out of his neck with every heartbeat and his open eyes looking up at him.

Timmy hesitated, then uttered "Sorry man." He squeezed the trigger a second time, sending a bullet into Vince's head. Blood and brain matter spattered the walls and floor.

Timmy stood over the fallen Vince, his legs shaking with the adrenalin rushing thru his system. After carefully placing the gun that Lorenzo had given him under a chair near the doorway into the kitchen, he turned to leave. Something in front of him on the floor moved, almost causing him to stumble. Instinctively kicking out with his foot to move whatever it was out of his way, he felt something hit his pants leg. Thinking nothing of it he went out the way he had entered, carefully closing the door behind him.

He casually walked away from Vince's house without a backward glance, noting with relief that nothing outside was stirring. By taking care of Vince, he had pretty much cemented his position with Lorenzo as a guy who could be counted on to get the job done. Walking towards where he had parked his car, he thought about those guys in those mafia movies who finally made their "bones," and afterwards began to get the respect they deserved. He was now a "hit man," and big things were going to start happening to him.

He began to feel a little pain in his right leg. He pushed it out of his mind as he got into his car and started the engine. Slowly he made his way onto Minnesota Avenue. After a few minutes, he sensed a burning pain in his leg and a gradual feeling of disorientation. Soon, his leg went completely numb. His tingling foot pressed down hard on the accelerator. He gripped the steering wheel, trying to steer down a street that seemed to be getting narrower each second. Something was seriously wrong with him. He had to get to Lorenzo's place fast. Racing down Minnesota Avenue S.E. towards its intersection with Pennsylvania Avenue, the car continued to pick up speed. At nearly eighty miles an hour, Timmy's car careened into the intersection as he slumped forward, his hands sliding from the wheel. It drifted to the right side of the road where it struck a parked car, became airborne and flipped end-over-end, finally coming to rest crushed against a street light pole. It took nearly ten minutes before a bystander on the deserted street phoned the police.

CHAPTER FOURTEEN

After the others had gone, Tony attempted to get some sleep on one of the tiny cots Frank had placed in the basement hideaway. He took off his shoes and settled back on the stiff canvas. Bone tired, sleep evaded him nonetheless. Thoughts about the recent developments in their investigation, along with the near-fatal snake incident, kept him awake and fidgety. Finally, suffering from sheer exhaustion, he was able to drift off into a troubled sleep.

When he woke up the following morning Tony felt like a new man, and after a quick shower and a change of clothes in the small bathroom that Frank had made available to them, checked in with his office. After identifying himself and asking to be put through to the captain, Anita informed him that the captain was waiting for his call.

"Tony, where are you?" Frank said anxiously when he answered.

"I'm still at our spot boss, and I feel like I need to be doing something constructive other than just sitting here. Do we have any new information?

"I haven't heard anything yet, but we've got a lot of feelers out with our local snitches. We're sure to hear something soon."

"I'll probably be coming in shortly unless you need me right away," said Tony.

"There's nothing major going on here right now," said Frank, "but Natalie just stopped by after making the funeral arrangements for Maurice and asked if we would help organize the wake. Of course I told her we would be glad to help in any way we could."

"Thanks, Boss," whispered Tony, overcome with emotion.

"No thanks necessary, Tony. He was one of ours. If you don't feel up to it right now I'll take care of it, and see you later on this afternoon."

"I'm okay," said Tony. "I'll be there as quickly as I can."

After putting his cell phone back in his pocket, Tony was suddenly filled with rage. He leaned against the wall, tears rolling down his face and his large fists clenched, and slowly slid down to the floor.

Sometime later, his emotions recovered, he weaved his way through an almost empty squad room towards the captain's office. He knocked on the door and heard Frank's grunt telling him to enter. Frank told him to sit and went to his desk and sat down across from him. He began to outline the plans for Maurice's wake. Tony was impressed. Frank had thought of just about everything. He had even included both Lina and Anita in his plan. Together, the girls would be in charge of the food, which was being provided gratis by a large grocery chain, in honor of the slain officer's sacrifice. When he finished, he sighed deeply and leaned across his desk.

"Tony," he whispered, "right after the wake, I want to start wrapping this whole thing up. We'll go with what evidence we have at that time. Since I last talked to you, I've been making some discreet inquiries. I have a friend who I've known since we were in grade school together that just happens to be a Federal court judge, and she's willing to work with us on this."

"Did you lay out the whole situation to your friend?" Tony asked, keeping his voice low.

"Yes I did, and she's given me a few tips that will help us make our case without either one of us stepping on our dicks."

"Can you trust her?"

"With my life. Is that good enough?"

"Yeah, Boss. That sounds great. I can't wait to get these slime balls."

"For right now," Frank added, still keeping his voice low, "I want you to go about your normal routine, and let everyone think you're still working those liquor store cases. Tony, keep in mind, the funeral and the wake will be over quickly, and then we'll start the ass kicking process."

Feeling a new sense of energy, Tony stood and shook his captain's hand.

"Boss, I'm gonna keep Lamont on Kirby until after the funeral, okay?"

"Yeah, keep the surveillance going, but tell Lamont to be extremely careful because we don't want him getting hurt, or them getting wise to us at this stage of the investigation."

As Tony turned to leave, he heard Frank quietly say, "Anthony, stay in touch—and watch your ass!"

Driving away from headquarters, Tony called Lina and confirmed that she was still on for their eleven thirty lunch date.

After sharing a tuna fish sandwich and a couple of cold beers at the bar, Lina and Tony moved from the club's bar area over to a unoccupied table where they could talk without being overheard. As soon as they sat down, she began to pepper him with questions about Maurice. Before answering her questions, he took a moment to admire the bright yellow dress she wore that showed off both her beautiful figure and olive complextion. He could also tell by the concerned look on her beautiful face that she was worried.

"Honey, I'm scared. What's going on? Why would someone kill Maurice? Do you have any idea who killed him? It happened at your house—were they after you, too? Are you in some kind of trouble?"

Tony tried to reassure her. "Listen, we've started to develop some good leads in the case, but we have a long way to go before this is finished. Baby, I wish I could tell you what's going on, but I can't right now because it might get people hurt. What I can tell you is, someone is coming after us, and we're going find out who they are and we'll deal with them. And you can stop worrying. I'm not in any trouble. Look, I'm scared too, but I think that right now, that's a good thing. I'm gonna be careful, and I'm gonna get whoever was responsible for killing Maurice."

Lina sat back in her chair, looked at Tony for what seemed like a long minute, then reached out and took his hand and squeezed it. Tony hoped she wouldn't break down in tears, but all she did was lean over and kiss him on the cheek.

"You be careful. I've gotten used to you being around, and I'd like to keep it that way."

CHAPTER FIFTEEN

Tony said goodbye to Lina and called Lamont to arrange a meeting in front of headquarters so he could be brought up to speed on Kirby's movements. Arriving in front of headquarters a few minutes later, he saw that Lamont was already there and sounded his horn to get his attention. Lamont waved and started towards Tony's cruiser.

"Tony, I've got some news," Lamont blurted out as soon as he got into the car.

"What you got?" asked Tony.

"Our boy Kirby had a meeting with a couple of dudes early yesterday afternoon. They met in a coffee shop just off of Maryland Avenue N.E. One of the guy's fits the description we have of this dude, Lorenzo. There was another guy with him that seemed to be some kind of bodyguard or something. Don't know who this other guy is, but I've got feelers out with some of the brothers and I expect to know something any time now."

"Good work. Were you able to get close enough to hear anything?"

"No way. It's a small coffee shop, and I didn't want to blow my cover. Anyway, your boy Kirby seemed to be real chummy with the Lorenzo guy, except for having some sort of argument towards the end of their meeting."

"What about the other guy that was there? What did he do?"

"He didn't take part in the meeting. All he did was sit on his ass at a nearby table and drink coffee."

"What did he look like?" asked Tony.

"He's a white guy, looked to be in his mid-forties, light brown hair and skinny. Anyway, I got a picture of him with my cell phone, so you can check him out later."

"What happened after the meeting?"

"The Lorenzo guy and his buddy left first, and then Kirby left. I decided that since I pretty much know where Kirby is because of our tracking bug, I would follow this Lorenzo guy and find out where his crib is, and then check on Kirby. Anyway, I got an address for our boy Lorenzo, but the other dude got away from me."

"Great work, Lamont. Here's where we are. First thing we have to do is get through the funeral and the wake. Frank and I are going to be tied up for the next two days, and we want you and Scopes to hold the fort while we take care of Maurice. After that, Frank has decided that we're gonna start kicking ass. We'll call right after the wake, and set up a meeting to plan how it's gonna go down."

"Sounds good. I'll tell Scopes and in the meantime, I'll stay on Kirby, but before I leave, Tony, I need to ask you something. Ain't it about time that I get a piece to carry with me?"

"Lamont," replied Tony, trying to stifle a laugh, "we'll discuss that when we get together again, ok?"

"That works for me," said Lamont as he exited the car.

Tony drove over to Natalie's house to discuss some of the details for Maurice's services. Leaving his car across the street form Natalie's place, Tony saw an even bigger group of young men gathered around the entrance to her doorway. Expecting a confrontation, he was prepared for whatever happened, but, other than a nod from the same young man who had spoken to him the first time he visited Natalie, nothing happened, except a pathway opened all the way to Natalie's front door. Once inside, Tony explained to Natalie about the police honor guard that would be made available for the funeral.

"Natalie, the department is going to have an honor guard at the funeral home, standing right by the casket the whole time Maurice is there. That's one of the honors available to a fallen officer. The chief will also be there, and would like to say a few words if that would be acceptable to the family."

"Tony, that's wonderful. Maurice would like that. Please let the chief know that we really appreciate him being there and consider it an honor for him to speak."

He discussed the gravesite ceremonies, along with details about the wake, which was scheduled to be held immediately after leaving the gravesite.

Natalie started to thank Tony for all the work he had done, but he quickly set the record straight, explaining that there were so many of his fellow officers volunteering to help that they had been forced to cut the list at fifty. He also told her about the response from the business community.

"Natalie, they've sent food, money, and even set up a hot line for tips from the community," said Tony. "Anyway, I have to get. There's a lot of work left to do before tomorrow, and I'm way behind." Natalie smiled and took his hand.

"Tony, before you go, tell me what's going on with the investigation. I need to know what's happening." Tony squeezed Natalie's hand, leaned over, and kissed her on the cheek. He spoke softly to her.

"Nat, it's gonna go down real soon. We're going to nail the bastards that did this. Keep this quiet, and don't say nothing to nobody until it's done, ok?"

Natalie nodded, hugged him and without another word being spoken, walked with him to the door.

CHAPTER SIXTEEN

Kirby sat in his livingroom, musing in his favorite overstuffed lounge chair with a cold beer in his hand. He was ready to walk away from the mess he had gotten himself into. Now that his wife was gone, the house, along with all its contents, meant almost nothing to him. Immersed in self-mockery and self-doubt, he forgot that he was in the best position of his life. Snapping back to reality, he figured he had enough money to completely disappear, locate a place where no one would ever find him, and where the banking laws insured privacy. He envisioned himself in bed with a young, long-legged girl who would fuck his brains out for a few pieces of cheap jewelry and some fancy dinners.

The house phone rang, shattering his reverie. He answered cautiously, since calls on his house line generally came from the office.

"Lieutenant Kirby." To his surprise, the voice on the other end was Lorenzo's.

"Yeah, this is me. What the hell are you doing calling me on my land line? You know better than that! Call me right back on the cell!" Kirby slammed down the phone and went to get the burner phone from his jacket pocket. He returned to his lounge chair to wait for Lorenzo's call. Moments later the phone vibrated in his hand.

"I'm here! "How many times have we talked about phone security?" snarled Kirby. "You and I both know how insecure phones conversations are nowadays, and you just broke one of my cardinal rules."

"Fuck you, man!" shouted Lorenzo. "I don't work for you, remember that! I'm calling to tell you that the situation with our mutual friend is being handled. I'm waiting for Timmy to call with the good news. In the meantime, relax and try to remember who's calling the shots here, ok?"

Mollified, Kirby softened his tone. "Yeah, I hear you. Call me when you get the word, ok?" It was too late; Lorenzo was gone.

He put the burner phone down on the coffee table beside his plush lounge chair, took a sip from his beer and began to rehash the short conversation. He was gratified that his suggestion to get rid of the snake guy was going to happen right away. He would need to make one more trip to the evidence room to collect the drugs and then get his share of the money. Then, he could disappear. He was acutely aware that Lorenzo, and whomever he reported to, would eventually need someone to take the fall when their operation was discovered, and the clown taking the fall wouldn't be him. He would make a clean break, with no strings attached to him or his money.

He went into the kitchen, got another cold beer from the fridge and returned to his chair. Taking a big swallow, he pointed the remote at the television and found a local news channel; reclining with his feet up, he started to doze off. Lost in that world between total relaxation and sleep, Kirby's subconscious registered a familiar name being mentioned on the television. He almost fell off the lounge chair. He had just missed part of a news report about someone by the name of Timothy Coglin being killed in a car accident in southeast Washington. He frantically began to switch channels to see if he could catch any of the other news stations reporting on the accident. When that proved unsuccessful, Kirby called the department's Accident Investigation Unit to get the information he needed. Using the name of a detective who worked for him in the Internal Affairs Division, he requested an update on the vehicle fatality that had recently occurred in Southeast. The officer on phone duty, his nerves shaken upon answering a call from the Rat Squad, was quick to supply the information; he was also relieved when the detective didn't ask further questions. In fact, the officer was so relieved that he failed to note the call from IAD on his phone log sheet.

Kirby collapsed in his lounge chair and tried to make some sense of what he had just learned. Timmy was dead. Was his death accidental, or did Lorenzo have anything to do with it? Had Timmy taken care of the snake guy? Was there anything in Timmy's vehicle that could point back to him? Kirby had a moment of sheer panic—things were starting to unravel. He'd better check with Lorenzo about Timmy's accident.

He grabbed the throwaway cell and punched in Lorenzo's number. After several rings, Lorenzo answered, shouting into the phone that he was very busy at the moment.

"It's me," said Kirby. "Timmy's dead. I just saw it on the news channel. They said it was some kind of car accident." He heard Lorenzo shout at someone in the background before he got back on the line.

"What the fuck are you talking about? Tell me what you heard," asked an annoyed Lorenzo.

"Sorry about interrupting your evening, but like I just said, Timmy was killed in an automobile accident over in Southeast Washington a while ago. I heard about it on the news channel. A reporter at the scene got the driver's name from somebody who found his wallet in the street, so I called down to AIU, and they confirmed that he had died in the accident."

"What the fuck is AIU? Talk in plain fucking English, ok?" Lorenzo was growing more impatient.

Kirby could hear more shouting in the background and took a deep breath. He gathered he was not the only one getting nervous about Timmy's death.

"AIU only means 'Accident Investigation Unit,' okay? They confirmed that a Timothy Coglin was killed in an automobile accident over in Southeast. Have you heard from Timmy?"

"Not since I sent him to visit our mutual friend. Hang up. I'll call you later."

Kirby started to say something, but quickly realized Lorenzo had already hung up.

CHAPTER SEVENTEEN

The funeral was held at the Grace Reformed Church on Fifteenth Street in Northwest Washington D.C., notable for the beautifully carved biblical scenes in its white stone façade, and the occasional historic attendance by President Theodore Roosevelt during his administration. The service went smoothly, if not a bit too long. Because this was a funeral for a murdered cop, covered by the national media, every two-bit politician and city official had to offer some remarks. They used this tragedy as a way for them to get their names in the papers, or on the evening news, and Tony hated it. In spite of all the bullshit spouted by the dignitaries at the church, Maurice would have been real proud of the send-off he received. The line of official vehicles stretched for over a mile as they made their way to the gravesite. Saying goodbye to his friend and partner was very emotional for Tony, but he held it together long enough to escort Natalie and her family to their limo right after the gravesite service ended.

The wake was held at the Fraternal Order of Police lodge hall, on seventh street N.W., in downtown Washington D.C.

The century-old gray stone building had recently been renovated and contained a small restaurant with a seating area, a bar, and several meeting rooms for lodge business. Immediately after Tony arrived at the lodge hall, Natalie approached him and asked about the investigation into her brother's death.

"Natalie," said Tony, "I'm working on it, and we're making progress. That's all I can say right now. Believe me, we're gonna get whoever did this."

"Is that the best you can tell me?" replied Natalie with anger in her voice.

"For right now, yes," said Tony. "I'm making progress, and the fewer people who know what I'm doing, the better. You've got to hang in there and let me do my thing, okay?"

Tearing up, Natalie suddenly reached out, grabbed Tony by both hands, pulled him close to her body and whispered to him.

"Tony, I want the fuckers dead, you understand me?"

Tony pulled himself away from Natalie, looked at her for a moment, nodded, and walked away. As he made his way across the room towards a group of Maurice's fellow detectives, he noticed his boss urgently waving for him to come over to where he and two other men were standing. Frank appeared highly agitated.

Tony recognizedthe same two detectives who had responded to Maurice's shooting. This was not going to be good.

"Hey, Captain. You need me for something?" he asked when he joined them.

"Sergeant, you know Fitzpatrick and Sipe, from Homicide; they're handling Maurice's case," said a suddenly formal Captain McCathran.

"Yeah, I know them. Thanks for coming, guys," Tony repied.

"Sergeant," said his captain, "they're not here for Maurice's wake; they want to talk to you about another case."

"Really? What case would that be, and while I'm at it, what's so important that you need to barge in on my partner's wake to talk to me? Couldn't it wait until tomorrow when I'm in my office?"

"Sergeant," said Frank, "why don't we go over to the kitchen to discuss this?" He quickly turned around and started towards the banquet hall's kitchen, followed by the two Homicide Detectives. Tony thought about telling the detectives to go fuck themselves, but instead followed along to see what they were up to.

As soon as they entered the kitchen, Tony's boss turned to the men and, in a voice dripping with sarcasm said, "All right, let's get to it."

The big detective, Fitzpatrick, looked at Tony. "Sergeant, we have reason to believe that you're a person of interest in a homicide case we're investigating."

"If this wasn't so stupid, I'd throw the both of you out of here on your asses," said Tony, his voice dripping with malice. Let's hear the rest of it."

Fitzpatrick took a step towards Tony, and with undisguised animosity said, "I don't have to take no shit from you, Sergeant. I only came here as a courtesy; I didn't have to do that."

"Sergeant, take it easy, and listen to what he has to say," said Frank, trying to ease the mounting tension between the two.

"Sure boss," agreed Tony. "Go ahead, Detective. Knock yourself out."

Fitzpatrick began to outline the circumstances surrounding a murder which had occurred in the Anacostia area of Southeast Washington the previous day. The deceased was a white male, approximately thirty to forty years of age, and the body had been found with a gunshot wounds to the head in a house full of poisonous snakes.

"What's this got to do with me?" asked Tony.

"We had the gun found at the scene tested for prints, and guess whose prints were on the murder weapon? Yours!" replied a smiling Fitzpatrick.

"*My* prints?" asked Tony.

"Yes, yours were the only prints found on the gun that we think fired the fatal shot," said Fitzpatrick. "We're still waiting on ballistics to match the bullet taken from the victim to the gun found at the scene. As soon as we get time of death from the medical examiner, we're going to need to know where you were during that time period. In the meantime, we'll need you to come down to the office and give us a statement."

Before Tony could say anything, Frank jumped in. "Sergeant, don't say a word. Let me handle this right now, okay?"

"Sure, Boss. I'll be happy to watch and listen."

Captain McCathran pulled himself up to all of his five-foot, eight-inch height and started in on the two men standing in front of him. "Both of you assholes should've done your homework before you came barging in here disrupting a wake for a fellow officer. Not only did you two sacks of shit show a complete lack of common sense coming here, you should have researched the weapon found at the scene of the homicide before you even thought about confronting Sergeant Spinella."

"Wait just a minute," said a visibly upset Fitzpatrick, "you can't talk to us like that. We're investigating a homicide, and I don't work for you, so don't be giving me a bunch of shit."

Captain McCathran's face was beginning to turn a bright red. He moved closer to Fitzpatrick. "Officer, if you say another word, I will suspend you right now for insubordination to a superior officer." Frank's voice was low and deliberately measured. "After that, I will document your complete lack of professionalism for not doing the required routine check of a weapon found at a murder scene before confronting an alleged suspect. If you need Sergeant Spinella to make a statement in regards to the issues that you pointed out to him today, I'll see to it that he appears at the Homicide office tomorrow morning, along with full legal representation. Is that clear?"

"I hear you," said a shaken Fitzpatrick as he turned to leave.

"I hear you, *what?*" demanded a totally pissed off Captain McCathran.

Fitzpatrick turned around. "I hear you, Captain, *sir.*"

"That's better. You're dismissed!"

Both detectives immediately left the kitchen. When they were gone, Tony gave his boss a look of concern. "That was awesome. What happens now?"

"What's gonna happen is exactly what I said was gonna happen. We show up tomorrow at Homicide, and before that, the first thing you do is cover your ass with a personal timeline. It should be easy for you to show where you were when this homicide took place. You know the drill. In the meantime, we get you a good lawyer, and it ain't gonna be one from the union either. I have some good friends who happen to be top notch defense lawyers that owe me a few favors. Once we get your statement done, we need to call a meeting of the crew with everyone there, including my ace in the hole."

"You're talking about your judge friend, right?" asked Tony.

"You bet your ass I am, and now we start to put all the pieces together. I'll let you know sometime tomorrow afternoon, after your interview, when to set up our meeting. Go out there and mingle while I reach out to my lawyer friends to see which one will be nominated to represent you, even though you don't need one. I'll be out shortly, and give you the skinny on tomorrow."

"Thanks, Boss. I owe you," said Tony.

"You don't owe me nothing. Get outta here and mingle," said a smiling Frank as he put his cell phone to his ear.

CHAPTER EIGHTEEN

Leaving the wake, Fitzpatrick, still fuming over his confrontation with Captain McCathran, fumbled for his cell phone. He had to let Kirby know what had just happened.

"Hey Fitz," said Dave, "That captain was pissed, and I've heard from people who know him that he's not someone to mess with. I know a couple of detectives who work for him and they say he's a bitch to work for if you don't play it straight. You know, it might be a good idea for us to think about taking some annual leave and lay low for a while."

Fitzpatrick lashed out with the back of his hand and struck his partner across the face. The blow caused Dave's head to violently strike the cruiser's side window with such force that it knocked him unconscious and caused the window to crack in several places. With his partner slumped in the front seat, Fitzpatrick frantically started looking for a side street to turn into.

After finding a suitable spot in a quiet neighborhood of single family homes to pull over and park, Fitzpatrick felt only a slight tinge of remorse for what he had done to his partner. He thought about how useless Dave really was to their plans. For a brief moment, as he was checking his partner's injuries, he thought how easy it would be, while he had the chance, to rid himself of what might become a problem for him down the road. Instead, Fitzpatrick, as gently as he knew how, began to pat his partner's bloody cheek. As Dave started to come around, the big detective attempted to wipe the blood from his face with an old napkin left over from a fast food outlet.

Once he came around, in between moans of pain, Dave asked what had happened.

"Man, I'm sorry," said Fitzpatrick, conveniently noting his partner's memory loss. "We almost got into a head on and I had to swerve to avoid it; then we hit a curb, and your head hit the window."

"I need to go to the hospital; I think my nose is broken, and I'm not seeing so good,"mumbled a barely coherent Dave while holding his head.

Sticking with his story about the near collision, Fitzpatrick contacted the police dispatcher, related what had occurred and asked permission to take his partner to the nearby Hospital Center. After assuring dispatch that his partner only suffered a blow to the head, the dispatcher replied that a fire department ambulance had already been dispatched to their location, and to stand by his location for its arrival. The dispatcher also informed him that his supervisor had been notified and was also responding. While waiting for the ambulance to arrive, he began kicking himself in the ass over the situation he had put himself into. He had acted too quickly in notifying the dispatcher about his partner's injury, and realized too late that he could have just dropped him off at a hospital emergency room. Dave could have received treatment as a walk-in, with no questions asked. *What's done is done.*

The fire department EMT's arrived in no time, and after evaluating Dave for injuries, decided they were going to transport him to the hospital center to be checked out. Just as the ambulance pulled away from the scene, a police scout car pulled up and two uniformed officers got out. They walked over to where Fitzpatrick was seated in the unmarked cruiser and informed him that they were there to take the accident report. The two officers left the scene as soon as they completed their report.

An older homicide detective, who had been patiently waiting for the uniformed officers to take their report and leave, walked over to the cruiser's driver side window, bent down and rapped to get Fitzpatrick's attention. Startled by the appearance of his supervisor, Fitzpatrick quickly got out of the cruiser and began to explain his version of what had happened.

Fitz was sure his sergeant wasn't fooled by the so-called accident. He wouldn't be a problem, though, because everyone in the Homicide Squad knew the crusty old Detective Sergeant was only months away from putting his papers in for retirement. He wouldn't be making any waves. As long as nobody did anything crazy, he didn't really give a shit as long as it didn't interfere with his coming retirement. After answering a few questions and being ordered to have a full report on his lieutenant's desk by the following morning, the old detective left the scene. Breathing a sigh of relief, Fitzpatrick immediately placed a call to Kirby. His other boss wasn't going to be happy with him.

CHAPTER NINETEEN

With Tony out of the kitchen, Frank called Lamont and told him that the time had come to begin putting all the pieces together. He instructed him to go back into Kirby's place when it was safe to do so, take all the safe deposit keys, cash, passports, and the gun, and bring them to their meeting place. He cautioned Lamont to stay in close touch with Scopes as to the whereabouts of Kirby before going inside his house. At the last minute, Frank remembered to tell Lamont to double-check that Scopes had made copies of all the pictures he had taken with his cell phone of the evidence in Kirby's place, especially the gun.

Frank then placed a call to his friend Virginia Gills, a sitting federal judge, at her home, and asked if she would be available in the near future to meet with him and go over the evidence they had gathered. When asked by the judge exactly when he wanted to meet, Frank replied, "As soon as possible."

The judge told Frank that she would consult her schedule and call him right back with her availability. Frank called

Scopes to notify him of the coming meeting, and told him to stay close and not to do anything stupid.

After leaving the kitchen, Tony walked over to where Lina stood drinking coffee, and began to bring her up to speed about what had just happened with the two homicide detectives.

"Honey, are you in trouble?" she asked with a puzzled look.

"No, I'm gonna be fine. I can account for my whereabouts during the time this homicide went down. For that matter, I distinctly remember enjoying your company for a good part of that time," said Tony, laughing out loud, as she turned bright red with embarrassment. Hoping to change the subject, Lina noticed Frank crossing the hall floor towards them.

"Here comes Frank."

Tony turned and saw his boss stop and put his cell phone to his ear. After a moment, Frank put his phone back in his pocket and with a grin on his face walked over to Tony and Lina.

"What's up boss?"

"Tony, my boy, tomorrow is gonna be a good day. I've got you one of this town's best lawyers. He'll meet us tomorrow morning in my office. We'll go over the situation with him, and then go and kick a little ass over in Homicide."

"Who did you get for me?"

"Angelo Torella, probably the best criminal defense attorney in the country."

"How did you pull that off? I mean, how can I afford someone like him to represent me? You know I don't make that kind of money, Boss."

"Don't worry about it, Tony. He owes me a few favors, and besides, we grew up together as kids. He was best man at my wedding. As a matter of fact, while we were growing up together, I was the only non-Italian that he ever hung out with, and don't worry, he won't charge you a penny. Anyway, listen up; I'll need you at my office at six a.m. sharp to meet with Angelo. Bring the information you'll need to document your whereabouts and anyone you were with, and make sure it shows the times."

"Thanks, Boss. I really appreciate this."

"No thanks necessary, just be on time—and by the way, the phone call I got just a minute ago was my ace in the hole. We're on for tomorrow afternoon. I want you to call the guys and set it up for three o'clock. Make sure they're all there," said Frank as he walked away.

"Gotcha. Consider it done," replied a relieved Tony.

"You want to go somewhere and just be alone, honey?"

"Got any place in mind?" asked Tony, mischief clearly in his voice.

"Let's get a bottle of cheap wine, go to my place, and I'll be your personal trainer for tonight," she said. "How's that sound, big boy?"

"You're on!" said Tony, with a big smile on his face. "I've got lots of kinks in my body that needs attention and I hope you're up to the task."

CHAPTER TWENTY

Kirby sat in his living room trying to piece his plan together. His house phone rang, and again, thinking it might be the office, he answered in his official tone, "Lieutenant Kirby." After a moment of silence, he heard Fitzpatrick's voice.

"Call me back on my cell, you idiot!" snapped Kirby, and he quickly hung up the phone. Moments later, his cell phone buzzed.

"Yes!"

After listening to a rattled Fitzpatrick explain what was going on, Kirby began to feel like a steel band was constricting his airway. His brain was struggling to process everything Fitzpatrick was telling him. He had better start making an immediate decision to separate himself from these assholes he was involved with, before they took him down with them.

"Meet me in thirty minutes at the coffee shop," Kirby said as calmly as he could.

"What coffee shop?"

"The one down the street from headquarters, on Seventh Street," said Kirby, ending the call.

Kirby pulled up in front of the coffee shop a few minutes later and saw Fitzpatrick sitting at a table by the front window. He waved, then pointed to his cup mouthing a question as to Kirby's desire for coffee. Kirby waved him off and waited for Fitzpatrick to exit the café. He paid for a go cup at the counter, walked out and got in Kirby's car.

The two men said nothing for a couple of minutes after Kirby pulled away. Fitzpatrick opened up first, spilling everything that had gone wrong earlier during his confrontation with Sergeant Spinella and Captain McCathran. He also related the details about punching Sipe and the story he cooked up.

Kirby was pissed, but reasoned that it was all coming to an end anyway, so why not go for broke and use this idiot to help him make his plan work. He forced a disingenuous grin, and noticing a grocery store coming up, he pulled into the parking lot adjacent to the store and parked. Turning to Fitz he said,

"It's all gonna be okay, Fitz. You and I just need to start thinking about ourselves, and how we can make more money from this deal. Lorenzo doesn't do anything, and he gets most of the money. I think from now on, you and me should start taking our rightful share of the profits, because we take most of the risks."

Fitzpatrick, sensing a new drift in their relationship, heaved a sigh of relief and nodded his head in agreement.

"We might have to take some drastic action to get where we need to be, so I want to know right now if you're with me all the way. I don't want any bullshit! Flat out, are you with me or not?" said a suddenly serious Kirby. He took his eyes off the other cars in the parking lot and looked directly at Fitzpatrick.

"All the way, boss, all the way," Fitzpatrick said, shaking his head rapidly in affirmation.

Kirby outlined his plot to remove Lorenzo from the whole scheme.

"We're going to take Lorenzo out, but before we do, we need to know who his contact is on the inside. I need you to start watching him right away, find out where he goes, and who he talks to. We need to know as soon as possible, because this is all coming to a head, and you and I need a big score before the you-know-what hits the fan and the whole deal falls apart."

"Boss, can I use Dave to help with watching Lorenzo?" asked Fitzpatrick. "I know he's not the brightest bulb in the box, but he can be of some use with the surveillance, and that way we can switch off and keep the coverage constant."

"Do you think he can be trusted after what went down between you two? Do you really believe he bought that crazy-assed story about the phantom car?" asked a skeptical Kirby.

"Yeah, Boss," replied Fitz. "He totally bought it, and he'll do whatever I tell him to do because he's scared of me, and he knows I'll kill him if he messes me over."

"Okay, go ahead and use him," said Kirby, "but don't tell him anything about what you and I discussed, understand? Also make sure that it doesn't cause any problems with your office because of his being on sick leave. And remember, we need this information as soon as possible, so we can figure out our next step."

"Boss," said Fitz, "no disrespect intended, but before I leave, I need to know how much I'm going to get out of this new arrangement."

Quickly calculating the amount he could offer Fitzpatrick without hurting his bottom line, Kirby deciding he could afford to be generous, at least for the near future, replied,

"How does forty percent of the money we get for the drugs sound to you?"

"G-g-great, Boss! Whatever you need, I'm your man," stuttered Fitz, taken aback by his partner's generosity.

Kirby told him to start his surveillance on Lorenzo the next day. "Stay in close touch," he reminded him. Kirby started his car, while again reminding Fitzpatrick to begin watching Lorenzo tomorrow, and to stay in close touch.

CHAPTER TWENTY-ONE

Tony awakened snuggled up close to Lina's back, feeling well rested and strangely at peace with himself. Despite his early morning meeting at the squad office with Frank and his new lawyer, he selfishly wanted just a few more moments of being close to her before he had to get ready. He relished the softness of her skin next to his, pulled her closer and began to relive their earlier lovemaking in his mind. He was becoming aroused and started to calculate the amount of time he would have before he really needed to be on his way. Hoping there might be just enough time, he began to gently rub her back. He caressed her, working his way to her stomach, just below her breasts. She stirred slightly when he stroked the underside of her breast and surprised him when she reached around and grabbed his erection.

"As much as I would like to pounce on you baby, you need to get this thing," and she gave his penis a squeeze, "and the rest of you in the shower and get ready. You know how important this meeting is!" She gave him one more teasing squeeze, then turned around, gave him a kiss, and pushed him out of bed.

Twenty minutes later Tony left Lina's apartment on his way to the meeting; he was greeted by a mostly clear early morning sky, with a hint of sunshine poking through the thin clouds. Armed with a cup of hot coffee in his hand, he couldn't help but think back again to last night. He had been in relationships before, but somehow this one seemed different to him. Almost all of his prior relationships had been about getting laid on a regular basis without any hassles, but since meeting Lina, he had been giving a lot of thought as to why he felt so at ease with her, and why their lovemaking seemed so natural and right. As he approached headquarters, Tony couldn't help but think that maybe this might actually be the girl for him. Quickly putting those thought aside, Tony pulled his car into the entrance to the underground parking for personnel.

He made his way to the elevator and up to his squad room. As he approached his captain's office, he could see Frank talking to a tall, dark- complexioned man dressed in a beautiful hand-tailored suit that Tony would have to take out a bank loan to buy. When he entered Frank's office, his boss introduced him.

"Tony, this is Angelo." Without saying a word, the tall lawyer walked over and stuck out his hand.

"Hi, I'm Angelo Torella. I'm going to be representing you, and hopefully, I'm going to get this straightened out today!"

Tony grabbed his outstretched hand. "Pleasure's all mine, and I hope you're right about taking care of this crap today."

"It should be a piece of cake! Did you bring the timeline and the police report about the burglary to your place?"

"Got it right here, sir," said Tony. He handed Angelo the papers.

"Why don't we just forget the sir crap, okay?" Angelo smiled warmly. "I'm just Angelo to you. If Frank says you're okay, that's good enough for me!"

"You got a deal," said Tony. After taking a few minutes to look at the documentation, Angelo turned to Tony and Frank.

"We've got everything we need right here. I think we can answer any questions that they might have about your whereabouts at the time of the shooting, and also about the gun they recovered at the scene. I don't see anything coming out of this hearing today. If it does, I think that we can handle it with no sweat."

Tony began to feel more confident about his upcoming interview with the Homicide detectives. He, his boss and his lawyer headed over to the Homicide offices—a short walk. The receptionist greeted them and pointed towards a nearby office occupied by three men who were talking in a huddle. When they entered, Tony recognized the two detectives and James Kirby, the IAD lieutenant whom Tony knew to be dirty. Frank gripped his arm, sensing that his anger was piquing. He leaned in to say something but Tony cut him off.

"I know, Boss. Now's the time we kill them with kindness and bomb them with bullshit. For right now I'm going to be 'Mister Congeniality.'"

Lieutenant Kirby left Fitzpatrick and Sipe and approached them in greeting. After brief introductions, he commented on a prior involvement he had had with Tony's lawyer when he was with the Homicide squad.

"It was quite a while ago, and I don't know if you remember it, but it was the case where a congressman's administrative assistant was out with his girlfriend at the National Theater; his wife found out and waited for them to come out after the show was over and shot the girlfriend. You represented the wife, and I responded to the scene and handled the case. I remember meeting you at the trial when I testified for the prosecution."

Unable to recall meeting the lieutenant, Angelo joked, "How did your case work out? Did my client walk?"

"I believe you won that one," Kirby replied.

"Anyway, I know you're here on official business, so I won't hold you up; it was nice to see you again." With that, Kirby left the office.

"Let's get this over with," Angelo said as he watched Kirby's exit. After he was introduced to the two detectives, who seemed slightly awed by the presence of such a big-time lawyer at a routine hearing, everyone sat down, and Fitzpatrick began the interview.

"Because this is a serious matter, Sergeant, I would like to explain how this hearing will proceed. I'm going to read the official statement of facts in this case, and then I'll ask you for a statement regarding your involvement, if any, with this matter. But before I do any of that, I'm going to read you your Miranda rights, okay?"

"I'm aware of my rights, but please, go ahead. Knock yourself out."

Fitzpatrick performed the perfunctory recitation and then began his questioning. "Sergeant, do you own a thirty eight revolver?"

"Yeah, I own a thirty eight revolver, and I reported it missing when my house was broken into."

"I didn't ask about any report; please do all of us a favor and just answer my questions without going into a lot of explanations, okay?"

"I was just making sure you had it on the record that I reported the gun missing almost two weeks before this murder occurred."

"I'll get around to that Sergeant. For now, just answer the questions I ask without elaborating. So when did you report this gun missing?"

"You've got the offense report right in front of you. Why are you wasting my time with this petty bullshit when you already know all this information? Just read the damn PD 251," Tony snapped.

"*I'm* the one conducting this interview," said Fitzpatrick, whose face was starting to resemble a ripe tomato. "I'll handle this interview the way I see fit. As far as I'm concerned, you're just another suspect in a murder case, and you'll sit there and answer all of my questions no matter how long it takes."

Tony's attorney attempted to diffuse the growing conflict between the two men by asking Fitzpatrick if he had received the ballistics report. "If so," he said politely, "could I review it?"

"Sorry, Mr. Torella, but I can't address that issue at this time. Just to remind you, this is simply a meeting to get Sergeant Spinella's statement about his whereabouts at the time of the shooting, his ownership of the gun in question, and any knowledge he might have about the offense in question. Any actions as a result of this meeting will be handled by the United States Attorney's office.

"You haven't even finished this so-called interview and you're already saying this case is being sent to the United States Attorney?" interrupted Tony. He stood up and leaned across the desk. "You and I both know this is all a bunch of bullshit! If you got a problem with me, why don't we get it out in the open right now!" The room was still.

"You call yourself a detective?" snarled Tony. "You're nothing but an asshole! You couldn't find a bleeding elephant in a snow storm, you piece of shit!"

Fitzpatrick sat stunned by the verbal assault. Tony was raging. He leaned farther over the desk, his face inches from Fitzpatrick's. He could sense the other men bracing themselves. Regaining his composure, he simply winked at his adversary.

"It was really good seeing you, Detective," he said in a low voice. "I'm looking forward to seeing you again—real soon."

Torella quickly grabbed him by the arm and pulled him away from the desk.

"Detective Fitzpatrick, you have clearly expressed your bias against my client, and I intend to personally see the Chief about your unprofessional conduct during this so-called pro-forma interview," as he, Frank, and Tony left the office.

When they had distanced themselves from the homicide office, Angelo stopped and turned to Tony.

"Tony, before I leave, I just wanted to explain that my outburst at the end of the meeting was just a little theater for Fitzpatrick's benefit. But don't worry about his forwarding the official report to the U.S. Attorney because that's pro-forma in these circumstances anyway. But I am going to send a note to the Chief about Detective Fitzpatrick's unprofessional conduct during the interview. I know it won't go anywhere, but it might get them focused on your situation. I'll stay in touch, but if you hear anything, give me a call."

After Angelo left, Tony thought that, all in all, it hadn't been such a bad day. Frank read his mind.

"You know, once the U.S. Attorney gets the report and reviews it, he'll probably shit can the whole thing. It's coming down to the wire Tony, and we'll need all the time we can get to make sure this is wrapped up tight enough to present to a grand jury. Don't forget our meeting this afternoon!"

CHAPTER TWENTY-TWO

It was a little past three when Tony arrived at the meeting place. Everyone else was already there when he arrived. Immediately, Frank was on his feet, asking Tony to come over and meet his friend, who was engaged in an animated conversation with Lamont. Tony was struck by how youthful the woman seated next to Frank looked, and wondered how someone who looked this young could be a federal judge.

Dismissing his thoughts as both silly and judgmental, he extended his hand in greeting as she stood to take his hand; Tony couldn't get over how different she looked compared to other female judges he had occasion to appear before while on duty. A quick appraisal told him she was very pretty, about five-feet seven, with a pretty damn good figure for a woman of her age.

"It's good to meet you, Sergeant, I'm Virginia Gills. Frank has spoken highly of you, and your work ethic." The judge's voice was strong and clear.

"Don't believe a word of it, Judge," said Tony. "It's a pleasure meeting you as well, and since we're kind of working together, please call me Tony."

"It's a deal," she replied, "and because Frank told me that you're pretty much in charge of this investigation, I'd like to ask if we could get started as quickly as possible. I have to prepare for a new trial I have starting tomorrow."

"Judge, I'll try and make this as fast as possible, but for the record, I'm not in charge of anything. All these guys are equally invested in seeing to it that these bums are put behind bars." Turning to the rest of the people in the room, Tony asked them to please take a seat so he could begin to bring the judge up to speed with what evidence they had up to this point in the investigation.

Beginning with Frank, and going around the seated group, everyone involved described their part in the investigation, and what they were able to uncover so far. During the briefing, she did not say a word. When everyone finished their reports, the judge got up from her chair.

"Other than violating several local and federal laws, you seem to have done a fair job so far. Make no mistake about it, I cannot condone the breaking of any laws, and I'll not be a party to anything of that sort."

A stunned silence settled over the group. Tony jumped to his feet and began to try and explain why they had done what they did. The judge motioned for him to sit back down.

"I know what you're trying to say, but it's not necessary. I think that I've got a pretty good grasp of the situation, and I honestly feel that you're on the right path, but you gentlemen need to refine your investigation. Document the money! Approach the surveillance of these suspects in a lawful manner! I can help you with that, so when you do drop the hammer on these sleaze balls, what evidence you have will stand up in a court of law." She looked over at Frank.

"Frank, call me tomorrow so I can fit you into my schedule. I'm very busy, but we need to start gathering some legal muscle for our team." Frank, looking like a teenage boy on a first date, was beaming. .

Hearing the judge use the term "our" really seemed to pump the guys up; from the looks on their faces, they were ready to do anything the lady said. Noting a momentary lull in the conversation, Tony took the opportunity to ask the judge if they could legally continue their surveillance of Lorenzo and Kirby without breaking any laws.

"That's a fair question. I think that it's permissible for one citizen to observe the movements of another citizen in a public environment, as long as it doesn't violate that citizen's privacy rights. Keep in mind," she continued, "that it doesn't mean you can peek in their windows, or tap their phones to get information to use against them. Frank, Tony, you both already know this, but I'm saying this for the benefit of all of you. There will be no shortcuts in this investigation if I'm to be a part of it! If any of you have a legal question, feel free to let Frank know so that he can contact me for an opinion. This is a very serious and complicated matter that could eventually involve several law enforcement agencies, up to, and maybe including the United States Attorney. I'm going to play this by ear for right now, but I'll start lining up the help we'll need if we're going to be successful in this."

She started to leave, but apparently had a second thought and turned to Frank.

"Frank, I think it would be a good idea, since this situation seems to be quickly evolving, that you stay in very close contact with my office. I'll let my secretary know that you're to be put straight through to me whenever you call. If I'm in trial, I'll get back to you as quickly as possible. In the meantime, do not discuss this case with anyone other than those of us currently involved. Got that?"

"Absolutely," replied Frank, as they walked, arm and arm, out of the room together.

Tony's cell began to vibrate. It was Lina.

"How about stopping by this evening? I've got some ideas that I think might help with your investigation," she said.

He mentally reviewed his schedule. "I'd love to stop by. How's pepperoni sound to you?"

"I'll make that worth your while if you make that a *large* pepperoni!" she quipped.

Tony laughed as he put his cell phone back in his pocket. It was turning out to be a great day.

The meeting being more or less adjourned, Tony started to leave. Scopes and Lamont intercepted him with some questions about their next assignment.

"Hey Tony," said Lamont. "Nobody told us what you want me and Scopes to do."

"Sorry about that, guys," he apologized. "I got side-tracked. Lamont, I want you to continue your surveillance of Lorenzo, and let me, or Frank, know if anything un-usual happens. Scopes, it's very important that you don't take any more chances without checking with me, or Frank, first. You got lucky last time. I also want you to make sure you let Lamont know where Kirby is at all times because we don't want any surprises. Is everyone clear with your assignments?"

Both men nodded in assent. "I'll be in touch with you guys later. Call me if you need me; I'll be at Lina's."

After he got in his car and left, he thought about going by his place to get cleaned up and change clothes. He still couldn't get the picture of the snake in his closet out of his mind. He' had better get over it real fast, because he had a lot of work to do.

As he headed over to his Capitol Hill home, he placed a call to Anita at the office. She answered on the first ring, which must have been a new world's record for the busy phones in the squad room. He could tell from the tone of her voice that she was a bit frazzled.

"Anita, it's me, Tony. I'm just checking in to see if there's anyone looking for me. Do I have any messages that need my attention?"

"Yes, you do. Assistant U.S. Attorney Sullivan left you a message. He wants you to call him in regards to that homicide case in Southeast."

"Did he leave a number where I can reach him?"

"Yes," she said, and gave him the number he requested.

"I'm on it," said Tony. "I'll be in the office tomorrow if anyone asks, okay?"

"Great," she said. "Look forward to seeing your handsome face, and maybe you'll take a few minutes to bring me up to speed on what's been going on around here."

"You got it," said Tony as he ended the call and continued towards his home. He punched in the numbers Anita had given him for the U.S. Attorney's office.

While he was on hold, Tony recalled several cases he had worked on with the attorney. Sullivan was a pretty decent guy, and he could more than handle Fitzpatrick's fabricated case against him. Sullivan's voice interrupted his thoughts. They spoke the usual hellos and then Sullivan got right to the point.

"What did you do to get Fitzpatrick all worked up?" he asked.

"Nothing that I know about," lied Tony. He listened to Sullivan reassure him that the report from Homicide was a bunch of bullshit and there was no cause for him to worry.

"I'm too busy for trumped-up cases like this. If I ever see another one like this from him, I'll personally let his chief know what I think," Sullivan said.

"That's good to hear, Sully, because it *is* bullshit and I really appreciate your looking out for me. Why don't we get together for lunch soon and catch up?"

After making some tentative plans, Tony thanked him again and hung up. He pulled into the parking spot across the street from his house and hurried inside. He was anxious to get over to Lina's, where hopefully his day would end on a happy note.

CHAPTER TWENTY-THREE

Frank had just dropped the judge off when Lamont called him. His voice was breaking up badly and he couldn't understand him.

"Call me right back. I'm in a bad spot and I'm going to change my location." A minute or two later, Frank's phone chirped once more.

"What's up, Lamont?"

"Frank, I've got eyes on our boy Lorenzo and he seems to be a very popular guy."

"What do you mean?" Frank asked.

"I'm watching him like you told me to, and what I'm seeing is that I'm not the only one watching him. Since I've been sitting on Lorenzo's place, I've noticed two other guys who also seem interested in our boy."

"Have you been able to make them?"

"Yeah, I know both of these guys. They're the same two detectives I saw you and Tony talking with at Maurice's wake. On top of that, the one guy, the big one, was in the pictures that Scopes took at the park meeting with Kirby."

"That's good work, Lamont. Stay on Lorenzo, and maybe he'll lead us to his boss," Frank said, growing excited.

"I need to tell you something else."

"Go ahead," said Frank.

"Boss, you remember you told me to snatch the evidence in Kirby's pad?"

"Yes, I remember, what about it?"

"Well, I got to thinking. After hearing that judge lady telling us to do the right thing about getting evidence, I decided to leave everything where it was for the time being. Like she said, if we need it later, we can get a search warrant and do it legal. Oh, I almost forgot, the thirty-eight wasn't there, and I looked everywhere for it."

"Good thinking about leaving everything there. I should've told you that myself. Don't worry about the gun. We know where it is, and it's out of play. Stay in touch, and be extra careful," said Frank and he ended the call.

CHAPTER TWENTY-FOUR

From his perch on the roof, the tall, heavily muscled man was confused. He had not only observed people in a van watching the same house he was watching, but there was also another guy farther down the block who also appeared interested in the location. He was having trouble figuring out was who was watching who, and for what reasons.

This latest development only added to the bad feeling he had since taking this assignment. He had been raised in communist East Germany during the post-war period, when jobs for young people were almost nonexistent. As a result, the young man was a non-entity in a country which offered little hope of a future for its citizens. Being a clever young man, he decided early on to make his own way, no matter what it took. That decision resulted in his becoming well known to the local police. After too many run-ins with the law, where he was frequently arrested and viciously beaten, he found himself in front of a no-nonsense judge who possessed an interesting sense of justice. He was sentenced to either the army or jail.

Though he might have been a petty thief, Vadin was not stupid. He chose the army, where he thrived under the harsh discipline. Later during his training, the young recruit's marksmanship caught the attention of his superiors. An exceptionally good shot with a rifle, his sergeant recommended him for advanced sniper training. To the continued amazement of his commanding officers, he excelled with virtually every weapon handed to him.

Though he loved training as a marksman, he never felt like the army was the place he really wanted to spend his life. After serving his imposed sentence in the army, he was released from his military obligation and immediately went to work doing odd jobs for some of the unsavory characters from his old neighborhood. A lot of his work required the use of brute force with those people who were unable to pay his boss what they owed. He became so good at collecting money for his handlers that his reputation for brutality, and good results, brought him to the attention of a man that his boss, Alex, referred to as "*the* Boss."

One afternoon, while sitting around a small bar owned by Alex, he was summoned to the back office where he was introduced to a man sitting behind Alex's desk. Noting the deference Alex showed the man, Vadin decided to be very careful in what he said. Alex introduced "the boss" to Vadin, and then he and the others in the room promptly exited, leaving Vadin alone with the heavily muscled man.

The man told him that he had heard good things about him, and that he was thinking about letting him do some special work for his organization—work that required someone with a particular talent.

"What type of talent are we talking about?" Vadin had asked.

"Shut up and listen," snarled the man. "When I want you to speak, I'll tell you." Then, in a softer voice, he went on to offer him a slot in his organization that required his taking care of special problems that might arise from time to time. It took Vadin only a moment to realize that he was being given the opportunity of a lifetime, and he quickly accepted the offer.

Over the next few years he became very successful in taking care of several high profile problems for the man he referred to as the "Big Boss," who rewarded him for his efforts, both with prestige and money.

One late summer afternoon while hanging out in the playroom in his boss's home, he was summoned to his office, where he was told that he would soon be going to the United States to do some work for their organization. The job would require the best shooter Big Boss had. Vadin was told that they had some major problems that needed to be handled quickly, and without any attention being drawn to them.

"No problem, Boss. When do you want me to leave, and whom do I contact when I arrive?"

"You will leave tomorrow. Don't worry about your travel arrangements; they've all been taken care of. All you need to do is follow the instructions you will be given. Once you get to Washington, I want you to call this number I'm giving you for your instructions. Don't lose it, and when you get there, don't ask any questions, just do what your contact tells you to do, and then get back here. Do you understand your instructions?"

"Yes," replied Vadin as he put the slip of paper with the phone number in his pants pocket.

That had been over a week ago, and after crossing into the United States through Canada, he had made his way to Washington, DC, where he contacted his handler, a woman, for instructions. Later that same day, he found himself on the dirty roof of an upscale townhouse in a middle class neighborhood, watching his target's house while also spotting several other people doing the same thing. He wasn't getting the whole story. He would call his contact and tell her about the other surveillance, and maybe get new instructions.

CHAPTER TWENTY-FIVE

Tony couldn't bring himself to start getting cleaned up for his date with Lina without first checking the whole house. Once he was satisfied that no snakes, or any other threats, were in the house, he undressed. Before he stepped into the shower he once again checked behind the toilet, just to be sure.

After getting cleaned up and splashing on his best aftershave, he stopped by Luigi's, his favorite pizza place, to pick up the large pepperoni he had promised Lina. Luigi's was a small, Italian restaurant located on the corner of a busy intersection in Southeast Washington where the Sousa Bridge crossed over to connect with the area known as Anacostia. He had found Luigi's while walking his beat as a rookie patrolman, and the first time he walked through the front door his sense of smell was overcome by the wonderful aroma of the cheeses and dough. He was hooked. Over the next several weeks on his beat he stopped in to visit Luigi who grew quite fond of him and always gave him a break on the price of his food—not only because he was a cop, but because he was *paisan*, Italian. Tony never felt comfortable with that arrangement, and he argued unsuccessfully with Luigi for several years about it. Once, after he and his former wife Debbie had finished eating a pizza at one of the several small tables inside the restaurant, Tony had asked for the bill and was told by the young waiter that Luigi said there was to be no bill for him. Tony became upset, left the table, and went to the kitchen where he confronted Luigi. After shouting at one another for a moment or two, Luigi grabbed Tony, kissed him on the cheek and told him everything was okay while shooing him out of the kitchen. Since that time, Tony always paid for anything he got at Luigi's. As he waited for his pizza to arrive, a couple of the guys he knew behind the counter teasingly remarked about how nice he smelled, and wondered out loud if he was looking to get lucky. After swapping the usual insults with his buddies, Tony started to walk over to the cash register to pay for his order when he was intercepted by Luigi, who grabbed him in a bear hug and kissed him on both cheeks while muttering greetings in Italian which Tony didn't completely understand.

"Anthony, *Come stai*? I know it musta be hard for you to lose you friend. You must tell me if you need anything, okay?"

"Luigi, I'm doing pretty good," said Tony, attempting to change the subject, "and I'm really looking forward to enjoying your pizza with my lady friend in just a few minutes." Luigi glowed with that remark, and again embraced him, squeezing him so tight he had trouble breathing.

"Paisano," Luigi whispered in his ear, "please do not insult me by attempting to pay for your food. It is my gift to you and your lady, bene?"

Tony smiled at his friend. "*Si, Va bene, grazia* Luigi," he conceded and he left the pizza shop.To his surprise, Lina greeted him at the door wearing a light blue summer dress that accentuated her gorgeous figure, and holding a very expensive bottle of 2007 Fattori, Amarone Classico, to go with their pizza. That evening, after drinking all of the wine and eating most of the pizza, there was no discussion of his investigation of Maurice's murder. Later, to his delight, Tony found himself lying naked in her bed waiting for her to leave the bathroom and join him. Lying there, he couldn't help but think about Maurice and what a shitty mess he had left behind for him and others to clean up. Those thoughts quickly vanished, though, when he heard the bathroom door open and soft footsteps coming towards where he lay, waiting with anticipation.

CHAPTER TWENTY-SIX

Prior to securing his hiding place, Vadin had gained access to a common roof atop a group of adjoining townhouses directly across the street from the target's house. Making sure he wasn't seen, he checked the surrounding roof area for the quickest and easiest escape route from the kill zone. He checked several roof access hatches and finally found one that was unlocked. He carefully lifted it and saw that someone had removed the inside hasp where normally there would be a pad lock to secure the roof access hatch from the inside. The hatch opened and closed without making any noise—good. He silently lowered himself down to the second floor hallway, and listened for any signs of life. All was silent.

He padded to the kitchen area, where he found a back entrance to an alley running directly behind the row of town houses. Comfortable with his escape route, he returned to his rental, parked in a one hour time zone and drove around the neighborhood until he located a legal parking spot. He parked the car and went back to his rooftop perch.

Vadin pulled his cell phone from his jacket pocket and called his contact. The light from his cell broke the evening twilight.

"What's he up too? Has he had any visitors?" asked the same female voice from earlier.

"He's not doing anything, and he has had no visitors," he answered. "I need to know what is going on. Why did you not tell me that my target is being watched by others?"

"What?" said his contact. "What are you talking about? What people? How many? Describe them to me."

"There are three of them. Two are white men and they are in what I think is police car with no insignia. The other is a black man in older, four-door blue car."

"It's nearly dark. How do you know it's a police car, or does it just look like one?" the woman probed.

"No, I know police car when I see it. I have been around police all my life—it is police!" Vadin nearly shouted into the phone.

"Okay," said the woman. "Keep watching our man. I'll get back to you in a couple of minutes. Stay off the phone until you hear from me," she ordered and hung up.

Vadin looked at his phone, angry at the way she had spoken to him. He considered himself a professional, and wasn't used to people not showing him the respect he deserved. Feeling his anger mount, he thought to himself that maybe when this job was over he might just find out who this bitch is and kill her too. Of course, if he did do that, his boss would probably have him killed as well. With nothing better to do than wait for his contact to call back, he went over to the spot where he had stashed the case containing his Dragunov sniper rifle, checking to make sure it was in working order. He reflected on his home and how much he missed the security of being around people he could trust. His cell phone vibrated and he hit the talk button.

"Your target will be leaving his home within the next ten minutes. Take him out! You've got a description of him, correct?"

"Yes, I know what he looks like."

"Good. When the job is done, follow your exit instructions to the letter and you should be okay. You won't hear from me again." The line went dead.

Vadin was elated: there would be no more waiting. He could take care of business and get back home to a nice payday. With deft hands he lifted the sniper rifle from it protective case and snapped the suppressor onto the end of the barrel where it fit nice and tight. He loved the feel and balance of his Dragunov. While in the army he came to admire the sheer beauty of the Soviet-made weapon, as well as its ability to hit and destroy any target.

Cloaked in the evening darkness, he crossed the roof back to his position behind a brick chimney situated near the roof's edge, got down into a kneeling position and carefully sited the front door of the target's house for the third or fourth time. He was very precise in following a set routine whenever he took a job of this nature. For him, being a professional meant being extremely careful. He always carried an all-purpose clasp knife strapped to his leg, along with a small neck knife on a string around his neck.

He looked through the rifle scope at the front door across the street, mentally reviewing his escape procedure once he took the shot. He was startled to see the front door suddenly open. His target stood in the doorway, talking to someone inside the house.

Vadin sighted in on the back of the man's head and took aim. He could feel the strength of the rifle in his hand as he paused. This was always the moment when he felt God-like. The power of life or death in his hands almost always gave him a powerful sexual release. He slowly squeezed the trigger, rewarded with a soft, popping sound as the bullet left the barrel. Through the rifle's scope, he saw the bullet strike the target's head about an inch and a half above his right ear, causing his skull to shatter. Blood and brain matter sprayed as his body arched into the air, coming to rest in the doorway. For several moments Vadin remained almost completely still as a strong climax rocked his body.

He quickly broke down the rifle as screams echoed from across the street. Methodically, he packed the Dragunov in its case. Without rushing, he walked over to the roof hatch, let himself down onto the second floor of the townhouse and made his way through the kitchen and out to the back alley. He walked casually, gun case in hand, to where his rental car was parked, got in and slowly drove away.

CHAPTER TWENTY-SEVEN

That same evening, Frank was in the living room of the two-story Cape Cod that he and his deceased wife had designed and built nearly thirty years ago. Located in an older neighborhood in Chevy Chase where residents walked along neatly-kept sidewalks bordered by ancient, imposing trees, his home was a safe haven and a refuge from the less savory demands of his job. He sat in his favorite chair and sipped a glass of single malt scotch. He gazed out his big picture window into the semi-darkness, taking in the final scenes of the day as he listened to his favorite oldies. He heard the low vibration of his cell piercing through an old doo-wop melody by the Platters of "Only You."

"This is McCathran." A hysterical voice was on the other end, shouting.

"Who the hell is this?" he demanded. Tuning in more closely, he recognized Lamont's voice.

"Take it easy, Lamont, and slow down. I can't understand a damn thing you're saying," he said.

"The shit has hit the fan here, Frank. The guys I was watching, you know, the two detectives? They were watching this guy Lorenzo's house, and just now he got blown away, right in his front door!"

"Lorenzo?" Frank put his glass of scotch down on the table.

"Yeah, I think it was him," answered Lamont.

"Did you see the shooter?"

"No. All I saw was the guy's brains sprayed all over the place."

"What did Fitzpatrick and Sipe do?"

"Just like me, they beat feet outta there."

"Ok, you head on home, and I'll call you later. You done good Lamont," said Frank and he hung up.

Frank finished his scotch in one gulp and called Tony. There was no answer, so he called Scopes and Lamont to set up a meeting at the farmhouse right away. He tried Tony again—still no answer. He searched his wallet and found Lina's number. When he dialed it and she answered, he wasted no time.

"Lina, put Tony on—*now*."

"What's up, Boss?" asked Tony, sounding more relaxed than he had been. Frank felt a brief pang of guilt.

"Lorenzo's been whacked. We need a meeting. I've already called Scopes and Lamont. Get there as soon as you can."

CHAPTER TWENTY-EIGHT

Kirby was home about to sit down and relax when his cell rang.

"This is Kirby." He pushed the speaker button on his phone.

"Lorenzo's dead, and I think it's about time you and I get acquainted," a female voice said.

"Who the hell is this?" he replied.

"We'll get to that later. What I want you to do right now is listen to what I'm telling you. I'll call you tomorrow and give you instructions as to where to meet; until then, don't do anything."

"Just wait a second! I don't know you—you're just a voice on the phone. How do I know this conversation isn't a set-up?" Kirby kept his voice low.

"You don't, but who do you think Lorenzo was working for? I'm going to give you a great opportunity—don't screw it up. I'll call you tomorrow.

"What d—?" Kirby started to ask, but it was too late. She was gone.

Kirby collapsed into his overstuffed lounge chair trying to process what had just happened. Whoever she was, she knew about his connection to Lorenzo. That made her the person he was looking for. He needed to play his cards carefully, but if this worked out, it could be the final move before his big score and his disappearance. He would wait for the call, say as little as possible in case it was a set-up, and make a decision at that point. If he needed to disappear sooner, that is, if the shit hit the fan, he was prepared.

He had barely regained his composure when he heard someone banging on his front door. Being cautious, he opened the drawer of the table alongside his chair and withdrew a small, snub-nosed revolver. With the gun held at his side, he unlocked the door only to have it pushed open by an excited Detective Fitzpatrick, who barged into the foyer babbling about someone being shot. Kirby shut the door and grabbed Fitz by the arm.

"Fitz, stop for a minute and take a deep breath. Tell me what's going on."

"We were watching Lorenzo like you told us to do, and as he was leaving his house he was shot."

"Did you see who shot him?"

"We didn't see anything or anybody. One second he was standing in his doorway, and the next he was lying in the doorway with his head blown off," said Fitz, still shaken.

"Is Dave with you?" Kirby asked, pulling back the drapes in the front window and peering out.

"Yeah, he's out in the car."

"How's he doing? He didn't freak out or anything did he?" asked Kirby, turning back to Fitz.

"No, he seems to be doing okay, but as far as I'm concerned he's a nutcase."

"Okay, for right now don't discuss any of our conversation with him. We need to keep him motivated but out of the loop. Get outta here and go home—I'll contact you tomorrow."

After Fitz left, Kirby paced the room in agitation. Those two guys were becoming a liability. He was scared, but as he reflected back to the conversation with the unknown woman, he began to regain his confidence. He would out-think whoever this person turned out to be.

He settled down somewhat and in a few minutes went to bed and fell asleep—dreaming about that young island girl with her long legs wrapped around his back.

CHAPTER TWENTY-NINE

It was almost eleven o'clock when Tony arrived at the farmhouse. Frank wasted no time in bringing everybody up to speed about the hit on Lorenzo. Scopes reminded them of his aversion to guns, but before he could work himself into his usual anti-gun rant, Frank intervened and told him to take a seat and listen. He quickly took the hint and sat down.

"Lamont, are you still good with helping us with this investigation?" asked Frank. "And while I'm at it, I've gotta ask, does anyone here want out? If you do, I'll understand."

For a moment no one said a word. Then, all at once they all had something to say. Frank raised his hands for quiet, and again asked them if they wanted to stay and help, or leave with no questions asked. One at a time, they all agreed to stay.

"Lamont, with these new developments, I'll need you to really sit on Kirby, because I believe he's going to do something real soon. He's got to know that his shit is getting weak, and I expect he'll try and run before it all blows up in his face. Remember, he still has a lot of cash stashed at his house, as well as those boxes at the banks. If you need me to explain to the wife what you've been up to lately, I'll be happy to give her a call. It'll also give me a chance to say hi to junior and see how he's doing with all that metal in his mouth."

"Please do that," pleaded Lamont, "because she's been giving me a fit about not being around to help out at the house. Besides, she loves you, and if you tell her you need me, she'll go along with it."

"Consider it done," said Frank. "Scopes, since Lorenzo's murder, I might need you to help Lamont with surveillance on Kirby. We'll need to be on him constantly because I think he's going to make a move any time now."

"That's okay with me," said Scopes, "but I get to pick where we get our food while I'm working with him, and it ain't gonna be no half-smokes either," he said with a smile. Lamont grinned and gave him the finger.

After putting Scopes and Lamont together to set up their surveillance schedule, Frank pulled Tony aside and told him that he was going to see the judge tomorrow and hopefully bring in some muscle from the U.S. Attorney's office.

"Tony," said Frank, "I'm sorry about tearing you away from Lina, but we both know that this shit is coming to a head, and we need to stay in front of it."

"I understand, Boss, but I gotta tell you, your timing stinks!" Both men laughed, and after setting up contact times for the next day, went their separate ways.

The following morning Kirby woke up refreshed and looking forward to what he hoped would be a new chapter in his plan.

He went to the fridge, got two eggs and put them in a frying pan. As the eggs popped and sizzled he considered various scenarios. He would make sure, for his own safety, that any meeting with the woman caller would be in a public place—somewhere with lots of people around. He was about to turn the eggs when his house phone rang.

"Did you sleep well?" she greeted him abruptly.

"Well enough," he replied and waited.

"Meet me at the Mayflower Hotel restaurant at exactly eleven forty-five—and be on time," she warned.

"Wait a second! How will I know you?" he asked, only to be left with a dial tone and the smell of burning eggs in the air.

Cleaning up the mess, Kirby rehashed every word of the conversations he had with whom he now referred to as, 'the voice'. His upcoming meeting should be relatively safe, because they would be in a very public place frequented by an upscale clientele.

It was Tuesday, and Tony made his usual visit to his office to push some papers around and bullshit with some of the other detectives in Robbery Squad. He asked some general questions about the liquor store robberies, and got so caught up in reading the case reports that he actually developed a plan to find the guys who were hitting the stores. He would implement the plan as soon as he returned to his usual routine.

He looked up from his desk and noticed Anita staring at him. He gave her a half-hearted wave and went back to reading the reports. An hour or so later Tony's stomach was letting him know it was time to eat. Thinking he might get Lina to meet him at the police lodge, he pulled out his phone and called her office number. While waiting for Lina to pick up, he noticed that Anita was no longer at her desk. He heard his girlfriend's voice on the other end.

"Hi, baby. I was just thinking, there's not much going on right now and I thought you might like to meet me at the club for a sandwich."

Lina launched into a long explanation about working on a big presentation for her boss and playfully asked for a raincheck. After some harmless phone-flirting, she changed the subject.

"Remember when I told you I had thought of something that might help with your investigation?"

"Sure, I remember. What's your idea?"

"I think you should have Lamont video everything that might have to do with the case. It might come in handy later."

"That's a great idea, honey. I'll call Lamont and tell him to do just that. In the meantime I'm going to have a very lonely lunch. Call you later?"

"You better," she replied with a low laugh and hung up.

Tony contacted Lamont and passed on Lina's idea for catching Kirby on video if anything important went down. Lamont loved the idea.

"Maybe I'll even win an Oscar," he joked.

"You wish," said Tony, ending the call. Before leaving the squad room to head over to the club for lunch, he called the judge's office and set up a meeting for later that afternoon.

When he got to the lodge Tony ordered a double cheeseburger and a draft and found a table in the corner. He waved to several police officers he knew from his academy days who were sitting nearby. He hadn't been seated long before Jess, the club's perky young waitress, placed a cold draft beer in front of him. He took a long drink and over the top of his mug spotted Matt Hollis, another old acquaintance from his police academy days, sitting across the room by himself. Several years back Matt had left the department and gone to work for the Drug Enforcement Administration as an investigator assigned to south Florida. Matt was built like a fire plug, about five nine and around two hundred pounds, with the face of a movie star and the disposition of a junkyard dog. Tony fondly remembered Matt as always being the first in their academy class to crack a joke while being lectured by some self-important guest speaker. As a result of his antics, he was usually in hot water with the academy staff even though he finished third in the class.

Tony waved for him to come over and sit with him. Matt caught Tony's raised hand, picked up his beer and sauntered over to his table. After the usual greetings the two men began to discuss the old days and mutual friends who had passed on. Their food arrived and they continued brief exchanges between bites.

After swallowing the last bite of his cheeseburger, Tony quipped,

"You know, my girlfriend would kill me if she knew that I had a cheeseburger. She's on some kind of crusade to keep me from dying from too much cholesterol. I don't know what it is about women."

"My wife is the same way. I wonder if all women subscribe to the same health magazines."

"Damned if I know," said Tony, laughing. "What I do know is, I like cheeseburgers, and I'm gonna keep eating them when she's not around."

They talked about old cases and old associates for another twenty minutes or so.

"So, what have you been into lately? Anything interesting?" Tony asked.

"Tony, I can't really discuss any of the stuff we're working on right now, you know how it is. But one thing I can talk about is an investigation that I'm involved in that might involve drug trafficking in the city. We're looking into a local thug that you might know—someone who's involved in moving large quantities of narcotics in the city."

"What's the guy's name?" asked Tony.

"Right now, all we got is the name 'Lorenzo,' and from what our sources tell us, he appears to be the number-one man operating in town. He's our target."

Tony narrowed his eyes and said nothing.

"You know this mug?" Matt asked, eyebrows raised.

Tony had known Matt a long time. He was a good cop. He instantly decided to trust him with details about his case.

"You know, I might just have some information that could help you with your investigation, and maybe after we exchange information, we can get our bosses to agree to let us work together on this."

"Sounds good," replied Matt, somewhat surprised. "Tell me what you got."

Tony spent the next thirty minutes laying out the details of their investigation. Matt was excited about the information Tony and his crew had uncovered, and began to explain the DEA's interest in Lorenzo and his organization.

He explained that they knew that Lorenzo was moving large quantities of drugs, but couldn't pin down who was supplying them.

"Lorenzo's dead, Matt."

"What?"

"He was shot last night—in the doorway of his house."

"No shit!" said Matt. "I hadn't heard about that. That changes everything! We should still share our information about this case, and maybe find his source. What do you think about that idea?"

"I like the idea," said Tony, "but I'll have to check with my boss. For right now, though, we have to agree that this conversation never happened, okay? I'll get back to you by tomorrow afternoon with an answer."

"Sounds good to me," said Matt.

After they paid their bills and said their goodbyes, Tony headed over to the courthouse to meet the judge. With the DEA joining the investigation, they might have a good shot at finding out exactly who the players were in this case. He needed a good explanation for the judge as to why he discussed the case with Matt, after she explicitly told everyone not to do so. His best bet, he concluded as he parked outside the courthouse, would be to just tell it like it happened and let the judge decide if Matt should be included.

CHAPTER THIRTY

It was mid afternoon and the bright afternoon sun beamed down as a slight breezed moved the bushes in front of the courthouse. Tony entered the imposing, gray stone building. He was suddenly nervous when he arrived at Judge Virginia Gill's second floor office. Normally, at least for a working cop, being in a judge's chambers usually meant you'd messed up—or worse.

After being announced by the judge's secretary, Tony entered her office to find it somewhat crowded. He first recognized Assistant U.S. Attorney Sullivan, who was talking to Frank. Over in the far corner of the office, sitting in an oversized leather chair, was Inspector Billings from IAD, talking with the Chief of Police. *I'm definitely the low man on the totem pole in this meeting*, he thought. He resolved to let his boss do all the talking, unless he was directly asked to speak.

"Tony, welcome to my inner sanctum," said Judge Gills, walking over to him. "I hope you've got lots of news for us because I've just begun to describe a rough outline of the information you have for these gentlemen."

"Judge," said Tony, "I think that maybe Frank should lead off with what we've discovered so far."

"That will be okay, but you must realize that you're not going to get out of here without sharing your insight into this matter."

"Yes, Judge, I know that. If you need me to elaborate on any details just let me know."

"That should do," she said. She asked everyone to have a seat.

Almost two hours later, after most of the questions had been asked, Judge Gills asked Tony to describe the attempt on his life. He described the break-in and snake attack to the mesmerized group. Revulsion appeared on all their faces as they congratulated him on being alive.

Attorney Sullivan then took the lead in the meeting. "To get the ball rolling in my shop, I'm willing to start putting together a rough outline of the case even though I understand that it might be a bit premature. I think that it could help us all get a better grasp on the overall picture if I can put our information into some sense of order. I'll get on that right away, and I'll keep everyone up to speed. If anyone here needs to get in touch with me, I'll see that you have my private number before you leave here.

"That sounds good, Sully," said Inspector Billings. "I want you all to know that I've got a couple of detectives working for me in IAD that I can vouch for. I know you might have some reservations about them, but I've known them since they came on the job, and I know they're both honest cops. Frank, I'll have them get in touch with you and Sergeant Spinella right away. Since you already have people watching Lieutenant Kirby, I suggest it might be a good idea to have these two keep an eye on the property room and the personnel assigned there."

Tony studied the old cop. This whole mess had taken him completely by surprise. He reached out to shake his hand.

"Inspector, I really appreciate your help with this. We've got to get these guys before they do any more damage to our department—or hurt any more cops."

"Sergeant, I've got almost thirty years on this job, and thought I'd seen it all. This takes the cake. The chief said for me to help in any way I can, so all you or Captain McCathran gotta do is ask."

"Inspector, I'll stay in touch with you and keep you up to date," Frank interjected. "Can you give me a call in the morning with the names of the two guys you want me to use?"

"You bet. I'll call as soon as I get in the office."

"Don't forget gentlemen, this stays with us," Judge Gills announced. "We need the utmost secrecy on this until we're ready to move. My secretary will be in touch with you to set up another meeting within the week. Until then, please do not discuss this matter with anyone not a part of this investigation." As the men began to file out of her office, Judge Gills pulled Frank aside and asked that he and Tony stay for a moment. After the others had left, the judge shut her door and motioned for them to take a seat.

"Gentlemen, I think we are very close to being able to issue search warrants in this case. But before I can do that, I need you to bring me solid probable cause to justify those warrants. What we have right now are many pieces of a puzzle that we need to put together to be able to use those warrants to our advantage."

"I understand, judge," said Tony, "and we're working on it as best we can."

"Tony," she said, looking squarely at him, "I know all that, and I also know how much you've put into this case. I'm not criticizing you, or your effort. All I'm saying is get me some probable cause to issue the warrants, and I'll do so. Anyway, the reason I had you both stay behind, is that I have this idea I'd like to run by you. Have either of you given any thought to maybe attempting to put a wedge between this Fitzpatrick and his partner?"

"No, we haven't," said Frank, "but that might not be a bad idea. If we can turn one of them, it could bust this thing wide open."

"You know who I think we should concentrate on," said Tony, "that little rat Sipe. I think he's the weak link between the two."

"I agree," said Frank. "I think we might be on to something. Thanks, Judge. We'll keep you posted."

"See that you do," she said with a big smile as she ushered them out of her office.

"You know, Boss," Tony remarked as he and Frank left the courthouse, "that gal is something else. She's got balls the size of grapefruit, and she ain't afraid of nothing. Matter of fact, she's not hard on the eyes either. But I guess you haven't noticed that." He looked at his boss out of the corner of his eye.

"Not a bad guess, Detective. Yeah, she and I have been seeing each other for the last several months. We kinda like to keep it low profile if you know what I mean. You know, Tony, I'm beginning to think that she might just be the one."

Tony was floored by Frank's abrupt revelation. "It's about time you found somebody to hang out with, Boss. I'm really happy about this news and I'll be sure to keep it to myself." *Excepting Lina*, he thought to himself.

"Real quick, before we go our separate ways," said Frank, "I need you to find out where Sipe lives, and what shift he's working. We'll make plans to snatch him and see if we can get him to give it up."

"No problem," replied Tony as he headed for his car., "I'll have it for you by the time you get in tomorrow morning."

Walking away, Tony got to thinking that the whole time he had worked for Frank, he couldn't remember ever seeing his boss with a woman. He had been a widower for quite a while, and from everything he had heard around the office, Frank had been devastated by his wife's death. This thing with the judge was really good news.

As Tony drove away from the courthouse, he decided to use a little deception to get the information about Detective Sipe's working schedule. He pulled out his phone and called the Homicide Squad. Impersonating Lieutenant Kirby, Tony found out that Detective Sipe was supposed to be working the day shift, but had called in sick. After ending the call, Tony phoned an old friend who was a supervisor in personnel. After making sure his friend would keep it quiet, he got Sipe's home address and phone number. It suddenly dawned on him that he had not mentioned his discussion with the DEA agent to the judge, or Frank. He would have to fess up sooner or later, but for the moment, dismissed it from his mind.

CHAPTER THIRTY-ONE

Later that morning Kirby, right on time, walked into the Mayflower Hotel. After asking the doorman for directions to the restaurant, he headed towards his meeting with the unknown voice. He was nervous, but determined to see this through.

He stepped inside the restaurant and looked around. He noticed a woman waving at him from a table in the far corner. She acted as if she knew him. Returning the wave, he made his way over to her table.

Oh shit! That's the girl that works in Robbery, and she's made me. Any thought of a secret meeting with the person he spoke with on the phone had just gone out the window. Kirby put a smile on his face.

"Hello, it's nice to see you. It's Anita, right?" he said casually.

"Yes it is," she said, smiling broadly. "It's nice to see you, too. Would you like to join me?"

"I'd really like too," said Kirby, "but I'm meeting someone for lunch. Maybe another time."

"Just shut up and sit down," hissed Anita, glaring at him with indignation. "*I'm* the person you're meeting."

Speechless, he took a step back. Then he pulled himself together and slowly sat down.

"You gotta be kidding me! What is this, some kind of joke?"

Anita leaned across the table. "When the waitress comes over, you'll order some lunch, and while she's here, don't engage me in any conversation. When she leaves, I'll need you to listen to what I have to say, and then I'll ask for your input. Understand?"

Kirby nodded, still stunned. *This pretty woman was the mastermind behind all this?*

"Good. Let's enjoy a nice lunch, and then we can discuss some business that should be mutually beneficial." Kirby nodded again, feeling sick to his stomach.

After placing their lunch orders, Anita quietly outlined a plan whereby the two of them would execute one more visit to the property room, only they wouldn't take just a portion of the stored drug evidence, but all of it.

"Can I ask a question?" Kirby interrupted.

"Yes, go ahead, but keep your voice down," replied Anita.

"Are we going to wait until there are enough confiscated drugs in the property room to make it worth our while? Because, after this one, I think we need to think about disappearing while we still can."

"Do you think I'm stupid?" snarled Anita. "I planned this out long before you came along. I know what I'm going to do, and I suggest you start planning for what you're going to do after we make this last score."

"How can I trust you not to throw me to the wolves when this is over?"

"You idiot! What good would it do me to expose you? I'd only be exposing myself if I did that. Start thinking rationally or we'll both end up in jail. Think about it—I've been working on this for a long time, and it's worked like a charm the whole time; there's no reason to think it won't continue to work if we both pay attention to what we're doing. Anyway, before I go, I need you to understand something, so listen very carefully. If you attempt to play me, or deceive me in any way, what happened to Lorenzo will happen to you. Do not fuck with me! I'll call you in two days at your home to set up our next meeting."

Anita quickly got up from the table without so much as a goodbye, wove her way through the restaurant and was out the door before Kirby could gather his thoughts. He couldn't believe that this woman was the person he had been looking for the whole time. He was still in a bad position if she decided to sacrifice him to save herself. He needed to refine his contingency plan for a quick escape.

The waitress appeared, placed both orders of food on the table, and after a quick "Enjoy your lunch!" walked away, nearly colliding with a slightly built black man carrying a camcorder who appeared to be just another one of the thousands of tourists who converged on Washington, D.C. this time of year. Kirby looked at both plates of food.

What the hell, it look's good.

After he finished his lunch and ate part of Anita's, he left the hotel and called Fitzpatrick, telling him he had some great news and to meet him right away at his house.

Anita drove away from the Mayflower thinking about her early days with the department. Back then, she had enjoyed the job and the people she worked with. The detectives had treated her with the respect she had earned through her hard work and dedication. Numerous times over the years, she was invited to various family functions held by members of the Robbery Squad. She began to feel like they were part of her family. In the last few years, however, she began to notice a major change in the squad as people came and went. The new breed of detectives had no personalities and no appreciation for the work she did for them on a daily basis. Their only concerns seemed to be kissing their boss's ass, trying to get weekends off, or using her as a source of free labor.

There were a few good ones who seemed to appreciate her, but they were few and far between. She would have gone on doing her job the same way she had always done it, except for that piece of shit, Mark, who had ruined her life. The handsome young detective from the Morals Division had waltzed into the Robbery Squad one late summer afternoon, taking both her heart and her virginity in their first week of dating. Two months later she was pregnant. When she told him, he had confessed to her he was married and had a child. After the initial shock, she realized that he would never leave his family broke off the relationship, and had an abortion. Afterwards, the few who knew her best couldn't help but comment on a certain sadness about her.

Not long afterward, Anita began to hear rumors floating around the squad about large amount of narcotics held in the property room. Many times, she overheard the detectives sitting around the squad room joking about the lax security and how easy it would be to replace the drugs with anything from powder to sugar and simply walk out with the real stuff. After that, all it took was some planning on her part, along with the seduction of a detective from the Narcotic Squad, who, before resigning from the Police Department, set her up with an eager, local street dealer named Lorenzo. It was Lorenzo who had eventually convinced Lieutenant Kirby to help with the theft of the drugs, and he, Kirby, later blackmailed Detective White to assist him with removing the narcotics from the drug evidence room. At the time, she thought bringing Kirby on board had been a smart move, but now she was beginning to regret that decision. It could all come back to haunt her if she wasn't careful, and she didn't like that feeling one bit.

Driving back to headquarters, she smiled at the thought of those smart assed detectives at the Robbery Squad eventually finding out that the supervisor in charge of their office staff had outsmarted them all, and disappeared. She parked across from the main entrance and pulled her phone from her purse. The voice on the other end answered on the first ring.

"I need his services one more time. I'm willing to pay the same figure we discussed before. Is that acceptable to you? Good, have him call me as soon as he gets here; tell him to use the same number he used before, and be prepared to stay for at least two days. I will send your fee immediately." She put the phone back into her purse and smiled to herself as she exited her car and headed for her desk.

Vadin had just turned off the highway into a truck stop to get something to eat when his phone began to vibrate. He quickly pulled into a parking space and put the phone to his ear.

"Vadin."

His boss explained that there had been a change in plans. He would need to return to Washington D.C. to take care of another situation that had come up, and he would have to be there for at least two days. He would contact the same person he had dealt with previously, and do exactly what they asked. While his boss continued to talk, Vadin fumbled in his pants pocket for the slip of paper that contained the contact's phone number. Relieved to find it still in his possession, he went on listening. He was told that when he got home, there would be some extra money waiting for him.

After getting something to eat, Vadin began the long drive back to Washington, D.C. He was a little angry at having to return after driving all this way, but smiled at the thought of another chance to use his beloved Dragunov. He wondered what his new assignment could be. No matter. Whatever it was, he would get it done quickly and get home as fast as possible. After he was paid he might ask for some time off. A more appealing thought was that, if he were successful in pulling off this additional impromptu assignment, his boss might consider giving him his own crew. He sped down the interstate, looking forward to his future.

CHAPTER THIRTY-TWO

Not long after leaving Frank at the courthouse, Tony's cell phone rang. Keeping one hand on the steering wheel, he punched the speaker button and heard Lamont, who could hardly contain himself.

"You want to hear some serious shit?" he said, his voice cracking.

"You bet I do," replied Tony. "I need to hear something good."

"Well, here it comes. I followed Kirby like you told me, and guess where he went, and who he met?" asked Lamont.

"Okay, I'll bite. Who?"

"First, I gotta tell you how this all went down. I tailed Kirby as soon as he left his house, and followed him to the Mayflower Hotel downtown. After he went in, I had to find a place to park, which took me a few minutes, so I lost sight of him. Anyway, I finally found a lot for my car, went into the hotel, and started looking for him. I found him in the restaurant having lunch with somebody you might know."

"Hey Lamont, will I still be young when this story ends, or are you going to tell me what's happening?" Tony was growing impatient.

"Keep your pants on, Boss," said Lamont. "I promise it'll be worth the wait."

"Okay, but get to it, will you?"

"Anyway," continued Lamont, "they sat in the back corner of the room chatting like old friends, right up until the end of their conversation, when the woman sorta jumped up and left without even waiting for her food to arrive."

"Did you get a good look at her?"

"Yeah, she walked right by me as if I didn't even exist, and not only did I get a good look at her, I got both of them on video too!"

"Outstanding!"Tony hollered into the phone., "So, who is this mysterious woman?"

"Do you remember at Maurice's wake you introduced me to the lady that runs your Robbery Squad office?" asked Lamont.

"Are you talking about Anita, our office manager?" Tony was in disbelief.

"Yep, that's who it is. I remember you telling me she was the one who was responsible for making sure the office ran smoothly, and your guys wouldn't know what to do without her."

"Shit!" said Tony. "Are you absolutely sure? This is hard to believe. Keep your phone close because I'm gonna need to see that video as quickly as I can arrange it with my boss. I'll get back to you in a couple of minutes," he said. He hung up and called Frank's home number.

Frank had just walked into his house and checked his messages, pleased to see he already had a call from Inspector Billings with the names of the recommended detectives, when his phone rang once more.

It was Tony on the other end, and Frank had to sit down on the comfortable old couch he had inherited from his parents when he heard what Sergeant Spinella had to tell him. He struggled to wrap his head around what he heard. *Anita?* He had always looked at her as the glue that held the entire office together. She was the most important civilian in the office. It simply couldn't be. He let out a sigh, trying to pull himself together.

"Tony, did Lamont actually get the impression that they were conspiring?"

After he listened closely to Tony a minute or two longer, he was convinced.

"Tony, I'm expecting Virginia over in a little while. Can you get the video and meet me at my place, and we can all watch it together?" Tony said he would contact Lamont, and they would be at his place within the hour.

Frank quickly called the judge and told her about what he had just learned, and that Tony would be bringing the video over for them to view.

"It might turn out to be a long evening," she replied. "I've got a bottle of Merlot on hand. Why don't I bring it along and you and I can enjoy a small sample before the boys arrive?"

Frank didn't argue with the lady. He smiled to himself and hung up the phone.

CHAPTER THIRTY-THREE

Fitzpatrick made his way to his boss's front door and rang the bell. Kirby quickly opened the door and waved Fitz inside.

"What can I get you to drink? Beer? Wine?" asked Kirby.

"A cold beer would be great," answered Fitz. After handing him a beer, Kirby, with a smug look on his face, related to Fitz what had happened earlier that day between him and Anita. Fitz was floored.

"Is she for real, I mean, this is no bullshit, is it?"

"It's the real deal, and she is one scheming, nasty bitch," replied Kirby. "So what we have to do is play along, make our big score, and then lay low for a while. You know she was the one who had Lorenzo killed, don't you? She practically admitted it to me during our meeting, and I don't doubt for a minute she'd have me killed too, if I don't play ball her way," said a very serious Kirby.

"Boss, you sound like you really believe that shit about her having Lorenzo killed. Do you really think she's capable of all that, I mean, she's just a secretary for God's sake?"

"Fitz, I'm no dummy, and you weren't there, so shut up and listen," answered an irritated Kirby. "She's been planning this for years, and I really don't know how long she and Lorenzo have been raiding the evidence room. I think it's been at least a couple of years, and that proves *she's* no dummy, either. You had to be there to know she is one serious bitch. I knew when I looked into her eyes, that she wouldn't hesitate to have my ass if I didn't go along with what she wanted me to do."

"So what do we do?"

"For the time being, we go along to get along. She holds all the cards, and frankly, I don't know who else is in this with her. All I know is we're going to go along with her program, make our score, and then find a way to point suspicion her way. While I'm thinking about it, have you heard from Dave?"

"No, not for the past two days," Fitz replied.

"You know," said Kirby, "I think he might become a problem for us down the road, and we need to do something about it before it comes back and bites us on the ass. You and I both know he's the weak link here, so why don't you give him a call, set up a meet, and maybe arrange something for our little friend that won't point to us." Kirby paused, took a big swallow from his beer, and looked directly at Fitzpatrick. "Can I depend on you to take care of this for us? Remember, it's your ass on the line right along with mine if he decides to switch sides."

Fitz looked at his boss and slowly nodded his head.

Since his divorce, Dave had been living in an upstairs apartment in an old house that someone, back in the sixties, had converted into four rental apartments. From the beginning of his involvement with Kirby and Fitzpatrick, he had become progressively more paranoid about being thrown to the wolves. It had gotten so bad, he had begun parking his car a couple of blocks away from his apartment, to throw off anyone who might be watching his place. He regularly checked the street in front of his apartment for surveillance. It was during one of these routine checks that he noticed a car parked under a tree about twenty yards down the street with the big bulky figure of Fitz sitting in the front seat. Quickly backing away from the window, Dave went to the bedroom to get his service weapon from the dresser.

He returned to the living room where he sat down on the couch with gun in hand facing the front door. Truly scared for one of the first times in his life, he decided that instead of just sitting there waiting for Fitz to come for him, he would get out of there and get somewhere safe. He could just be overreacting, but a gut feeling told him differently and getting away seemed to be the smart thing to do. Checking the hallway to make sure no one was there, he made his way down the stairs to the basement storage area, where he forced open a door he hadn't used in many years. It led to an old attached garage that opened onto the back alley. He walked the two blocks to his car as fast as he could, got in and drove away.

He couldn't decide where to go—he was done for, no matter which way he turned. His partner was out to silence him, and that piece of shit Kirby had probably put him up to it. He headed over to Virginia, where he got a room at a reasonably priced hotel on Courthouse Road.

After getting settled, he asked the bellman who directed him to a nearby convenience store and he set out to get a little something to snack on while he figured out his next move. He deliberately chose an exit through a side door, seeing nothing suspicious as he walked up the hill to the small grocery.

He returned to his hotel room with a six-pack of soda and some potato chips. Grabbing one of the plastic cups provided, he poured himself some soda and put together a plan. After two cans of soda and a caffeine rush, he determined there were three ways out of his situation, none of them boding well for him.

The first plan was to withdraw all his savings from the credit union and run for it. His second option was to take out both Fitzpatrick and Kirby before they could get to him, but that might prove hard to pull off, since they both carried guns too. The third option was to reach out to Captain McCathran and convince him that he became involved with Fitzpatrick and Kirby only because they had threatened his life, and after witnessing them kill Detective White, he was absolutely certain they would make good on their promise to kill him if he didn't do as he was told. If Captain McCathran believed his story, he would even agree to testify for the prosecution, if it would help his position. This option was a bit thin, but if he could pull it off, he stood a good chance of walking away from this mess with only the loss of his job and pension. Though not entirely convinced he should trust McCathran, it was his best shot and he picked up the phone and called Robbery Squad. He left a message at the duty desk with Detective Jim Pratt, an officer he'd known for several years, stating he would call back in the morning.

Sitting in his car parked down the street from Dave's apartment, Fitz became suspicious. If Dave thought that someone was looking for him, he wouldn't be coming and going through the front door of his building, but would probably come and go from a back entrance.

Fitz drove his car around to the back of Dave's building. He cut his lights and slowly cruised down the alley running behind the apartment. He spotted a lone figure ahead, walking swiftly down the alley. He stopped the car and looked hard at the disappearing figure: the slightly bow-legged person walking away looked a lot like his partner.

Fitz backed out of the alley and drove around the block to where the alley intersected with the street. Just as he turned the corner, halfway down the block, he saw a car's lights go on as it slowly pulled away from the curb and drove away. Falling in behind the car, he recognized Dave's private vehicle, and he dropped a few car lengths back to avoid being spotted. As they both made their way through town to the Fourteenth Street Bridge, and then south into Virginia, Fitz frequently changed lanes to avoid suspicion. *Where was that idiot going?*

Sipe's car turned onto Route 50, and after a short ride, got off onto North Courthouse Road where he pulled into a hotel parking lot, got out of his car and went inside. Fitz parked his car where he could see the check-in desk through the lobby window and watched Dave check in. He would be patient and wait a while before he located his partner's room and paid him a visit. Right now, he was hungry, and he rummaged through his glove box for something to eat. Finding a couple of candy bars to hold him over, he settled in to wait for the front desk activity to die down.

CHAPTER THIRTY-FOUR

Vadin checked into a cheap tourist motel located in a mostly black neighborhood in Northeast Washington DC. He wasn't there long before his phone sounded. He heard his boss's voice asking if he had spoken to his contact yet.

"No, I just checked into my room; I'm going to call right now." His boss warned him to make sure the situation was completely handled and to not get caught. He shook his head in frustration, ended the call and removed the slip of paper with the contact number from his pocket.

"Are you in the city?" said the female voice after he dialed the number.

"Yes, I am here, and I'm ready for your instructions."

"Good. I want you to stay by your phone until I contact you again. There may be two targets."

"I can handle that. I will wait to hear from you," replied Vadin, and he hung up.

x

By the time Tony arrived at Frank's place, Lamont, Frank and Judge, Gills were all sitting and enjoying a glass of wine while they discussed the case. Tony turned down the offer of a wine, anxious to get to Lamont's video from the Mayflower.

As they watched the video, Tony felt like a part of him had been taken away. Over the years, he had placed so much trust in Anita. He couldn't believe the person on the video was someone he had worked with for so long. During the dark days of his divorce, he had confided in Anita, valued her advice. Despite there being no audio, he could see by the expressions on their faces that Anita was in total charge of the meeting. After it concluded, Lamont asked the question on everyone's mind.

"What do we do now?"

The judge pointed a finger at Tony. "The first thing we need to do, as I suggested at our last meeting, is find our Mr. Sipe, and if possible get him to turn on his friends."

"I'm working on it," said Tony. "As soon as we finish here, I'm going over to his place and try and scare him a little."

"Just be careful, Tony," said Frank, "because he's a cop, he knows what's waiting for him if he gets busted. He might do something crazy."

"Don't worry, Boss," laughed Tony. "I'm gonna take Lamont with me as insurance."

Lamont jumped to his feet, demanding to be given some "heat" to carry for his own protection. Tony was still laughing when the two of them left Frank's and headed over to Sipe's.

Tony located the address given to him by his friend in personnel, parking about half a block away. From this vantage point he had a full view of the front of the building, and knowing that Sipe didn't know what his personal vehicle looked like, Tony felt secure enough to attempt some surveillance.

"Watch for anything unusual," Tony told Lamont. "I'm gonna go check out the foyer and see if I can find out which apartment is his."

He made his way to the front entrance, scanning the area as he did so. Once inside, he walked over to a row of dilapidated mailboxes, sprayed with graffiti, and found Sipe's name crudely written in the slot for apartment four. Using the stairs, he went to the second floor where two doors accessed the landing. He stood and listened for a minute or so, hearing only the sound of his own breathing. Fearing discovery, he headed back down the stairwell.

Taking the stairs two at a time, he heard his cell phone go off. Ignoring the call, he exited the building and returned to the car.

"He lives upstairs, apartment four," Tony said as he jumped into the driver's seat. "There are two units up there. I didn't see or hear anything."

"I know," said Lamont. "I tried to phone you. Sorry. That was probably a mistake."

"That was you?"

"Yeah, it was me. I thought you should know that I didn't see any lights on in the windows upstairs. Didn't look like anybody was home. You know," he added, "I can easily get into his pad. Most of these old buildings have simple locks. I can be in and out in no time."

"No," answered Tony. "We're going to do this the way the judge wants it done."

"Sounds good to me," said Lamont. "It might be a good idea to check around the area to see if his car is here."

"That is a good idea. I remember seeing him not too long ago, in front of headquarters, driving an old blue four-door sedan with Virginia plates. I think he used to live in Virginia when he was married. Let's check a two or three block radius," said Tony, as he pulled away from the curb.

They searched a four block area for about an hour; finding nothing, they called it a night. Tony dropped Lamont off at his house and headed home. He remembered he hadn't phoned Lina since their earlier lunch conversation. He would probably catch hell about it, but pulled over to make the call anyway.

He put the phone on speaker and let it ring several times. It was kind of late—she was probably already in bed. He started to disconnect the call when he heard her breathless voice.

"Tony, is that you?"

"Yeah, baby, it's me," he replied in his most soothing tone.

"Where have you been? Are you ok?"

"I'm good. I'm sorry I didn't call. A lot's been happening."

"It's ok, sweetheart. I just miss our quality time. I wish this whole Maurice mess would just go away and leave us alone."

"We're getting close; it won't be much longer before we drop the hammer on these bums, and then we'll have all the time in the world to be together. Don't forget, I'm the guy who's had to walk away from your warm bed on *two* occasions now," Tony teased.

"Of course I won't forget," said Lina. "And we're gonna make up for it as soon as possible. We'll turn off all our phones, okay?"

"That sounds like a plan to me."

After saying goodnight Tony pulled away from the curb and continued on to his house. Twenty minutes later, he flipped down his neighborhood parking sign and headed for his front door. Before he got to the front gate, he took some precautions. He stopped near a large oak and listened for a moment, then went to check the rear door before going inside. He walked to the corner and then down the back alley and entered his backyard. The full moon lit up the vacant yard. No one waiting to kill him there. He went back around to the front and after checking that all was secure, went inside his home.

He made a beeline straight to his bedroom, flopped down fully clothed onto the bed, and fell asleep instantly.

Noise. Confusion. Tony fumbled for the ringing cell phone on the nightstand and barked groggily.

"Spinella. Whatever you have to say, it better be good!"

It was Frank. "You need to get your ass here as fast as you can. All hell has broken loose."

"What's going on?" Tony mumbled through a dry mouth, his eyes still closed.

"Sipe called and left me a message sometime last night, saying he was going to call me back this morning. It's a good thing I couldn't sleep last night and decided to come in early to clear up some paper work. I want you here when he calls. Get your ass moving."

"I'm on my way, Boss," replied Tony, hanging up the phone.

He got undressed, grabbed some clean underwear and a T-shirt, splashed some cold water on his face, threw on some deodorant and was out the door in five minutes.

CHAPTER THIRTY-FIVE

Tony gratefully poured himself fresh "office coffee"—it was early in the day—and walked into Frank's office. It wasn't long until the phone rang; Frank gestured for Tony to pick up a nearby extension.

"Captain McCathran!" There was a momentary pause on the line before they heard Dave's voice.

"Is it safe to talk?"

"Yes, it's safe. What can I do for you, Detective?" said Frank.

"I have information for you that will rock the department, and probably cause some people to go to jail. I'm scared, and if these people find out I've talked to you, they'll kill me. I've seen them kill before, and they won't hesitate to kill me. I need protection, and if you can protect me, I'll tell you everything that I know about these bastards," said a terrified Sipe.

"Where are you now?" Tony broke in.

"Who's that?" Sipe shot back, startled to hear a strange voice.

"That's Sergeant Spinella." said Frank. "He'll be working on this with me, and you can trust him to not let any of this get out before we're ready."

"Don't tell anyone else!" Sipe was becoming rattled. "I don't want anybody to know where I am. I'm in the first hotel you'll come to after you get off Route fifty onto North Courthouse Road in Arlington. My room number is two twenty four, and I'll wait right here for you. I need to know who's coming, or I don't open the door."

"Detective," interjected Tony, "we're on our way. Do *not* open the door for anyone other than Captain McCathran or me, do you understand?"

"Yeah, but hurry, I'm scared shitless," replied Sipe. He started to hang up but realized Spinella was still talking.

"Do you have your weapon with you, Detective?"

"Yeah, Sarge, I got it with me."

"Use it if anyone other than us comes for you," said Tony, "but when we get there, I want to see it in your holster, and nowhere else, you got that?"

"Yeah, I got it," said Sipe hanging up the phone.

Frank high-fived Tony. "Now we can get the hard evidence the judge wants, and there's no reason, if Sipe cooperates and gives us what he knows, that we can't get those warrants."

"We better get going," said Tony, "because traffic into Virginia is usually a bitch this time of day, and the sooner we scoop him up the better I'll feel."

Tony drove the unmarked cruiser while Frank got on the phone with the Judge's assistant. They headed for the Fourteenth Street Bridge into Virginia.

"The judge is in trial at the moment," said Frank after he hung up. "Her assistant will get a note to her right away since I told her it was urgent. I think she'll be pleased at the latest developments, and when I talk to her, I'm gonna ask her to contact Sullivan. If she calls him, it'll carry more weight than if you or I called. Anyway, the ball is moving and we gotta keep after it until we finish this mess—get those pieces of shit off the job and in jail."

"You realize, Frank," said Tony, "we're going to get our asses kicked by the media when this whole mess comes out. I'd like for us, and by that I mean our impromptu task force, to be the first ones exposing the corruption story to the press. That way, we can shape it to our advantage and show the public that we enforce the law no matter who's involved— even the police."

"That works for me," said Frank.

They took the turn off Route 50 and onto North Courthouse Road. Tony made a left into the parking lot of the hotel and parked near the entrance. They went inside and took the elevator to the second floor.

After searching the hallway in both directions they found Sipe's room number. Tony, with his hand on his weapon, knocked loudly.

"Who is it?" Sipe called through the door.

"Captain McCathran and Sergeant Spinella," replied Tony. "Open the door."

Sipe slowly opened the door, stepping back to let the men enter, his hand on his service weapon. Moving into the room, Tony quickly approached Sipe and removed the detective's weapon from its holster and handed it to Frank, who, after clearing the weapon, put it in his coat pocket. Sipe was showing signs of a complete breakdown: Unshowered, unshaven, and the haggard look of no sleep.

"What do you guys want to know? I'll tell you whatever," he said anxiously.

"Right now, all we want you to do is take it easy. We're gonna take you someplace safe where we can all relax and discuss how you can help us," Frank answered.

"Where are you taking me?" Sipe's head swiveled back and forth as he shot looks at Tony and Frank. "Who else knows about this? You guys have got to keep this quiet or they'll find out and try and shut me up."

"We'll answer all your questions in a little while, but for right now, let's get you outta here," said Tony, trying to sooth the agitated Sipe.

After collecting his personal belongings from the room, the three of them made their way down to the lobby. Tony went ahead, instructing Frank and Sipe to wait inside the lobby until he pulled up in the cruiser. They waited until Tony rolled up to the front entrance and made a quick dash for the car, both of them jumping into the back seat. Tony sped away as soon as he heard the rear door slam.

The sound of a nearby car door slamming woke Fitz from a deep sleep. He had been asleep most of the night. He checked the parking lot for Dave's car, noting it was in the same spot as where he had last seen it. Maybe he had lucked out after all.

He wiped the sleep from his eyes, got out of the car and headed for the hotel lobby. It was starting to get busy with people checking out—a good time to get Dave's room number without drawing a lot of attention.

He walked inside and noticed the bell boy, a kid not much over eighteen, standing by the elevators. He removed a twenty from his wallet and approached the young man, giving him a story about his old high school buddy being registered there and wanting to surprise him. It took another ten bucks to persuade the kid, but finally he walked away to get the information Fitz needed. After waiting what seemed like forever, he returned and told Fitz the room number.

Fitz thanked the boy, took the stairs to the second floor and located room two twenty four. He put his ear to the door and listened for any signs of activity. Nothing. The lock on the door was electronic. He would have to wait for the cleaning crew to make their rounds, then slip in. He went to the end of the hallway and called Kirby.

"Boss," he began when he heard the lieutenant's bark, "I'm over here in Virginia. I've been here all night keeping an eye on Sipe."

"Virginia? What the hell, Fitz!"

"You told me to take care of some loose ends, and I'm glad I did. I think he's running," Fitz reassured his boss.

"Call me back on my other phone!" Kirby groused.

When Fitz called back, Kirby was speaking in a whisper. "Tell me what's going on." Fitz could hear Kirby's door closing in the background.

"Last night I followed Dave over here to a hotel on Courthouse Road. I haven't seen him leave, and I've been watching all night. His car is still parked in the same spot.

I have a plan to get into his room. I'll call you as soon as everything is taken care of."

"Don't take any chances," the lieutenant warned. "Make damned sure no one sees you. If it gets dicey, back off. We can take care of things later."

"Playin' it real careful, Boss. Don't worry—it'll be over shortly. I'll call you." Fitz hung up, taking a deep breath and exhaling. Kirby was placated, for now.

He headed back toward Dave's room and spotted the cleaning crew, who were just starting their rounds at the opposite end of the hallway. He figured it would probably take them an hour or so to reach Sipe's room, so he left the hotel in search of a place to grab some breakfast.

He located a diner within a few blocks and wolfed down some eggs and fries. He lingered a while, enjoying a couple of coffee refills, before he returned to the hotel.

His timing was perfect. The cleaning cart was stopped right in front of room two twenty four. He stuck his head in the door and called out.

"Hello, it's me. This is my room and I think I forgot my cell phone…."

No response. The bed was unmade—someone had slept there, anyway. Other than that, there was a half-empty bottle of scotch. Nothing else—no luggage, clothes, anything.

Walking back to his car, Fitz dreaded the call he would have to make to Kirby. He would be blamed for this no matter what he said. He would buy himself some time, delay the call. Instead, he phoned his office and asked his sergeant for some compensatory time off—and got it.

As soon as Frank, Tony, and Sipe got onto the Fourteenth Street Bridge, the mood in the cruiser changed dramatically. Frank, sitting in the back seat looking straight ahead, began to grill Sipe.

"Listen up, Detective. We're taking you to Sergeant Spinella's house, where you'll be safe. You'll be protected around the clock. You'll be Mirandized before we begin with any questioning. I'm warning you that anything you tell us had better be the truth, because if we think you're bullshitting us at any time, your ass is going straight to jail." Sipe started to open his mouth but Frank raised his hand. "Don't say anything, just listen. We're gonna need you to give us the name of all police officers involved, as well as the particulars: who gives the orders, who grabs the drugs, and who they sell them to. For right now, just keep quiet and relax. You're gonna have plenty of time to tell your story before this is all over."

Tony watched Sipe in the rearview mirror. Sinking down into his seat, looking like a whipped dog, he remained silent.

Frank placed a call to Virginia next.

"Virginia, we have Detective Sipe in our custody and we're headed over to Sergeant Spinella's place. Do you think you can contact the others and arrange for them to meet us there later this evening?" After a short pause, he said, "No, we haven't questioned him and don't intend to until everyone gets to Tony's place later." He spoke to her a minute or so longer, then hung up. He leaned forward over the front seat.

"The judge is going to contact everyone on the team and arrange a meeting at your place this evening. She also told me not to interrogate Sipe until everyone was there, just to make sure we dotted all the i's and crossed all the t's to make sure everything was done legally."

Tony was relieved. He wasn't looking forward to grilling a fellow officer—even though he *was* a piece of shit and deserved to go to prison. When he pulled up in front of his house, he handed his house key over the seat to Frank.

"Go on in while I park the car. There's cold beer in the 'fridge. Get me one, too."

Fitz waited an hour before calling Kirby. Dave had somehow slipped past him, and his car was still in the same spot from the previous night. His mind was in such turmoil he didn't hear Kirby answer.

"It's all gone to shit," Fitz said, snapping back to reality. "He's disappeared, and I don't know how he did it. I've checked inside his room, and no one was there. The bed had been slept in, but there was no other trace of that little rat other than a half empty bottle of scotch. His car is still where he parked it. I don't have a clue."

"Get to my place as fast as you can!" Kirby barked and hung up.

Before he headed for Kirby's, Fitz checked with the front desk to see if anyone had noticed Dave leave. When he returned to his car, he was ashen. He drove back into the city, his face contorted with worry. If Sipe turned on them, his chances of saving his job and his pension—let alone avoiding jail time—were very slim.

CHAPTER THIRTY-SIX

Anita had spent the last few days gathering everything she would need to disappear. She was a great advocate of the Peter Principle, and a true believer in proper planning and preparation, if one hoped to be successful in life. She was also smart enough to see that right now, there were too many variables in play: all it would take to expose her would be a single misstep by anyone working for her.

Standing in her bedroom, she looked at the beautiful window curtains she had purchased with her first paycheck from the department, and remembered how proud she had been to put them up without help from anybody. She couldn't believe that as a young single girl, all alone, and new to Washington D.C., she had managed to buy and furnish a beautiful, thirty-year-old, three bedroom home in a mixed neighborhood in Southeast. She recalled hitting her finger with a hammer when she put her brand new bed frame together. She looked down at the array of false documents spread across her bed and marveled at how far she had come.

At best, there were only one or two weeks left before all hell broke loose. She had already made most of her arrangements, and only needed one more visit to the property room to grab one final batch of narcotics. After that, she could leave with enough money to live the rest of her life in a reasonably comfortable style.

Checking her documents one more time, she had obtained two of almost everything she might need to build her new life. She had two different state drivers' licenses, one with an official picture of her as a blonde, and the other as a brunette; she had two birth certificates, two Social Security cards, library cards, several credit cards, and two passports, one from Australia, and the other a British issue.

Six months ago, using a false identity, she had paid cash to a private owner for a two-year-old vehicle in near-perfect condition, and stashed it where she could easily get to it. A plastic surgeon in Brazil was ready to change her appearance as soon as she arrived. She had it down to the last detail.

She picked up her cell to phone Kirby. It was time to set the final date for the narcotics move. It suddenly occurred to her, however, that Lorenzo was dead. *How would they move the drugs?* Placing her cell phone back on the nightstand, she went to the kitchen, fixed herself a generous bowl of chocolate almond ice cream, and sat down to think. She needed someone with the right contacts to help her move the drugs—someone whom she could trust, and then later, could be quietly disposed of.

Vadin was bored out of his mind and pissed off at the same time. There had been no call from his contact for the last forty-eight hours. Needing to stretch his legs, he left his dingy motel room and walked along New York Avenue, in the direction of downtown Washington. He got to the intersection of Florida Avenue and spotted a seedy-looking neighborhood bar. He needed a cold beer and some company.

Once inside, he saw a few patrons seated around a couple of rickety tables. There was one man sitting at the bar. Vadin grabbed a barstool, sat down and ordered a beer. The bartender, who could easily have weighted four-hundred pounds, studied him for a second or two.

"What kinda beer you want?" he asked.

"Anything cold," replied Vadin.

The bartender reached into a cooler behind him then turned around, putting the tall bottle on the bar in front of Vadin.

"That'll be five bucks," the bartender said.

Vadin took a long pull from the bottle first, then reached into his pocket and threw a twenty on the bar. As the bartender picked up the money and went to the register, he felt the presence of someone behind him. He turned to see a heavy-set black man standing there staring at him.

"How are you today?" Vadin said, eyeing the man cautiously.

"How 'bout you buying me a beer?" the man replied with a smile.

Vadin studied him a moment, then shrugged. "Sure, I buy you a beer. Sit. We can talk."

The man took the barstool to Vadin's right. "Man, we can talk. ' Long as you keep the beer comin'," the man said.

The bartender approached them. "Reggie, drink your beer and get on home, ok?" he addressed the man in what sounded to be a familiar manner.

"I don't got to go *anywhere*," replied Reggie in a raised voice. "I'm a man, I do what I want. Don't be tellin' me to go home!"

Vadin took a final drink from his beer and rose from his barstool to leave. Reggie reached out and grabbed his arm.

"I'm not through drinkin,' Whitey. Sit yo ass back down and buy me another beer."

Vadin jerked his arm away. "Sorry, my friend. I've got to go now. It was nice to meet you."

Suddenly Reggie grabbed him and wrapped his beefy arm around his throat, choking him and screaming something about a "white devil." Vadin wasted no time. Within seconds the neck knife appeared from inside his shirt. Vadin in one swift move snapped open the blade and sliced Reggie's arm, opening a large cut that began to bleed profusely. Reggie screamed and let go.

The bartender, clutching a large towel, ran from behind the bar and called out to Vadin. "Get the hell outta here before the cops come!" He twisted the towel into a tourniquet and began to wrap Reggie's arm to stop the bleeding from his severed artery.

Vadin exited the bar quickly, dodging cars as he crossed the busy street, and went behind a building where he removed his bloody jacket and threw it, along with his baseball cap, into a dumpster. Needing to get out the the neighborhood as fast as possible, he hailed a cab. He instructed the cabbie to drop him at a spot roughly six blocks from his motel. He would walk the rest of the way to his motel, so as to not give away his location.

Once back in his room, he berated himself for breaking his cardinal rule of not interacting with anyone while on the job. *No help for it now.* He washed away his attacker's blood, changed his clothes, and checked out.

CHAPTER THIRTY-SEVEN

Tony walked into his kitchen to find Frank and Sipe seated at his table. Frank was sipping a beer, while Sipe had opted for a soda.

"Did you get one out for me?" he asked.

"Sorry," said Frank. "I didn't know how long it would take you to find a parking space, and I didn't want your beer to get cold."

"That's okay," replied Tony. "I can get it myself." After grabbing a beer, Tony sat down at the table and began to ask Frank a few questions about how this would all go down after everyone got there. Frank then explained that he was going to leave all of that up to Assistant U.S. Attorney Sullivan, and Judge Gills, to figure out, since they were the legal brains of the bunch. Dave, who had been sitting quietly drinking his can of soda, became animated.

"I want immunity, or I don't testify!" Tony turned to look at Dave, and before he or Frank could say a word, Dave went on. "I have information that can close a lot of cases, and

I need some kind of protection from these killers before I'm saying a damn word."

Frank spoke first. "Listen to me you, little shit! You're not telling us anything—no demands, no nothing—until everyone's here, and we can work out how this is gonna go down, got it?"

"Yeah, I got it," said Dave, recoiling. "I didn't mean no disrespect, but I'm scared, and these fuckers are killers."

"We know that," said Tony, "but for right now, just take it easy, we'll protect you."

"Are you sure you can protect me?" asked Dave in a subdued voice. "Remember, these are cops we're talking about, and they know how to find people."

"As far as we know, nobody knows that we have you," answered Tony, "or where you are. We intend to keep it that way until the last minute. So don't worry yourself about them. Right now, all you have to worry about is telling the truth about what's going on. Remember, you only have one shot at seeing some light at the end of the tunnel, so if you have any brains at all, you better work with us."

"I plan to," said Dave, choking down a big gulp of soda. . "Why the hell do you think I called you if I wasn't gonna cooperate? I'm scared, and they threatened to kill me!"

"Okay, as long as we're all on the same page, but for right now, just relax. They'll all be here shortly, and we can get started. For right now, no more discussion about the case. We need you to be rested and clear-headed so you can answer all their questions," said Tony.

Two hours later Tony answered the door and, to his pleasure, Inspector Billings entered. He ushered him inside, took a quick glance toward the street, and shut the front door. He explained to the inspector that, in order to save time, they wouldn't discuss anything until all the interested parties were present. After seating him in the living room, he went to get him a drink. When he returned, the inspector had let in two more people: Sullivan, and a woman carrying a large bag whom he didn't recognize. They were engaged in animated conversation when Tony walked into the room.

Sullivan smiled and extended his hand to Tony. "Hey pal, looks like we might end up with a case after all."

"We might have a shot, Sully, but we need to wring every bit of information we can get out of this little bastard before he changes his mind," he replied..

"I agree," said Sully, "and I also think it would be a good idea for us to have a pow-wow before we question the witness, to decide exactly what we need to know, and in what order. Oh, by the way, I must apologize; I didn't introduce you to Mrs. Martin, our stenographer. She's been with me for over twenty years and I trust her implicitly," added Sullivan. He turned and gestured to the woman who was yet engaged in conversation with the inspector. She walked over to Tony and Sully, held out her hand, and in a soft voice said,

"Hi, I'm Cathy Martin, and I've heard a lot of nice things about you, Sergeant."

"Don't for one minute, believe any of it," said Tony. "It's nice to meet you, Mrs. Martin, but I must admit, I'm somewhat curious about why you're here."

"That was my idea," interjected Sully. "I decided that we might need a record of this interview with Detective Sipe, and Cathy is the best we have. She'll do a great job. She's been sworn to secrecy, and she's also brought her video equipment to augment her written report. That way, we cover all the bases at one time."

"So that's what you have in the bag?" asked Tony.

"Yep, everything we're going to need to document this interview is 'in the bag,'" laughed Cathy.

Tony heard the front door bell chime and went to open the door. Opening the door, he greeted Judge Virginia Gills, who entered carrying a large grocery bag.

"Welcome, Judge," said Tony, bending down to take the bag. "What have we here?" he asked, leading her into the living room.

"Oh, just a few snacks we can all enjoy later," she replied. She strode over to the other people assembled. After shaking hands and being introduced to Mrs. Martin, the judge suggested that they all take seats, and work out how they plan to approach the witness. Before they started, Judge Gills asked Tony where Frank was.

"Judge, he's in the kitchen with the witness. We need to have somebody with Sipe at all times, because we don't really know what he'll do. He's desperate and scared to death of those other rogue cops. I'll go and relieve him, so he can be part of the planning session.

"What was all the laughing about?" Frank asked when Tony entered the kitchen.

"That was me, I'm a hit!" he replied facetiously. "Maybe after I leave the job I'll pursue a career as a stand-up comedian."

"Yeah, right, you're already a comedian," said his boss. "Is everyone here?"

"Yeah, they're all here and waiting for you in the living room. I'll stay here and keep our guest company. Do me a favor boss, keep me posted on what's going on, okay?"

"Will do," said Frank as he left the room.

"What happens now?" asked Sipe.

"They're all in there trying to decide what they want to ask you," said Tony. "If I was you, I'd make it a point to tell them everything you know, because, like I said earlier, if you have any hope of ever seeing the end of this, your only way out is to tell the truth."

"I know, man," whispered Sipe, "and I intend to tell everything. Just promise to keep me safe from them, and I'll help you break this wide open."

Fitz walked up to his boss's front door, dreading the confrontation about to take place. Kirby opened the door before he had a chance to knock and invited him into the living room.

"Take a seat," instructed Kirby, "and tell me what's going on."

Fitzpatrick related all of the details of his unsuccessful search for Dave, except for the information he was able to obtain at the last minute.

Kirby studied him for a minute. Fitz's palms were sweaty and he rubbed them together. "What haven't you told me?" his boss asked, finally.

"Boss, I think it might be time for us to shit and get. After I talked to you the last time, I decided to check one more time with the front desk crew, to see if any of them remembered seeing someone fitting the description of Dave in the hotel."

"Well? What the hell did they say?" snapped Kirby.

"The young girl on duty remembered seeing him leave with what she thought were two plainclothes cops," said Fitz. "She remembered because she had just come from the restaurant with her coffee, and they were blocking the doorway between the front entrance door and the restaurant door, and she had to walk around them."

"That's it? That's all you got?" Kirby's impatience was mounting.

"Boss, there's more," whined a reluctant Fitz. "She also remembered them getting into an unmarked police cruiser. She knew what one looked like, because she used to date a detective from Arlington. Someone's got him, and we don't know who." Fitz could see Kirby's face lose most of its color—he looked like he might collapse.

"You okay, Boss?" asked Fitz. Recovering slightly, Kirby mumbled something about a license plate.

"What did you say, Boss?"

"*Did* she catch a license plate?" yelled Kirby.

"No, I asked her that. She said she only saw two guys running towards a black cruiser after it pulled up in front of the lobby doors. She did tell me that they both got into the back seat. That's all she could remember about it."

"Fitz," said Kirby, "this changes everything. We need to make plans to be out of here within the next couple of days, and I need to call the bitch and tell her the bad news. This means that we will have to make a move on the drugs within the next twenty-four hours, get our money and disappear. The way I figure it, even if they've got him, and we're not even sure who 'they' are, they won't be able to do anything right away. They'll need to follow protocol to the letter with this, because it involves police officers, and that will take some time. Shit, it'll take days before they can even get any warrants issued. I think we've got some time before the shit hits the fan. Just do what I tell you to do, Fitz, and we'll both get out of this smelling good."

Fitz was numb. It was all crumbling down around him, and he didn't know what to do. He had been a cop a long time, and for most of that time, he had been a damn good one. But now, if he didn't get the hell of there pretty quick, he would only be remembered as the dirty cop sent to jail for whatever charges they might be able to bring against him. Then it hit him. *What if that little bastard Sipe blamed the killing of Maurice on him?* Killing a police officer was some serious shit— he could conceivably get the needle—or at least spend the rest of his life behind bars. He knew what happened to police officers who were sent to prison, and he made up his mind right then, that he would much rather die, than spend one day in jail surrounded by those animals. His pity party was abruptly interrupted by Kirby.

"I'm calling her now. Don't say anything while I'm on the phone, just listen."

"Gotcha, Boss," answered Fitz. He leaned back in Kirby's recliner and took a deep breath, once again wondering how he had ended up in this mess.

CHAPTER THIRTY-EIGHT

t took over twenty minutes for Anita to calm a frantic Kirby when he phoned her about the latest developments. The moment for decision-making had arrived a little sooner than she expected, but her plan was in place. She didn't panic, but was keenly aware of what little time she had to make her last score and run. It was probably McCathran and Spinella who had gotten to Sipe. She instructed Kirby to have both of them watched. If they could find out where they had taken him, they still had a chance of keeping the lid on the whole deal.

She gave Kirby final instructions and then placed a second call. The same monotone voice from before answered.

"Do you know who this is?" she asked. Without waiting for a reply, she went on. "I will require you to be on standby for the next twenty-four hours. Your target is guarded by more than one police officer, so be extra careful. It's imperative that the subject be taken out completely. You need to be ready at at moment's notice, and you *cannot* be caught. Do you understand?"

"I understand," said the man.

Anita hung up the phone. At least she had part of this mess under control. All Kirby had to do was locate Sipe before he spilled his guts. Her next hurdle was Lorenzo's replacement. She recalled his bragging about someone he knew in Morals Division, someone with whom he had worked a couple of deals before she became involved. She racked her brain while she put the rest of her things in order. As she pushed a suitcase out of her path, it hit her.

"Charlie!" she said aloud. "Charlie Thomas." She pumped her fist, grabbed her phone and placed a call to Morals Division.

"Morals Division, Detective Duke."

"Detective, this is Anita from Robbery Squad. Is Charlie Thomas available?"

"No, I'm sorry. He's on the street. I can get a message to him if you want me to," the detective replied.

"Please, I would appreciate your having him give me a call if you would, but I'm at home, and I don't want my number to go out over the air, okay?"

"No problem, I'll take care of it right away. What's your number?"

She gave him her home number. "Anything else?" he inquired.

"No. Thanks a lot, detective. Good bye."

There might be a way out of this after all, she mused. If Charlie cooperates and helps her move the drugs, and if her man can get to Sipe, it becomes a whole new ball game. Her mood was lifting by the minute. She continued her preparations while waiting for Detective Thomas to call. An hour later she was starting to get anxious when her phone rang.

"This is Anita," she said, hitting the speaker button.

"Anita, this is Detective Thomas. I'm sorry it took so long to get back to you, but we got busy, and this was the first chance I got to call. What's up?"

"Detective, I'm sorry to bother you," said Anita, "but something came up that might be mutually beneficial to us both, and I thought that we should try and get together to discuss it. Just so you know, I've got you on speaker phone because I'm working on something and need my hands free."

"No problem. You had mentioned something in your message about a mutually beneficial situation. What are you talking about?"

"I really can't talk about it over the phone, but believe me you might be able to make a nice piece of change, if you'll take the time to meet me, and listen to what I have to offer," said Anita, in her most sexy voice. He took the bait.

"Now you've got my curiosity in high gear. I'm working four to twelve today; how about we meet tomorrow for lunch somewhere?"

"That sounds like a plan," she said. They agreed to meet at eleven thirty the following day at Flaps Restaurant, on the southwest waterfront. She finished her packing, went to her fridge once again and pulled out the carton of chocolate almond ice cream.

Sipe felt like his head was going to explode. Ever since they had Mirandized him, they had been hammering him non-stop with questions about Kirby, Fitzpatrick, Lorenzo, and some chick named Anita. They wanted to know about a lot of shit that he didn't know anything about. He tried to explain to them that he was just an innocent bystander who had been forced to help them under the threat of death. When questioned about the killing of Detective White, he gave them his rehearsed version of how he saw Detective Fitzpatrick hide behind a tree out in front of Sergeant Spinella's house, and when Detective White came out, shoot him in cold blood. He explained to his interrogators just how terrified he was of being killed just like Detective White, if he didn't continue to follow orders from both Kirby and Fitzpatrick. Much of the questioning centered around someone named Anita. For some reason, they didn't believe him when he told them he didn't know anyone named Anita.

He led them step-by-step through the routine they established for getting the drugs out of evidence and taking them to a local dealer named Lorenzo, who moved them through his contacts on the street. As he prattled on, he got the impression by the looks on various faces that his "scared gofer" defense was working. He told them how both attacks against Detective White and his brother-in-law, had been ordered by Kirby. Assistant U.S. Attorney Sullivan then insisted that he tell them all he knew about the hit on Lorenzo. Dave tried to convince them he knew nothing about it, because he had seen the man shot from half a block away, but no one appeared to believe him. They pummeled him with more questions until it dawned on him that he had an ace in the hole that might buy him some good will. As the others were discussing his answers among themselves, he raised his hand like a kindergarten student. Sullivan stopped in mid-sentence.

"What now, Sipe?"

"I just thought of something important concerning Sergeant Spinella."

"Please," said Sullivan, "enlighten us."

"Do you remember the guy that got shot over in Southeast last week?" he asked. His question was met with silence from everyone in the room. He started from the beginning.

"Let me start from when I first heard about this 'snake guy,' who was allegedly some big-time professional burglar—one of the best on the East Coast. He was also one of the biggest collectors of exotic snakes in the country."

"What's this got to do with what we're discussing right now?" interrupted Sullivan.

"If you'll just give me a chance, I'll tell you," pleaded Dave, continuing. "The snake guy was hired by Lorenzo, who'd used him before, after Kirby suggested they put a hit on Sergeant Spinella because of his involvement with the investigation. The guy was supposed to plant one of his poisonous snakes inside Spinella's house, and then get out."

"Wait a minute," interrupted Sullivan, "why would Kirby want to have Sergeant Spinella killed?"

"Simple," answered Dave. "They knew from their wiretap of the chief's office that he was Captain McCathran's best investigator, and that he would eventually get the case. Kirby also knew that Spinella had a reputation for being a bulldog when he got into an investigation, and wouldn't stop until he finished it. On top of that, everyone knows that he's a straight-shooter and you can't bribe him."

"Okay, that explains some of it, but where are you going with this?" asked Sullivan.

"If you let me finish, I'll try and make it simple for you," said Dave. Sullivan was becoming slightly irritated, but gave him a nod.

"What happened was, this nut case snake guy, I think his name was Vince, not only left a poisonous snake in Spinella's house, he also took an old thirty-eight revolver, which he wasn't supposed to do. Anyway, his stealing the gun turned out to be a stroke of luck as far as Kirby was concerned. After the snake idea didn't pan out, Fitzpatrick told him about the gun after reading it in the police report. Kirby then calls Lorenzo and convinces him to get the gun back from the guy because he thought it could tie them to the burglary. Lorenzo, who liked to mess with Kirby, offered to give the gun to him as a gift, but Kirby refused it. Several days later Kirby decides that this snake guy is a loose end, that somewhere down the line, he could help put him away. Kirby's pretty slick, and he knew that Sergeant Spinella's prints had to be the only prints on the gun, because Lorenzo made sure the snake guy always wore gloves whenever he did a job for him. So Lorenzo has the snake guy killed with Spinella's gun, which was left at the scene of the murder. Fitzpatrick would make sure he got the case. At the time, it seemed a good bet that, at the very least, Spinella would be placed on administrative leave until things were cleared up. It would get him out of the way for a while."

"Who killed this snake guy?" asked Sullivan.

"Timmy was the guy that did it," said Dave. Sullivan demanded to know who Timmy was and how he fit into the picture.

"He worked for Lorenzo," Dave explained. "He was his right-hand man."

"So where is this Timmy person right now, and how can we get to him?" Sullivan pushed.

"He's at the morgue! He got killed in an accident over in Southeast, after he killed the snake guy."

"Shit!" said Sullivan, turning to his assistant. "Cathy can you check on that for me?"

"Yes sir," said Cathy, as she got up and left the room.

"So, do you think the accident that killed your friend Timmy was really an accident?" asked Sullivan.

"First off, let's get this straight: he was *not* my friend! I hardly knew him. As far as the accident is concerned, who knows? I wasn't there, and the only two people people who might know would be Lorenzo—and he's dead—and that nut job, Kirby."

Sullivan looked over at Frank. "Let's take a short break and see where we're at."

"Good," said Sipe, "I gotta take a piss."

Sullivan's eyes followed Sipe as he headed for the bathroom. Clearly disgusted, he left the kitchen, followed by the rest of the group.

"What did you find out, Cath?"

"It's kinda weird. The medical examiner who did the autopsy said that this guy was dead before the accident happened."

"What? Did he explain how that happened?"

"Yes," she replied. "He said that the cause of death was from a venomous snake bite." The judge, seated on the sofa next to Frank, spoke up.

"According to the witness's statement, that makes sense. The deceased was obviously in the snake guy's house prior to his death, and somehow got bitten while involved in the killing of this Vince person."

"Yes, that could have happened, and he could've made it to his car and left the area before the venom took him out," said Inspector Billings, who hadn't spoken more than a dozen words the whole time.

"I'm starting to see this a bit more clearly," said Sullivan, "but we need to put more pressure on Sipe about this Anita person. He's got to know more than he's telling, and I personally think she's the center piece in this whole mess. We need to know everything about her role in the operation, and the only one who can give us that information is Sipe, so let's go back and hit him hard."

Judge Gills, who had listened to Sullivan's theory without saying a word, interrupted him. "Mr. Sullivan, I would suggest that we not push Detective Sipe too hard. He might just stop talking altogether, and we don't want that to happen at this stage of our investigation." She went on. "Maybe we should try a slightly different approach. Why can't we offer him something in return for the information you need? That might be just the thing to get him talking."

Everyone but Sullivan seemed to agree that it was a reasonable approach to take, and that it would help their case if he took the offer. Sullivan, who wanted to be in complete control of the interrogation, paused to give some thought to the judge's suggestion.

"Okay, it's worth a try. I can offer him immunity if he agrees to tell us everything he knows and testify against all other persons involved in these crimes. I'll also have to get it cleared by my boss, but I don't think I'll have any problem once I fill him in on what we have."

"Wait just a minute," Frank piped up. "I thought that we agreed that we would keep this whole thing secret until we had it sewed up.

"Frank," Judge Gills said, "I don't think at this stage of the game that bringing Sullivan's boss in on our investigation will compromise anything we're doing. As a matter of fact, if you think about it, we may be able to gain access to a lot more resources than we now have."

"Makes sense," said a mollified Frank. "Okay, I'm in."

Judge Gills, by her beaming expression, revealed her satisfaction that Frank was able to see the benefit of their liaison with the U.S. Attorney's Office. She stopped everyone before they returned to the kitchen to continue their questioning.

"I would like to remind all of you that my presence here is solely for your guidance, and that I cannot be a participant in the questioning of this witness. With that, I think it's time I left and let you all do what needs to be done."

Everyone offered her their understanding and said their goodbyes. After Judge Gills left, they went into the kitchen. Tony walked over to Frank.

"Since you don't really need me in here, I need to take a break. I'll be back in a minute." Frank shook his head, taking Tony by the arm.

"Hold off for a couple of minutes," he whispered. "We're gonna offer the little rat immunity if he gives us all the information that he has, and I want you here to witness it."

"Okay, Boss," said Tony. Frank nodded and went over to stand by the table next to where Sipe was sitting.

"Okay, Detective," said Assistant U.S. Attorney Sullivan, "here's where we are: I'm prepared to offer you immunity in this matter, subject to the approval of my boss, the United States Attorney, for your complete and truthful cooperation with this investigation. Any hint of evasion or lying on your part will nullify our deal. I'll have everything drawn up for you to sign by this afternoon, and if you wish to have an attorney present to represent you, we can make that happen. But, remember one thing, we will revoke this deal in a New York minute if I think you're not telling us the truth. Are you prepared to make this deal?" asked Sullivan.

Sipe, looking like a scared rat, nodded his head.

"No, that won't do. We have to hear you say that you understand and accept the deal offered to you," said Sullivan.

Sipe looked up and in a clear voice said, "I accept the deal."

CHAPTER THIRTY-NINE

Anita sat alone in her parked car in front of Flaps. She had arrived twenty minutes early, a deliberate move. Exiting her vehicle, she went inside, where a pleasant young hostess seated her at a booth. Soon she saw a man standing in the doorway, craning his neck as if he were looking for someone. She waved to him and he spotted her and moved toward her table. She took a moment to appreciate how handsome Charlie Thomas was. Five ten, wearing a tailored suit, reasonably fit with salt and pepper hair—and a great smile. *No wonder he thinks of himself as a ladies man. Maybe I can use that to my advantage somewhere down the line.*

"Hi, I'm Charlie Thomas, and you must be Anita."

"Yes, I'm Anita. It's nice to meet you," she said. "Please, sit down. I'll bet you're hungry, am I right?"

"You got that right. I've heard that they make some outstanding crab cakes here," said the detective.

"Okay, that's what we'll have then. Lunch is on me since I asked you here to meet with me."

"That works for me," said Charlie.

Anita observed his looks of visual appraisal. His eyes kept dropping down to her cleavage, and the twinkle in his eye gave away his thoughts.

"What is it that you want from me, I mean, you were pretty vague over the phone, so, why did you want to meet with me?" Charlie said with some skepticism.

"Let's order our lunch first, and then we can get down to business," she answered. After placing their orders, Anita and he discussed her relationship with Lorenzo. She pointed a finger at him, gently brushing his throat just above his loose tie.

"Lorenzo told me a lot about you. How you helped him out with a big problem once. He said you were a very, um… capable man."

The waitress bringing lunch interrupted her coercion of a demonstrably nervous Charlie. She sat the plates on the table, asked if they needed anything else, and when Anita impatiently told her "No, thank you," she walked away.

"May I call you Anita?" asked Charlie, leaning across the table.

"Of course," said Anita, "that's what everyone calls me. May I call you Charlie?" she flirted, eyebrows raised.

"Sure you can," he said. "Anyway, Anita, I want to say thank you for inviting me to lunch. I'm really enjoying these crab cakes. But I also want to say, that I don't know what the hell you're talking about. You got me scratching my head trying to figure out what's going on here. I'm not trying to be a smart guy or anything," he said, "but, is this some kind of joke?"

"No," replied Anita, "this is no joke. I'm deadly serious. I need for you to listen to what I have to offer—and the offer is exceedingly generous—and then you can decide whether you want to help me or not." *If he didn't go for it right away, it wasn't going to happen*, she thought.

His expression changed from bemused to opportunistic. He shook her hand.

"Okay, let's talk money," he said, taking a big bite out of his sandwich.

"Charlie, we'll talk money in just a minute; first, I want you to understand what it is I want you to do for me. When I'm finished, if you can't do it, just tell me and this conversation never happened."

"I think I can live with that," said the detective.

During their conversation, he attempted to make his role in her plan seem bigger than it actually was. Anita was annoyed.

"Listen, all I want you to do is just set up the meeting between me and your contact, and I'll do the rest. But this has got to happen within twenty-four hours or no deal."

"How the hell do you think I can set this up in the next twenty-four hours? These guys don't keep regular office hours; I need to tell them what's in it for them. On top of that, there's something else you need to understand: I have to cover *my* ass, and make sure there's no way I can be connected to this."

"I completely understand your position, Charlie. All I want you to do is just set up the meet, and then you can forget about the whole thing—it never happened," said Anita, recovering her smile.

"Okay," said Charlie. "I can probably contact my man this afternoon, and hopefully set up a meet real soon."

"Not 'real soon,'" interjected Anita. "Within the next twenty-four hours, like I told you, or no deal."

"Alright, alright," he replied. "I'll take care of it as soon as I leave here. Is that soon enough?"

"That should work." She pulled a pen from her purse and wrote on a paper napkin. "Here's my cell number," she said, handing the napkin over to Charlie, who put it in his pocket. "Contact me when the meeting is set."

"You know," said Charlie, smiling, "we seem to have put the cart before the horse, don't you think?" Quickly catching on to what he was saying, Anita leaned across the table.

"The figure I'm going to quote is a non-negotiable number. You'll either take it, or leave it, understood?" she whispered.

"Gotcha," replied Charlie, with a grin. "Let's hear it."

"I think ten thousand dollars will make you very happy, don't you?"

Charlie pressed his lips together, nodding in satisfaction. He stuck out his hand once more. "It's a pleasure doing business with you, and I hope we can do business again in the future."

Anita, confident her fish was hooked, started to get up from the table when Charlie reached out and stopped her. She slowly sat back down.

"Wait a minute. There are a couple more things we have to discuss before you leave."

"What *things?*" asked Anita.

"The most important part, as a matter of fact. My money! I want it as soon as I give you the meet time and location."

"Done," said Anita. "Call me when it's set up and I'll meet you with your money."

"Will do, but I want it in cash. Will that be a problem?" asked Charlie.

"That won't be a problem—just get it done. Anything else?"

"Well, er…." Charlie leaned back and put one elbow on the back of the booth. "I thought that since we seemed to get along pretty good, we might enjoy each other's company sometime without business getting in the way. I'd love to take you to dinner."

"Maybe," she replied coyly. "Let's just see how this works out, and then we can talk about it. It might be fun."

Anita left money to cover the check and got up from the table. Charlie followed her out to her car. She thanked him again before she drove away.

What a schoolboy performance that was! she thought as she gunned her engine and swerved onto the main road. Having gotten her way, Anita was still a little uneasy. Charlie talked a good game, and his eyes had lit up at the money, but trusting him completely? Several scenarios played in her mind, the worst being that he would turn on her. No matter. She had made her pitch and he had accepted. If he followed through, all would go well. Her confidence bolstered, she drove on to headquarters.

CHAPTER FORTY

Parked down the street from Sergeant Spinella's townhouse, Fitz sat in his car thinking that his whole world was about to come crashing down. This business of Dave turning state's evidence against them had his blood pressure raised to the point where he felt like he might pass out. Reassuring himself that Sipe had only been missing twenty-four hours— he could be anywhere—it was still imperative that they find him, and fast. Watching Spinella's house was the best approach.

The sun sank behind Spinella's house; long shadows extended across the front yard. It was mild weather for late winter in Washington. His appreciation of Mother Nature was interrupted when he spotted Inspector Billings from Internal Affairs leaving Spinella's house, followed by Assistant U.S. Attorney Sullivan. Fitz sprang into action and fumbled for his phone. He hit the speed dial.

"Kirby here."

"I just saw Billings from IAD and U.S. Attorney Sullivan walk out of Spinella's place." Fitz spoke rapidly and Kirby made him repeat his words.

"Stay on it," Kirby ordered. "I want to know every person who comes and goes from there."

"Sure, Boss. I'll keep watching until you call me off. Are you gonna tell the bitch about this?"

"You bet your ass I am!" Kirby let out an incredulous laugh. "She thinks she's the brains behind this whole operation—let her figure out what we're going to do!" Kirby abruptly hung up, leaving Fitz to his reconnaissance.

Anita called Kirby back on her cell after he stupidly phoned her at her desk. She stepped outside the building and proceeded to berate him when he interrupted her.

"We have a big problem," he said loudly over her rant.

"What do you mean?" she replied.

"I think Fitz found out where they're keeping Dave. I've had him sitting on Spinella's house, and he just saw both Inspector Billings from IAD and U.S. Attorney Sullivan leave the house. He didn't see anybody else leave, but I think it's a pretty good guess that he's in there, and God only knows what he's told them. You need to take care of this right now!"

"I *will* take care of it!" Anita shot back. "Keep me aware of anything else Fitz sees." She hung up before Kirby could utter a response.

She was becoming rattled now, but steeled herself and went back into the squad room to quickly access Spinella's in-house file. She recorded his home address. Once again, she left her desk to make another phone call. Spotting an empty office, she stepped inside.

"I have instructions for you. Are you ready to write this information down?" she asked. There was a short pause, with some shuffling noise in the background, then the monotone voice came back on.

She gave the man his orders along with the address.

"This must be done immediately!" she concluded, keeping her voice low. "The target must be completely eliminated! Once you are done, you are to leave the area! Do you understand?"

Hearing the expected acquiescense, she hung up.

CHAPTER FORTY-ONE

Vadin gathered his meager belongings, left his shabby motel room, and began to scout the area for a suitable car. He searched for over an hour, but finally found a weathered, late-model gray four-door sedan parked on a quiet, residential street. The car looked like its owner hadn't moved it in weeks: in the thick layer of dust covering the hood, an unknown finger had traced the words, "Wash Me." He started the car in minutes and drove from the area.

The winter sun warmed his face through the windshield as he drove. He was becoming a little homesick. Putting sentiment out of his mind, he concentrated on his route. He made the unnerving discovery that he was headed in the direction of the U.S. Capitol building. His target's proximity to that location worried him for a minute or two. He found a parking space two blocks away and walked to the address indicated. He carefully studied the dwellings across the street.

He chose the house directly across from the target, ascended the iron front steps and knocked. A minute or two later, an elderly man opened the door.

"May I help you?"

"Yes, please," said Vadin, holding out a piece of paper. "I'm not from here, and I would be pleased for you to help me find this place."

"Let me see," said the man, reaching for the slip of paper. "Maybe I can he—"

As the man reached for the slip of paper, Vadin grabbed his arm, yanked him forward and wrapped his arms around the man's throat, quickly dragging him into the house. The old man in a desperate, feeble attempt at resistance scratched at his face, which only served to anger his assailant. Vadin viciously choked the man, then pulled his neck knife and stabbed him repeatedly in the neck and chest. Blood sprayed everywhere, leaving the man sagging in Vadin's arms.

Vadin let the lifeless body fall to the foyer floor and listened closely for any sounds of others in the house. Hearing nothing, he set about checking the house, gradually ascertaining he was now alone. Returning to the foyer, he stepped over the old man's body and flipped through the mail lying on a table. The old man lived alone.

Up on the second floor, he located a front-facing bedroom and checked the sight angle to the house across the street. His next order of business was to secure his exit from the area once he completed his assignment. The kitchen exited onto an alley that ran behind all the houses on that block. The alley provided efficient access to his car.

He went upstairs to the bathroom where he removed his shirt and proceeded to wash the blood from his face and hands. Refreshed after cleaning himself, he went into the front bedroom and unpacked his rifle. He repeatedly looked through his scope at the large front window of the target house. There was too much interference from the sun's brightness. He would have to wait for the sun to descend somewhat before he could see into the house.

His stomach began to growl and he went to the kitchen where he found lunchmeat, bread, and some milk in the refrigerator. Making himself two big sandwiches, he carried his lunch back upstairs to the bedroom, sat in a comfortable chair, and wolfed down both. He chugged a glass of milk and picked up his gun. Still unable to see clearly into the house, he decided to take a short nap while he waited for his view to improve.

Lamont circled the block around Tony's place in search of a parking spot, hoping to catch someone pulling out. As he rounded the corner a block or so down from Tony's, he spied an unmarked car parked along the curb with what appeared to be the corpulent Detective Fitzpatrick sitting in the driver's seat. He drove around the block a few more times, located a vacant space and parked. Doubling back, he crossed over to the opposite side of the street and approached the unmarked car. A large oak tree provided the perfect cover, and after peering around it carefully he confirmed that it was indeed Fitzpatrick. Backing away, he retraced his steps until he got to the alley that ran behind Tony's. Arriving at Tony's back gate, he ran to the back door and pounded. With the sound of locks unlatching, a frowning Tony opened the door.

"Hey man, what's with the back door thing?"

"Frank told me to come over and make myself useful, and you're gonna be glad I did, because you got company!" Lamont replied.

Tony gave him a puzzled look. "I know I've got company. What are you talking about?"

"Your boy Fitzpatrick is sitting down at the corner watching your house. I spotted him when I was looking for a parking space."

"Aw, shit!" said Tony. "Cathy was just getting ready to leave, and Frank offered to drive her home. We can't let him see both of them leave here at the same time. How long do you suppose he's been out there? Billings and Sullivan left not long ago."

Lamont shrugged. "I only just got here; I have no idea how long his big ass has been sitting out there. If he saw both of them leave, he's probably already told Kirby about it. As a matter of fact, he was on the phone when I first spotted him."

"We better go tell Frank about this," said Tony. "Then we have to figure out a way to get Cathy out of here without him seeing her. This is some bad shit. They've probably figured out we have Dave here, and we don't know what they might do. They've already killed Maurice, and he was a cop, so nothing is off the table for them. We need to be ready for whatever they throw at us. You might just get that piece you've been wanting— it ain't gonna be no picnic if they try and get inside. We're gonna need some help. Maybe it's time to talk to the chief."

Tony went into the living room, Lamont following right behind him. After talking with Frank and listening to Sipe's unsuccessful plea for a weapon, they all agreed that the smart thing would be to stay put for the moment. In the meantime, Frank would call the chief and ask him for some additional manpower. Frank picked up the phone, then hesitated with an afterthought.

"Wait a minute. We all know we can't completely trust our department right now. Why don't we call the judge? Maybe she can use her influence and get us some Federal help. We don't have enough people here to protect ourselves, much less a crooked cop. On top of that, if they come at us, Tony's place is gonna get trashed."

"Great idea," Tony said. "Maybe she can get the Marshals Service to take Dave off our hands."

"That sounds good to me," Lamont chimed in. I really don't want to practice my shooting skills on that big bag of shit outside." Lamont's remarks broke the somber mood that had settled over the room. Laughing, Frank picked up his phone again to call the judge, walking back towards the kitchen for some privacy. He returned a few minutes later.

"Judge Gills wants us to sit tight. Someone from the Marshals Service will be contacting me shortly to take custody of Sipe. That should get us out of harm's way."

A collective sigh was heard around the room. Frank put up his hand.

"We still have to protect ourselves until the Marshals get here. Lamont, you cover the back. Tony, get him a weapon."

"Are you sure about that, Boss? You haven't gone crazy or anything, have you?"

Frank stifled a laugh. "Tony, you and I can't be everywhere; we need all the help we can get, so just go and get him a piece. I'll watch the front. Tony, you go upstairs and watch the street. Shout if you see anything that looks suspicious."

"What can I do to help?" Cathy asked.

"First of all, I don't want you getting hurt," Frank said, putting his hand on her shoulder. How about you help me watch the front of the house? Watch for any cars that appear to be driving by too slowly."

"I'm on it," said Cathy. "Just so you know, I was raised in a house full of hunters. I know how to use a gun."

"Even better," Frank said, smiling.

Tony went upstairs and rooted around until he found an old three eighty automatic that hadn't been fired in over ten years. After making sure it was loaded, he called down to Lamont.

"Lamont, come on up here! I've got something for you."

"Be right there," Lamont hollered from below. In no time he was standing next to Tony.

"Lamont, this is a three eighty automatic and I want you to be very careful when you handle it. I'm gonna show you how to load and fire it, but for right now, I'm gonna unload it and let you get acquainted with the weapon. It's pretty simple." Tony removed the gun's clip and ejected the bullet from the chamber. Handing the automatic to Lamont, Tony explained how it worked and watched as Lamont practiced the loading and dry firing procedure.

"Man, I'm bad," boasted Lamont. "They better be ready if they want to mess with me because Lamont's got somethin' for 'em." He went back downstairs to his post.

Tony made sure his department-issue weapon, a Glock 9mm, was loaded and ready, and took up a position in front of the upstairs bedroom window overlooking the front yard and street. If anything were to happen, it would happen fast, so he made sure he had extra ammunition, and his cell phone, which he placed on the desk situated in front of the window. He was glad they had decided to temporarily put Dave down in the cellar, behind the furnace. Dave had reluctantly cooperated, even though he didn't like the idea and bitched all the way to the basement.

Wanting to get a better visual on the street below, he went to his closet and retrieved his binoculars, a birthday gift from his ex. He returned to his position and scanned the area. Everything looked normal, with the occasional neighbor walking his dog and people jockeying for parking. Something was nagging him, but he couldn't pin it down. He looked away long enough to grab a bottle of water he had brought along, and when he turned back to the window, it hit him: the venetian blinds in the upstairs bedroom of the house directly across the street were raised all the way up. In all the years Tony had lived in that neighborhood, he had never seen those blinds raised. His elderly neighbor had mentioned to him on several occasions that he always kept them down to keep out the sun, because it helped lower his electric bill. He focused his binoculars on the window and his heart leaped into his throat. Someone was there, in the window, looking through the scope of a rifle aimed at his house.

He threw down the binoculars and raced downstairs, shouting for everyone to take cover.

"What did you see?" hollered Frank as everyone assembled in the living room.

"There's a rifle with a scope trained on the front of my house—somebody's in the upstairs window of the house across the street."

"Oh, shit!" exclaimed Lamont.

Frank waved him off. "If the front is covered, the rear likely is as well."

"I'll go check it out," Tony volunteered. Frank reluctantly agreed, but implored him to be cautious.

"Cover your ass, Sergeant."

"No worries," Tony replied.

He slowly opened the back door, stuck his head out, his weapon at the ready, and after scanning in both directions, stepped outside. There was no one in the backyard and the alley was deserted. He stepped back inside.

"All clear," he said. "I've got an idea. We make a 9-1-1 call and report a burglary in progress across the street." All echoed their approval.

"I'll wait a couple of minutes," Tony continued, "giving the police time to respond. I'll then go out through the back, utilizing the alley behind my house and the one across the way so as not to be seen. I'll try to gain access to the house and see if I can take this guy out."

"I'll go along with you, Sergeant," said Frank.

"No, Boss." Tony shot a look at Lamont and then back to Frank. "You had better stay here and protect the witness— along with everybody else. When you report the burglary, make sure you let them know there'll be an office in plain clothes on the scene."

"I can go with you, Tony," volunteered Lamont.

"Absolutely not. Frank needs you here to cover the back." Tony looked at Frank again, who gave a patronizing nod.

Tony slipped out the back door and into the alley, walking down to the connecting street. Before he made his way to the opposite side, he used the neighbor's wood fence as cover and peered around, looking through the tall oaks that lined the thoroughfare, up towards the second floor window. Seeing no movement, he darted across and slipped into the alley that ran behind his elderly neighbor's place. His ears pricked up at every sound: someone nearby shouted at their dog, while screams of childen playing came from another direction.

His heart rate elevated and he took a deep breath. *I'm too old for this shit,* he thought as he stepped cautiously down the alley, keeping his back against the tall wooden fence that bordered the backyards of the homes on that block. In no time he was directly behind the house in question.

He inched open the back gate, his gun poised, and looked around. There were no signs of life. He spotted a basement door to the place and, after taking a quick look in either direction, ran over to it. The door didn't appear to have been used much recently. He grabbed the doorknob and turned it—the door made a creaky sound as he opened it gradually.

Stepping inside, he held his breath for a few seconds and listened. Hearing nothing, he approached the basement steps leading to the upstairs. Ascending the steps, he placed his feet on the outer edge of each stair tread until he arrived at the top landing. He put his ear to the door and listened. Still nothing. Slowly, he turned the door handle, gun still in position, pushed open the door and stepped into a narrow hallway.

He was grateful to discover the floor plan nearly matched his own. He took another deep breath, his heart racing, and tip-toed towards the front foyer. The stairway to the upper level was to his left, and as he quietly moved forward the body of his elderly neighbor came into view. He lay in a wide pool of blood near the base of the stairs. Tony was engulfed by fury.

Taking two quick, light steps forward he knelt and felt for a pulse. Recognizing his effort as futile, he stood up. In an instant he made a decision. No Miranda bullshit for this asshole. Justice would be served up, quick and final, no appeals.

He started up the steps, each footfall slow and gradual. After six steps he stopped and listened again, the Glock in his hand pointed upward, then proceeded on, looking from side to side. Once he was on the top landing, he crouched down. He heard someone moving in the front bedroom. His current posture was awkward; needing to get in a more strategic position, he saw a vacant bedroom across the hall and went for it. He rose and in three quick, light paces was in the room.

No one had slept there in quite some time. An old bed with a tired mattress and an antique dresser were the only furnishings, and they were both, along with the floors and window sills, generously coated with dust. He squatted down behind one end of the dresser, a position where he had a view of the hallway, and waited for the police to arrive. Hearing more movement in the front bedroom, he took a quick peek around the side of the dresser. The subject had entered the hallway and gone into the bathroom. He heard the water running, then it stopped. It was time to make a move. Tony got ready.

CHAPTER FORTY-TWO

Vadin spent several moments admiring himself in the bathroom mirror. As he washed his hands, he made the decision that he would start dressing more fashionably. He had always thought of himself as a ladies man, and now that he was an international assassin, he should look more professional.

He took one last look in the mirror, turned off the bathroom light, and headed towards the stairs to go down to the kitchen get something more to eat. As he passed a spare bedroom his reflexes became electrified by a disturbance in the air. He spun around and saw a man pointing a gun at him. He ducked, pulled the gun from his waist and after firing two shots in rapid succession crouched and ran for the safety of the front bedroom.

A hot, searing pain shot through his lower back and he fell to the hallway floor, just short of the bedroom door. He began to crawl, dragging himself into the room hoping to reach his rifle. His legs were immobilized and his pants felt wet. Pushing himself against the closest wall, he raised his gun and pointed it at the doorway. The gun grew heavy—too heavy. His energy was fading; he needed to rest his eyes. Struggling to keep his gun raised, his arm began to shake. The last things he heard was the gun's metallic clatter as it hit the floor, followed by someone shouting "Police!"

Tony sat on the floor of the hallway, leaning back against the wall. He breathed heavily—the impact of the bullet had knocked him off his feet. He pressed his hand, blood running through his fingers and down his arm, against the wound in his biceps. He felt around the back of his arm for the exit wound, and found the hole. It was a through-and-through. His Marine training kicked in and he removed his belt, wrapped it securely above the bullet's entry point and pulled it tight. All the while he kept his eye on the doorway. He had gotten off one shot—he hoped it hit its mark.

A banging noise came from downstairs as the front door gave way and several voices yelled "Police!"

"Police officer, police officer! I'm in plain clothes and I've been shot!" Tony hollered. "The shooter is armed and he's in the bedroom at the top of the stairs. He may be wounded—I think I put one in him!"

A police officer's head slowly rose above the balustrade. Tony pointed in the direction of the front bedroom.

"Right there," he said in a semi-whisper.

The officer, gun raised, waited for his partner to join him. The first officer slowly leaned his head into the bedroom and looked in.

"He's down," he said.

Tony tried to stand up—he wanted to see the asshole who shot him—but a wave of dizziness overcame him and he sank back down to the floor. Determined, he grabbed onto the banister and steadied himself as he rose. He staggered into the front bedroom and identified himself to the two officers.

"Sergeant Spinella, Robbery Squad."

Tony went over to get a closer look at the gunman, who was slumped against the adjacent wall.

"Officer," he piped up. "This guy is still breathing. Call for an ambulance."

"Fuck him, Sarge. We'll call an ambulance for *you*! This s.o.b. can wait!" replied the tall, red-headed officer.

"No, officer, I'm ok. Unfortunately we need this pile of shit alive, if possible, so he can answer a few questions. Call for an ambulance *now*!"

"Yes, sir!" replied the officer and he got on his radio.

Feeling queasy, Tony sat down on the bed to wait for the ambulance to arrive. He all at once heard Frank's unmistakable, gruff bark telling someone downstairs to "move the hell outta my way!" The sounds of multiple footfalls thumped up the stairs. Frank, Lamont, and Cathy appeared in the doorway behind the officers, the ambulance crew following after them.

"Tony! You alright?" Frank shouted as he ran over to him.

"Yeah, Boss, I'm ok. Just leaking a little bit. The medics'll take care of it." Tony looked around. "Hey, who'd you leave with Dave?"

"Lamont locked him in the basement; he can't go anywhere," answered Frank.

"Man, you look like shit," said Lamont. "But you got the bastard!"

"Maybe I did, but he got me, too," said Tony, letting out a weak laugh. He grabbed his arm and grimaced.

After the gunman was loaded onto a gurney, one of the EMTs approached Tony.

"Everyone move back," he said.

He took a look at Tony's wound and removed the tourniquet. As he dressed the wound, he told Tony he was lucky.

"The bullet missed the bone. Tying off the wound was smart. You could have lost a lot more blood. Can you walk or do you want us to put you on a gurney?"

Tony was caught off guard by the question. "I don't need a gurney. I'm fine, I can walk. Boss," he looked at Frank, "can you follow us to the hospital and give me a ride back?"

"You bet," said Frank affirmatively. "I'll see you there. In the meantime I'l make some calls and get some input on what to do with our friend, if he lives."

CHAPTER FORTY-THREE

When Frank brought Tony back to his place, he was surprised to see most of the original group from earlier all assembled in his living room. Everyone expressed their concern for his well-being as well as their eagerness to hear the play-by-play. He went over the events inside his neighbor's house as the others listened, wide-eyed. Judge Gills interrupted him.

"What did the doctor say about your wound?" she asked.

"He told me I was pretty lucky that the bullet missed anything vital. He said the wound was in and out, and after he stitched me up, he gave me some antibiotics and pain meds, and here I am. It's no big deal."

"The fact remains," said the judge, "you've been shot and you need to take it easy for a few days." She turned to the Assistant U.S. Attorney. "Mister Sullivan, have you been able to formalize the immunity deal with the U.S. Attorney, and if so, how soon can we expect the paperwork?"

"Judge," said Sullivan, "the deal is done. My boss is pretty excited about bringing down some crooked cops, and he assured me we would have the signed paperwork hand delivered to me here within the next thirty minutes."

Various sighs and words of relief came from all corners of the room. Now they could request warrants for everyone involved in the scheme. Judge Gills was making her recommendations to Sullivan as to which judge to choose for the warrant process when Tony heard his house phone ring. He answered and heard the voice of the officer assigned to guard the wounded prisoner. He had introduced himself to the officer before he left the hospital, asking him to keep him apprised of any changes. He listened to what he had to say, then thanked him and hung up.

"That was the hospital," he said, turning back to the group. "The guy I shot is still alive, but it looks like my shot severed his spinal cord and he's paralyzed from the waist down. Right now, it seems his condition is critical, but stable. Because of the large loss of blood, the doctors are not sure if he's going pull through. They'll know more tomorrow."

"By late tomorrow, I should have the warrants in hand, and by early evening, we can start executing them," Sullivan said. "We need to get all the information Detective Sipe has as quickly as possible, so that we can use it to justify the warrants. Tony, do you feel up to getting Sipe and bringing him to the kitchen so that we can get started?"

"Don't worry about me, I'm good," said Tony, leaving the room. He detoured to the kitchen before heading to the basement. Lamont was sitting at the table eating a sandwich.

"Lamont, I forgot to ask what happened with Fitzpatrick after the shooting."

Talking through a mouthful of tuna fish sandwich, Lamont replied, "After they took you away, I checked the area but he was nowhere to be seen. I think he heard the commotion and took off."

"You're probably right, but we still have to be on our guard just in case he comes back. These guys have to know that it's all coming apart, and I'm sure they're desperate, and that makes them dangerous, so be careful," said Tony, leaving the kitchen to get Dave.

Taking the stairs carefully because of his wound, he hollered out, "Hey Sipe, it's me, Spinella. Come out, it's all over!"

Dave emerged from behind the furnace, looking scared.

"Hey man,' said Tony, "everything's cool."

"What the hell happened?" asked Sipe, brushing a cobweb from his shirt. "First, they lock me in here, then I hear sirens, and now you show up with your arm in a sling."

"Later, Sipe. We have more important matters." He motioned for Dave to follow him up the stairs.

Everyone had moved to the kitchen. Sullivan gestured toward a chair and Dave sat down. The attorney walked him through the immunity deal for several minutes, and after a few questions whereby Dave got some reassuring answers, the just arrived paper work was placed in front of him and the deal was signed. No sooner had Cathy swept the papers from the table did Sullivan turn around and start grilling Dave with questions.

Dave was nervous and struggled with his answers. He tried to remember his earlier responses and repeat them verbatim, still afraid any slip-up could foul his immunity deal. When it came to questions about Anita, he became frustrated and repeated that he knew absolutely nothing about her. Sullivan finally ceased his questioning and motioned for Tony and Frank to follow him into the living room.

"Mrs. Martin has already made out the affidavits for arrest warrants for Lieutenant James Kirby, Detectives Harris and Ortiz of Internal Affairs, Detective Fitzpatrick of Homicide, and Officers Giles, Elliott and Stevens, of the Police Property-Evidence Room."

"You know," Frank interrupted, "it might be a good idea to apply for a search warrant for all of the suspect's bank accounts, and in Kirby's case, his safety deposit boxes."

"Already got that covered," answered Sullivan. "Those warrants will be served first thing tomorrow morning. I'm having a major problem, though, with what to do about this 'Anita.' We don't have any direct evidence tying her to this operation. Maybe when we get the others, we might be able to force some information linking her to this whole thing, but for right now, I don't have enough for a warrant."

"I've been thinking," said Tony. "Lorenzo's dead, and I seriously doubt that Fitzpatrick has ever met Anita, unless he bumped into her at the office, so that leaves us with Kirby. He's the guy that probably worked directly with her after Lorenzo was killed. It just makes sense, if she is the brains behind this mess, she wouldn't be dealing with the likes of Fitzpatrick. I really think we should target Kirby before anyone else. In my opinion, he's the key to getting Anita."

"I agree with Tony," said Frank, "and I also think we better act fast because he's a cop, and he's gotta know we're on to him. He might beat feet if we drag ours."

"Okay," said Sullivan, "his will be the first warrant to be served. But before anyone leaves, the U.S. Marshal's are on their way over to pick up Sipe. Tony, I know it will be a big relief for you to have your house back, and I want you both to know that I truly appreciate everything you've done, even though we've still got a lot of work to left to do."

CHAPTER FORTY-FOUR

Sitting in his car down the street from Spinella's house, Fitzpatrick was startled to hear gunshots. He took a quick look around; nothing was out of the ordinary on the street. He shrugged it off and resumed his surveillance, turning on some music and getting comfortable.

All at once a Police Scout car pulled up and double-parked directly across from him. Two uniformed officers bolted from the vehicle and ran over to the house across from Spinella's. They took the iron steps two at a time hollering "Police Officers!" Seconds later they forced open the front door and disappeared inside. Next, Fitzpatric heard sirens and that was his cue. He started his car and drove away as fast as he could. When he got a safe distance away, he grabbed his phone and dialed Kirby.

"What's up, Fitz?" Kirby answered.

Fitz rattled off what he had just witnessed, and after a couple of impatient questions and some confusion on Kirby's part, Kirby ordered him to head back to the scene.

"I'll make some inquiries. It could be a simple domestic disturbance. I'll get back to you before you reach Spinella's."

After he concluded his call with Fitzpatrick, Kirby placed a call to the Police Communications Division.

"Police Communications, Officer Dove, how can I help you?"

Kirby identified himself, then asked about the police activity in the one hundred block of Sixth Street southeast.

"Lieutenant," Officer Dove replied, "we dispatched a marked unit to that location for a breaking and entering call, and upon their arrival on the scene it turned out to be an officer-involved shooting with one suspect down and a police officer shot. The off duty officer involved is Detective Sergeant Anthony Spinella who is currently assigned to the Robbery Squad. The responding unit requested an ambulance. Precinct officials have been notified and are responding to the scene. At this time we know the condition of the suspect is critical, and the officer involved sustained a gun shot wound to the arm and should be OK. Both have been transported to the Hospital"

Kirby thanked the officer and hung up. A quick call to the Hospital confirmed the information he was given by Police Communications. He was completely baffled and tried to wrap his head around what he had just heard. Before he called Fitz back, he had to make one more call. It took one ring for Anita to answer.

"This is Anita. Whom am I speaking with?"

"Anita, this is Kirby. Something has come up, and I need to talk to you."

"So talk," she replied.

"Spinella has been involved in a shooting across the street from his house," said Kirby, "and he was wounded. I don't know much more than that, except the perpetrator was also shot and is in the hospital with critical wounds."

"Did they identify the shooter?" she asked. "It's important that I know. Get that information to me as fast as you can, and at the same time, see if you can find out how badly wounded Spinella is."

"I already know that," Kirby replied. "I contacted the hospital. He's fine. He took a bullet through his arm, and was treated and released. He's probably already home by now."

"Shit!" she hissed. "Get back to me with what you find out—as quick as you can," and she ended the call.

Anita put the phone down. Tomorrow, she would send Kirby into the evidence room for the last time, and immediately after delivering the drugs to her new contact, put her escape plan into action, leaving as fast as possible. She placed a call to Detective Thomas, hoping to get the information on the meeting with his contact.

"Morals Division, Detective Trasatti."

"Hello," said Anita, in her most sexy voice, "may I speak with Detective Thomas?"

"One moment," said the detective. She could hear his muffled words, picturing his hand cupped over the receiver.

"Thomas, it's for you! Sounds nice." Another phone was picked up.

"Detective Thomas, can I help you?"

"Hi, it's Anita, and yes you can help me, by telling me the meeting with your friend is on for today."

"Good morning to you, too," said Thomas. "Yeah, we're on for noon today, and I'll meet you at eleven thirty at Sixth and Maryland Avenue Northeast. By the way," he said, lowering his voice, "don't forget to bring my money, and just so you know, Joe-Joe insisted that I be at the meet with you, or it don't happen. I think he has some trust issues."

"Actually," said Anita, "since I don't know any of these people, I'll probably feel a lot safer with you there."

"Okay," said Thomas. "See you at eleven thirty," and hung up the phone.

She had no sooner put the phone down when it began to ring. She recognized the number and answered.

"The shooter's still critical. He didn't have any identification on him when he was brought to the hospital. The officers confiscated a sniper rifle at the scene."

Anita paused for a few seconds, digesting what she had just heard. "I want you to make one last trip to the evidence room first thing tomorrow morning. I've made a new contact that I'm meeting with today to make the arrangements, and tomorrow I'll get the money, meet you with your share, and then we both disappear, okay?"

"Yeah, that sounds good. I'll be glad to have this over, and even happier when I'm out of here. Where do you want to meet me after I leave headquarters?"

"I'll be parked in front of the coffee shop around the corner from there. You know the place?"

"Yes," he said. "See you there around ten tomorrow morning."

Fitz's jaw dropped when he saw a black van with a U.S. Marshal's service logo on the side pull up in front of Spinella's place. Two men in SWAT uniforms got out and went to the front door, where he recognized Captain McCathran as the one who ushered them in. He got a sick feeling in his gut.

It was now a sure thing that Sipe was being held in Spinella's house. Time to call Kirby with the bad news. When he answered and Fitz spilled the information, he instructed him to leave the area immediately and meet him at noon the next day.

CHAPTER FORTY-FIVE

After bringing the two Deputy Marshals into the living room and introducing them to everyone, Sullivan gave the Marshals instructions to allow no access to the prisoner by anyone other himself, or other members of the U.S. Attorney's Office designated by himself. As he was being led away, Sipe stopped and thanked everyone in the room for saving his life. He also reassured them that he would cooperate fully with the investigation. Once he was gone, Tony was relieved that he finally had his house back.

"Tony, I'll be leaving now," said Frank, "but remember, take your medicine, and don't forget if the pain gets too bad, take the damn pain meds, okay! One more thing, have you talked to Lina since the shooting? If not, you better get on the horn and let her know what's going on. She's special, and you don't want to mess up now."

"Thanks Frank. I need to call her. I'll bet she's really pissed right about now, but after I explain everything, I think that she will understand," said Tony.

"I'm outta here," said Frank. "Call her now! I'll call you later to check on how you're feeling," as he closed the front door.

After Frank left, the others packed up their notes and records and quickly made their exits. When everyone had gone, Tony called Lina at home. The phone rang several times and he almost gave up hope of catching her when she answered.

"Hello, stranger! Mind telling me what's so important you couldn't take a few minutes to call me?"

"I'm sorry, baby. There's been a huge break in the investigation and I've been completely swamped. They've been hiding a prisoner in my house and a crowd of officials are hanging out in my kitchen. It's been crazy. I miss you," he said.

"So, when am I going to see you?"

"Soon, I hope. There's something else I gotta tell you, though."

Tony told about the episode across the street from his house, and as soon as he related to her that he had been shot, Lina became hysterical.

"What?! I'm coming over there *right now* and take care of you! Tony! How could you not have called me sooner about this?"

Lina went on raving for a minute or so more. Tony smiled to himself as she chastised him. There was no arguing with her feisty Italian temperament. He waited for a break in her remonstration.

"Ok, baby. Come on over. I'll be here waiting for you."

After he hung up, he headed for a much-needed shower. He never made it to the bathroom: *Scopes!* He phoned Frank.

"He's out at the farm," Frank reassured him. "I've kept him up to date, and he wanted me to tell you to stop getting shot! Now, quit worrying, hang up, and have some fun with Lina—but not *too* much fun! I need you in one piece! I'll talk to you first thing in the morning."

"Right, Boss."

Tony rushed through a shower and was just getting dressed when heard knocking. He looked out the bedroom window to the porch below and saw Lina. He hurried downstairs to let her in. When he opened the door, she fell into his arms, laughing and crying at the same time as she peppered him with questions about his well-being. Her enthusiastic embrace caught his injured arm and he let out a moan.

"Oh my God! I've hurt you!" she cried and fresh tears rolled down her cheeks.

It really did hurt, but Tony fought off the nauseating pangs for her sake. "Come here baby, I'm fine, just a little twinge of pain, but it's gone now."

Lina took his good hand. "Are you sure you're okay? Please don't try and be brave for me, I'll understand. Why don't we sit down and relax on the couch for a little while, and if you're hungry, I'll order us a pizza from Luigi's. Then, *maybe*," she took a cautious look at his arm, "I'll let you make it up to me for not calling me like you should."

Later, when Tony was polishing off the last of a large pepperoni and sausage pizza, Lina looked at him thoughtfully over her glass of wine.

"Honey, is it over yet? I mean, are you going to be in any more danger before this whole thing is finally done with?"

"Baby," he answered, looking right at her, "the warrants are supposed to be served tomorrow, and we know we're gonna get most of their crew, but I can't promise anything except that it's coming to an end real quick. Look, I don't want to get hurt, and I'm going do everything in my power not to get hurt again, but, in my business, you know bad things happen, and I can't predict when, or if, something might go wrong. I promise you that I'll be very careful, because I plan on spending a lot more time with you."

Lina responded with a smile, straddled him and, while making a conscious effort not to hurt his injured arm, covered his face with soft kisses.

"I've missed you," she said, "and I think, if we're careful, we might just be able to work around your bad arm. What do you think about that idea?" With his good hand, Tony pulled her mouth to his and gave her a long, soft, deep kiss. Pulling his head slightly back, he looked at her lovingly.

"What bad arm?" he teased.

Later, lying in Tony's bed upstairs after they had made love in a manner more passionate and intense than Tony had ever known, Lina lifted her head from his shoulder and looked directly into his eyes.

"I think I fell in love with you the moment I first saw you, and I want you to know that I will always love you."

"Ditto," whispered Tony. He pulled her to him with his good arm and began to show her.

CHAPTER FORTY-SIX

The phone awakened Tony from a dead, pain drug-induced sleep.

"I hope this is important," he answered groggily, swallowing and licking his lips.

It was Sullivan telling him to meet him at his office no later than 7:30. The first warrants were about to be served on the property room.

"How are you doing? Do you think you can make it?" Sullivan voiced concern.

"Of course I can make it," Tony said with increased animation in his voice. "I'll be there," he said, and hung up the phone. Wiping the sleep from his eyes, he looked over and saw a note on Lina's pillow.

Tony, I love you, and I want you know that just because I've made the decision to love you doesn't mean you owe me anything in return. The last thing I want to do is put pressure on you. Give me a call later, and please try and not get shot today, okay?

Tony was overcome by a host of emotions. He promised himself he would make the time to phone her later and tell her how he felt. He glanced at the bedside clock: it was not quite six thirty. He showered and threw on some comfortable clothes, no easy process with his arm in a sling. He went down to the kitchen and made some instant coffee, but emptied it into the sink after one sip. There would be better coffee at Sullivan's office, for sure. Before he walked out, he picked up his house phone and called Frank at headquarters. An unknown voice answered and put him through.

"How's the arm? Are you ready to go to work?"

"I'm fine, Boss. I'll meet you at the property room when they serve the warrants."

"Sounds like a plan. I'll see you there."

Tony went out and got in his car. Before he drove away, he took a look at the old man's house across the street. He could still see the crime scene tape attatched to the iron fence in front of the house, with a few pieces lying on the ground near the iron steps leading up to the front door. As he gunned the engine and sped off, he cursed the actions of a few greedy pieces of shit.

Kirby left the house extra early. He wanted to get in and out of the evidence room before things got too busy. Pulling into the Detective Division's parking lot, it occurred to him that he would likely never see headquarters again after that morning. The finality of it was ominous.

He took the elevators up to the evidence/property room and went through the usual sign-in procedure. He made his way back to the section where drugs and paraphernalia were stored. There was an unusually large number of evidence envelopes. He was glad he'd brought his large attache case.

After a quick look down the corridor in either direction, he sat the attache case down on one of the tiered shelves and opened it up. He got to work taking bags of drugs, emptying them into the bags he'd brought, and replacing them with various powders and placebos as needed. When the case was crammed full, he locked it and headed back to the front desk. The officer on duty gave him the usual nod and he exited the property room.

As he rounded a corner toward the elevators, he saw a large group of men, some in uniform, and some in plain clothes, exit the elevators and head in his direction. He did an abrupt about-face, ducked into a men's room and entered one of the stalls. When he ceased to hear voices, he exited the stall, opened the men's room door slowly and stuck out his head. The coast was clear—he made a dash for the back stair and in another minute he was driving out of the parking lot. It was time to call Anita.

"Yes, what's going on?" she answered when he called.

"There's something you need to know," Kirby said.

"Go on."

"As I was headed out of the property room I nearly collided with a bunch of cops who were headed for the property room. I hid out in the bathroom for a few and then went out the back way. Looks like the shit is hitting the fan."

"Was our usual man on the desk?" Anita asked casually.

"Yeah, he acted the usual, but—"

"Good. Then I'll see you at the coffee shop."

Kirby tried to go on, but the phone was dead.

Anita was packed and ready to go. She had plenty of money on her person, and more stashed in two off-shore accounts with secure passwords known only to her. In her mind, she had worked hard for that money. It dawned on her that the money for Charlie Thomas was stashed under the front seat of her car. She'd better make sure Kirby didn't see it.

En route to the coffee shop, ahead of schedule, the pressure started building inside of her. Despite the bright sunshine painting a beautiful picture on the street and trees around her, Kirby's words about the cops at the property room echoed in her head. She gripped the steering wheel, telling herself to be calm. She had to follow through with her plan, and stay on her game. She had planned things perfectly. All she had to do was mark the details as she always had. The words "Murphy's Law" popped into her head and she shook them off.

Anita parked in a spot facing the lot entrance so she could see Kirby pull in. Checking her watch, she went inside the coffee shop, ordered a latte and returned to her car. She sipped the hot, creamy beverage slowly through the plastic lid, not taking her eye off the lot's entry. *Kirby was a weak link. Could he hold it together?* Suddenly, there he was, pulled up next to her blowing his horn. She could have smacked him. Angrily she rolled down her window and motioned to him.

"What are you doing? Do you want to draw attention to us? People are looking for you, you idiot!" she hissed. "Go park out on the street and get back here!"

"Ok, ok," he said impatiently and backed away. Minutes later he opened her passenger door and got in, a large attache case in his hand. Anita was fuming.

"What the hell is *wrong* with you? Have you gone completely out of your fucking mind? What the hell were you thinking, blowing your horn? Don't you realize they might have warrants out for your arrest even as we speak? Let me make one thing very clear to you, I'm not going to jail because of your stupidity. Is that clear?"

The look on Kirby's face was one of both astonishment and irritation. He mumbled something about blowing the horn not being such a big deal.

"Well it *is*," she shot back. "We need to stay below the radar because this is it. Today is our last day with this, and all we have to do is stay outta sight, get our money and go." Nodding towards the attaché case, she asked, "Did you get it all?"

"I took as much as the case would hold," he said, "and it's a lot more than we usually take. Here, lift it and see how full it is."

"I'll take your word for it," she replied. "Tell me a little more about those cops you saw by the elevator."

"I only got a quick look, but I did see Sullivan from the U.S. Attorney's office, as well as Billings from IAD."

"Did any of them see you?" she asked.

"Nope, I saw them first, and ducked into the bathroom like I told you, and when the coast was clear, I used the stairs down to the ground floor, and left the building."

Anita backed off and softened her approach. "You did good Jim, but you need to remember, that the only way we get out of this is to use our brains. We're smarter than they are, and we'll out-think them. Anyway, here's the plan. I'm gonna be leaving in a couple of minutes to go and meet the contact that'll take me to our new buyer."

"What time are you gonna meet me and give me my share?" interrupted Kirby?

"My meeting with the buyer is set for twelve noon, and I figure it shouldn't take more than forty-five minutes to make the deal, and then I'll come meet you. Let's say I meet you right here around one, and please, no more horn-blowing!" She started her car.

Kirby shook his head. "Okay," he said, which sounded more like "Whatever." He got out of her car and she drove off.

Kirby was pissed. He was over that bitch's attitude and couldn't wait to shake her. He phoned Fitz, who answered on the first ring.

"Did you get our money," he asked anxiously.

"Hold your horses, man. Yeah, it's done. She's on her way to move the stuff, and then I'm meeting her at one to get our money."

Fitz let out a long sigh. "Great," he said.

"Fitz, you gotta know something. I saw cops and feds at the property room this morning, including Sullivan and Billings. Looks like the jig is up. I'm ready to get the hell out, and I hope you are too."

Fitz was silent a moment. "All I need is my money," he said.

"Right," said Kirby. "I'll let you know when I have it and we'll meet up."

CHAPTER FORTY-SEVEN

Tony and Sullivan rode the elevator up to the property/ evidence room. They were alone, as the others had taken a separate elevator. Tony took the opportunity to ask Sullivan some questions that were on his mind.

"Why are we serving the first warrants on the officers in the property room, Sully? Don't we have enough to catch some bigger fish?"

"It's easier to arrest those whose positions are known, get them out of the way. Those people are also our sources for getting to the brains of the operation. The more they talk, they quicker we can find the others, who right now are in the wind. We'd be guessing where to find them at this point."

"Are we going to arrest all three of the officers assigned to the property room?"

"You bet," Sullivan said. "There are two arrest teams headed to their homes as we speak, and we should have all three in custody within the hour.

"Sounds good. Let's do this." The elevator stopped with a slight jolt and the doors parted. Tony and Sullivan joined Frank and the others who were waiting outside in the corridor.

The group headed for the property room. Frank hit a call button and a buzzer sounded, allowing them entry. Two DEA agents walked ahead of the group, wearing identical black windbreakers with bright yellow insignias. They approached the sign-in desk where the officer on duty looked up from his crossword puzzle and became wide-eyed. One of the agents took his position directly behind the officer.

"What th—" the officer said, his head swiveling back and forth.

The agent in front of the desk identified himself and then asked "Are you Officer Stevens?"

After he answered in the affirmative, the officer inquired if he should call his boss.

"That won't be necessary, Officer. We have a warrant for your arrest. Please stand up and put your hands behind your back."

The officer's face turned white and he glared at the agent. "This is bullshit!" he cried. He catapulted from his chair, shoving it backward into the agent behind him, knocking him to the floor. He then reached for his weapon.

Tony, standing off to the side, reacted. He dropped to the floor on his bad arm. Excruciating pain ripped through him as he fumbled for his holster. Shots rang out. He rolled closer to the desk for cover. All around him was chaos.

He looked under the desk. He could see the shooter's feet on the other side. Finally freeing his weapon from the holster, he fired off two rounds, praying he missed hitting the bottom of the steel desk and causing the bullets to ricochet. A scream rang out.

There was moaning, shuffling, several men calling out. Someone shouted for an ambulance. Tony tried to stand, and as he struggled he felt a wetness in his shirtsleeve. He had broken open the stitches in his arm when he fell. Suddenly Frank was at his side.

"Tony, are you hit?"

"No, I'm fine," he said wincing. "Did somebody get his gun?"

"I got it!" yelled one of the DEA agents, holding up the suspect's service weapon.

Holding his arm, Tony walked around the desk and bent over the fallen officer.

"What the fuck were you thinking? You could've killed someone."

"I'm bleeding. Get me to a hospital," said Officer Stevens. Tony glanced down at the man's ankle: a piece of shattered bone protruded through his sock.

"The ambulance is on the way," Tony said in a low, soothing voice. "They'll be here in a minute or two. Just take it easy for now. You might think about the trick bag you've gotten yourself into, and maybe do yourself some good by cooperating with us." The wounded man looked up at Tony.

"I'll think about it," he whispered, and closed his eyes.

CHAPTER FORTY-EIGHT

It was eleven thirty and the morning was filled with sunshine. A few billowy clouds drifted in the cerulean sky over Sixth and Maryland. Anita soothed herself as she waited with the mild breeze coming through her car window. The neighborhood where she was parked was in a transition phase. Several old row houses were in various stages of renovation, some cloaked in scaffolding, others surrounded by workmen carrying tools in and out of the structures. She had seen no sign of Charlie yet and was becoming anxious. Everything, all of it, rested on his taking her to meet this Jo-Jo person. She looked at her watch for the tenth time.

"Looking for me?" a voice said to her right. She nearly jumped out of her skin. Charlie grinned at her through her passenger window. *Bastard must have been an Apache scout in another life.* She found her smile quickly.

"There you are! I thought maybe you changed your mind," she said, trying to not to sound glib. "Get in."

Charlie gave her the directions and they pulled out. As she drove through the city, the detective ran through the protocol of what was going happen when they got to Jo-Jo's.

"Make sure you get all of your money at the time you give him the drugs. He'll want to check them out—he'll probably have one of his flunkys do it. It's all part of the dance so don't be alarmed. Another thing, you should have a number in mind before you go in there, because this dude is not much on negotiating. Make sure you don't show any weakness, because he will exploit that to the fullest. Anita, this dude is not a nice person, and he's dangerous, so watch your ass."

She reached over and patted Detective Thomas on the leg. "I'm really grateful for your help, Charlie. Look under your seat."

He hesitated a moment, then did as she asked and retrieved a bag containing ten thousand dollars. He opened the bag and pulled out a bundle of bills.

"Pleasure doing business with you, ma'am," he said, a broad smile sweeping across his clean-shaven face.

"Count it if you like, it's all there."

"Not necessary," he replied. "I do hope, though," his eyes wandered over her, "to spend some of this money on a very nice dinner with you."

"I think that's a great idea—I'll look forward to it. But first, let's get this meeting out of the way, and then we can make plans for later."

"Well then," he smiled, "let's get this over with. Pull over. We're here."

Anita pulled up and parked in front of some run-down brick row houses. There was trash strewn in the yards and beat-up cars sitting on blocks. Charlie pointed to a house with a forties-style fascade. They got out of the car, Anita carrying the attache case, and walked up to the front door. An enormous black man, who weighed all of four hundred pounds, stood on the porch.

"I gonna frisk ya," he said in a flat monotone. "Just be still, and we can get this shit over with." He then proceeded to thoroughly check them both, spending some extra time running his hands over Anita's ass. He then told her to open the case, but she resisted.

"Your boss might not like you making me open this case out in public; maybe you should check with him first."

The big man gave her a nasty look and then turned and spoke to someone through the front door, which was ajar. There was mumbling inside and the door closed.

"The inside guy is asking permission for you to bring the case in without its being searched," Charlie whispered in her ear. A moment later, the front door opened again and the black guy inside motioned for them to come in.

Anita marveled at how nicely appointed the interior of the house was, with beautiful tan leather furniture accented by plush wall-to-wall matching tan carpet, as opposed to the ramshackle look of the outside. Walking into the living room, she saw a handsome, well-groomed white man about five-ten, forty-ish, with a slim build, wearing a beautifully tailored blue pin-stripe suit and seated on the couch.

"Please have a seat," he said. "Thank you for coming; I hope we will be able to reach a mutual accommodation here today. Anita, is that correct?"

"Yes, that's right," she answered.

"Okay," he began, "here's how this works. I need to see what you've brought, then, if it tests out okay, we will discuss price. I will offer you what I feel is a fair price for your merchandise, and, if you accept, we do business. If not, you are free to look for another buyer. How does that sound to you?"

Anita was taken by the professional, business-like proposal offered by the handsome man. Having bright blue eyes and dimples, along with a big friendly smile, didn't hurt her appraisal of Jo-Jo either and served to put her more at ease with the unfamiliar situation she was now in.

"That sounds fair to me," she stuttered. The man quickly raised his hand and a black man appeared in the doorway to the living room.

"Marko, please be kind enough to check the contents of this case for me."

"Right away, Boss. Be right back." He disappeared down the hallway with the attaché case.

"May I get either of you something to drink?" he offered. Thomas, who up until this moment had been completely silent, said,

"I would really like a cold beer if you have one."

"And Anita, how about you? What would you like? I have soda, wine, or whatever you want."

"Some water would be nice, thank you," she answered.

The man stood and walked to the hallway and issued instructions to someone to fetch the refreshments. He then returned to his seat.

"So," he said, "If today's transaction proves to be beneficial to both of us, would you be interested in doing more business in the future?"

"Absolutely," she lied. "I think if we can reach an agreement on price, we can do a lot of business in the future."

Their drinks arrived carried by yet another man they had not seen before. As she took a drink of the ice cold water given to her, she wondered just how many people this guy had working for him.

"Are you new to this business, Anita?" His words rattled her. She cocked her head and looked Jo-Jo right in the eye.

"I'm only new to this end of the business; I've been handling the other end for several years now. I'm only here because I lost my other contact," she asserted.

"Yes, I heard about that. It seems Lorenzo may have irritated someone who took it personally. For me, no disrespect intended, Lorenzo was an uncultured slob who never knew that this was simply a business, and not some mafia movie. Sorry, but I think that we're all better off with that man no longer around to draw unwanted attention to our enterprise."

Anita started to say something when Marko re-entered, walked over to his boss, leaned down and whispered into his ear. Smiling, the man clapped his hands together.

"We can do business. Marko tells me that it's all excellent quality, and he's weighed it. I am prepared to make you an offer."

Anita abruptly turned to Detective Thomas. "Charlie, I hope you won't mind, but I would appreciate it if you would wait for me outside while I finish my business with Jo Jo."

If looks could kill, the look he gave her would have qualified as a deadly weapon.

"I'll see you outside," he said with feigned politeness and left the room. After he had gone, Jo-Jo looked at Anita.

"I think that was a smart move on your part. He doesn't need to know your business."

"I agree. So what's your offer?"

"Two hundred and fifty thousand," he replied." She nodded and stuck out her hand.

"It's a deal, but I do require that payment be in bills no larger than fifties."

Jo-Jo nodded his head once in assent. "That shouldn't be a problem, but it will take a few minutes for my people to put it together for you. Do you want to use the same attaché case you brought here for the money?"

"That will be fine," she replied.

He got up, walked to the doorway, and once again issued instructions to someone in the hallway to get her money ready. As he came back around the couch and sat down, she flattered him.

"I didn't' expect to meet such an obviously educated gentleman in this situation. As a matter of fact, I heard you were a very nasty piece of work who uses"—she paused—"excessive force to get his way."

Jo-Jo studied her for a brief moment before he replied.

"In answer to your question, and it was a question, I have been successful in acquiring higher education, and this has translated into my being able to run a successful business enterprise. I don't make any apologies for methods I use to control either my work force or others who may cause me harm. You understand, of course, that this is a violent world we live in."

Anita began to warm up to the articulate man sitting across from her.

"I hope you won't think harshly of me," he went on, "but I firmly believe that just because you are in an unconventional business, you do not have to be an uneducated lout. I take pride in being able to converse in three different languages, and have business interests in four different countries. Occasionally, I do have to take harsh measures with some of the people that I do business with, because they always make the mistake that my civility is an indication of weakness, and that, I cannot have."

"I guess I can understand that," she replied, "but don't you get tired of the unrelenting pressure of doing business while worrying about your safety?"

"It's just a part of it. Let's face it, I'm in a very competitive business, and most of my adversaries are uneducated street thugs who only know one way to operate: through fear and intimidation. I prefer the subtle approach if possible. If that doesn't work, than I employ other means to get my point across. In answer to your question, yes, I do sometimes get weary of the constant pressure."

Anita was enjoying her conversation with Jo-Jo, and was almost sad when Marko entered the living room carrying the attaché case with the money.

"Is everything in order?" Jo-Jo asked.

"Yeah, boss, it's all there." he answered.

"Would you like to count it before you leave?" asked Jo-Jo. Anita felt reasonably certain that the charming man sitting across from her wouldn't cheat her.

"That won't be necessary. I actually do trust you, and I have enjoyed our meeting. I think we'll be able to do a lot more business in the future. I'll look forward to seeing you soon."

She started to pick up the case, then realized that it was very heavy and quickly sat it down on the couch. Jo-Jo laughed.

"Money's heavy, and a lot of money is *very* heavy. Marko will carry it to your car for you."

"That won't be necessary," countered Anita. "I think I can manage it by myself, and if it becomes too heavy, Thomas can take care of it for me."

"Absolutely not," answered Jo-Jo. "I won't hear of it. Marko is a big, strong young man, and I want him to give you a hand. As a matter of fact, I took the liberty of telling Marko to go outside and inform the detective that it was okay for him to leave, because you would be under my personal protection until you reached your destination. That's a lot of cash, and you can't be too careful nowadays."

"Okay, that sounds good to me," she replied, taken aback. She wondered how Charlie had left. Jo-Jo turned to Marko and motioned toward the front door.

"Take the car and follow her. Once she's safely at her destination, get right back here, because I'm going to need you."

"Okay, Boss," said Marko, picking up the attaché and walking out the door, Anita close behind. As the two of them crossed the street to her car, Marko spoke.

"Just for your security, how about me keeping the case with me for added protection until we get to wherever you're going?"

"Do you think because I'm a woman I'm stupid?" Anita was becoming irritated. "Just put the damn case in the front seat of my car like your boss told you to do, and let's get outta here."

Marko quickly put the case on the front seat of her car, and with extra force, slammed her car door, muttering obscenities as he walked across the street and got into his car.

Anita wasted no time in getting out of the neighborhood, trying to decide where to go. She didn't have many options, but chose to head for her place, hoping the police hadn't caught on to her yet.

As she pulled into a parking space in front of her house, Marko, who had followed her the whole way, pulled up and double parked several feet behind her. He got out of his car and walked over to her driver's side window. She rolled it down.

"Want me to take the case inside for you?" he smirked.

"No, thank you. I can manage it from here," she replied, hoping he would get the hint and leave. Instead, he squatted down by her car window and with undisguised hostility in his voice said,

"I want you to reach over and pull the case towards you, and I'm going to relieve you of the burden of worrying about all that money."

"What the hell are you talking about?" barked Anita. "You've done what your boss told you to do, and you can leave now."

"I am doing what my boss told me to do, bitch," he snarled, showing her a big knife that he seemingly pulled out of thin air. "You can give me the case, or I'll cut your fucking head off! It don't make no difference to me either way, so make up your mind, which is it gonna be?"

That bastard Jo-Jo had set her up and now she might have to pay with her life. She wasn't about to give up what she had risked everything to get to a thug with a knife.

"Please don't hurt me! I'll do what you ask," she said, adopting a frightened look. She slowly reached into the purse by her side and found the small, automatic pistol nestled inside.

Keeping up her vulnerable woman act, she made an attempt to pull the case towards her, but quickly turned to Marko.

"It's too heavy; I can't lift it sitting down. If you want it, you'll have to come around to the other side of the car and get it yourself."

He stood up, walked around to the front passenger door, opened it, and leaned in to grab the case. Anita fired twice, hitting him both times in the chest. She quickly pushed his body out of the car and drove off.

CHAPTER FORTY-NINE

Later, Tony was sitting in Captain McCathran's office with Sullivan, Inspector Billings, and Matt Hollis, his friend from the DEA. Matt, in the beginning, had been a little miffed at him for not leveling with him when they first talked about the case the day they met at the policemen's lodge; Tony explained Judge Gills' request not to discuss the case without anyone outside their group and he soon came around. They had just heard that Officer Stevens was in surgery, and might lose his foot as a result of the serious wound to his ankle. No one in the room felt a lot of sympathy for him.

"The son of bitch deserved what he got. He could have killed one of us, and when he pulled his weapon, all bets were off," Tony said. No one disagreed, of course.

The phone on the Captain's desk began to ring. "I told them to hold all my calls," groused Frank, as he picked up the phone.

"Captain McCathran." After a moment or two of listening, he said, "Thanks for the information, send me a copy of your report," and placed the phone back in its cradle.

"The shit keeps getting deeper. That was the detective in charge of the two arrest teams that went to arrest Officers Giles and Elliott.

"The first team went to Giles's house, and he wasn't there. His wife, who appeared to be very unhappy with her husband, happily volunteered information that he was probably with 'that bitch' he's been screwing for the last two years, and gave the team the address where he could be found. They went to the address the wife gave them, and attempted to serve the arrest warrant. A stand-off ensued, and he barricaded himself in one of the bedrooms in the house, and when SWAT entered the house, he shot himself in the head. He's dead."

"What about the other one, Officer Elliott?" asked Sully.

"They grabbed him while he was packing his suitcase. He'll be in booking shortly," answered Frank.

"Good news!" said Sully. "Now we need to pick up Ortiz and Harris from your shop, Inspector."

"Yeah, I know." Inspector Billings said. "The chief must have called me at least ten times today demanding to know what I'm going to do about the rotten apples in my squad, and raising hell because he feels like we haven't kept him in the loop. I tried to explain to him that this whole thing evolved very fast, and we were so busy rounding up these dirty cops that we hadn't been able to stay in close touch with him."

"I'll call him," said Sully, "and stroke him a little. His only real interest is being included in any press conference we might have, and I'll make sure he's kept up to speed on where we are with the rest of the arrests. Right now, let's get back to your shop, Inspector— how do you want to handle it?" he asked.

"I checked, and both of those detectives are working four to twelve today," said the Inspector, "and they should be here for roll call in about an hour. I thought I'd personally arrest them in front of the other officers at roll call to make a point. I'll also suspend them at the same time."

"Inspector," interrupted Frank, "would you like us to be there to help with the arrests?"

"Yes, Captain, I would appreciate the help. After all, you guys have worked on this a lot longer than I have, and you deserve to be there," said the tired looking Billings.

Matt had been quiet during the discussion. All at once he stood and waved his hand to get the others' attention.

"Does anyone have a problem eating pizza, 'cause I'm starving and I'm gonna order us a couple. Also, since I'm the only Italian in the room, I'm gonna be the one picking the place to order the pizza, and secondly, it's on me."

Tony looked at his friend and shook his head. "You're about as Italian as Moscowitz over in Sex Squad."

Everyone began to laugh. Matt had wanted to lighten the mood a bit, and he had succeeded.

Roll call at IAD usually consisted of a small, informal sharing of information about ongoing investigations among the detectives working the various shifts, and the occasional handing out of assignments by the official in charge at that particular roll call. When Tony accompanied Inspector Billings, along with Frank, Sullivan, and Matt Hollis, to the roll call room, everything got very quiet. Detective Harris, a seven-year veteran of the department, two with Internal

Affairs, was sitting in the back of the room wearing a rumpled gray suit which appeared to be doing a heroic job of trying to contained his large frame. When he saw his boss enter the room, he leaned over and whispered to his partner, Ortiz, who was seated beside him.

"This don't look good, 'Tiz. What's going on?"

Ortiz, a distinguished-looking man in his late thirties, was referred to by some in his squad as "The Model." He was dressed in a dark blue tailored wool suit and a red silk tie. He didn't hear what Harris said, exactly, as his attention was focused solely on the newly-arrived officials. He simply shrugged his shoulders at his partner's inquiry.

"Good afternoon, men," said Billings. "I know this might seem a bit unusual for me to be at your roll call, but circumstances require that I be here today, to send the message that this department will not tolerate criminal behavior of any sort by members of this squad, or any member of our police department. Detectives Ortiz and Harris have taken it upon themselves to dishonor both this department, and themselves, by their behavior."

Tony, along with Matt, took a position near the two disgraced officers, quietly instructing them to hand over their service weapons. Mouths agape, they reluctantly relinquished their weapons. Inspector Billings continued his speech.

"You are both suspended from duty pending a full review by the Department, and you are both under arrest. The charges against both of you will be explained later to you and your attorneys, if you engage them. Right now, I want Assistant U.S. Attorney Sullivan to explain to you your Miranda rights."

As Sully informed the gentlemen of their rights, Frank asked them for their badges and then handed them to Tony and Matt. Tony and Matt approached the visibly shaken inspector, and attempted to hand him the guns and badges. Billings waved them off and pointed to the IAD official in charge of that shift.

"Give them to Sergeant Leong."

Later, back at Frank's office, the team was having coffee, recapping the earlier arrests. After the usual self-congratulations, Sullivan took the floor.

"Okay," said Sully, "let's tick off the names of the players who are no longer an issue in this investigation. First, Lorenzo, dead; his hit man Timmy, dead; the snake guy, Vince, dead; Officer Giles, dead; Officer Elliot, in custody; Stevens, in custody at the hospital; Sipe, in custody; and finally, Harris and Ortiz, in custody. By my reckoning, that leaves us with Lieutenant Kirby, Detective Fitzpatric, and Anita.

"What about the dude that shot me?" asked Tony. "We know he fits into this somehow, and we need to find out who his contact was."

"I think we might have answered that question," answered Sully. "We found a slip of paper in the shooter's pants pocket with a phone number on it that traced back to Anita's cell phone. Before you ask, we tried the number and no one answered it. As an aside, we've heard from the hospital that the guy who shot Tony is going to make it, although he'll be paralyzed for life. Also, thanks to the chief, we have both Kirby's and Fitzpatrick's houses covered, and a BOLO has been issued for both their cars. I've also arranged for their bank accounts to be frozen, so their access to funds has been eliminated." The group considered Sullivan's words for a short while.

"Do any of you have anything to add before we all go home and wash off this stink?" asked Frank, breaking the silence. When no one offered a reason to extend the meeting, everyone left with the understanding they would meet the next morning in the chief's office to discuss the future direction of the investigation. As they were leaving, Tony pulled Frank aside and pleaded with him not to call him unless it was a true emergency, because he had some making up to do with Lina.

"That goes both ways, Anthony; I have a certain lady judge who is demanding a little more of my time"

Tony smiled. "By the way, Boss, is there a BOLO or anything out on Anita? Have they frozen her accounts too?"

"Sully neglected to mention her," Frank replied, "but her accounts are being frozen just like the others, and she is also listed in the BOLO, so don't worry. Go have some fun, and forget about this investigation for right now, okay?"

"I think I can handle that," Tony answered. "I hope that you and the judge can do the same. See you tomorrow morning, early."

On his way to Lina's, he made a quick call to Natalie to let her know all that had transpired. After answering her stream of questions, he promised to call her back as soon as anything had changed.

CHAPTER FIFTY

Kirby was furious. He had waited at the coffee shop for almost two hours. *That bitch stood me up!* His tires squealed as he exited the parking lot and sped away. His phone rang for the tenth time in two hours. Time to finally answer the call from an anxious Fitz.

"Boss, I'm gonna kill that bitch the next time I see her, and I mean it!" Fitz was rabid when Kirby broke the news.

"Fitz, if you're lucky, you'll never see her again. Don't be stupid—you only have a few hours before they find you. Use that time to get outta here. I don't know where you're going, and I don't need to know. This is the last time I'll be talking to you. When I end this call, this number will no longer be active. Good luck, Fitz. Keep your head down." Kirby threw the cell phone out the car window.

Kirby's head was reeling. Without the money from Anita, he was coming up short in his escape plans. He would have to visit his bank—a risky scenario at this point—and retrieve cash he had in one of his safety deposit boxes. He had no choice. He headed for his bank, all the while his eyes darting up into his rearview mirror. Someone could be tailing him at any moment. He noticed on two occasions a vaguely familiar civilian car had popped up behind him. Kirby pulled up at a red light, stopped, then slammed the pedal to the floor and charged through the intersection. He nearly collided with a garbage truck. In his mirror he could see the truck driver giving him the finger and shouting. He also saw the suspicious car swerve around the garbage truck and close the distance between them once more. He would have to draw the car into a less congested area in order to have a chance of out-running whoever was driving—or better yet, lure him or her into an area where he had a chance of surviving confrontation.

I just killed a man. Anita kept replaying the scene of Marko's lifeless body falling to the pavement. She drove onward on auto-pilot, barely aware of her surroundings. *I need to get to my other car and transfer all of this money and the other stuff I'm taking with me.* In what seemed like no time she arrived at a dilapidated garage in a rough section of Southeast.

She selected a key on her key ring and opened the lock on the garage door. When she stepped inside she peered around to make sure everything appeared normal. Then she walked back out to her vehicle and began bringing in the money and the rest of her belongings. She had decided earlier she would transfer the money from the attache case into a heavy-duty carry-on bag, which she would then ensconce inside the spare tire well in the trunk. She made ready all of her false identification and then dumped her purse onto the front passenger seat of her new transportation. She saw the gun she had used to shoot Marko fall out onto the seat. Recalling a dumpster loaded with construction material about a quarter mile back, she mentally checked that off her list.

She was taken aback when she examined her hands. They were spattered with small droplets of blood, as was her clothing. She opened a small suitcase and got out a change of clothes—jeans and a pullover sweater—and then retrieved some pre-moistened towlettes from her purse to wipe her hands and face. When she was dressed and refreshed, she backed the new car out of the garage and pulled the old one inside, locking up the garage once again. Scanning the area for anyone watching, she headed for the dumpster. She wiped the gun thoroughly before she got out and tossed it in.

Back inside her car, she began breathing a bit easier. She tuned her radio to some soothing music and proceeded to I-95 south. Her plan was working and she would soon be in Florida, boarding a plane and heading for Brazil—and her new life.

Unable to shake the car chasing him, Kirby headed for an old, rarely used industrial park he knew, about half a mile away from his current location. When he would look up in the rearview mirror, he could see the other driver waving and gesturing frantically. He pulled into an area surrounded by a chain-link fence and then parked his car between two large trailers in front of a loading dock outside of an old warehouse. Pulling his weapon, he opened his car door, rolled out and crouched down behind the open door. He could hear the blood pulsing in his ears as he tried to listen. As he tried to pace his breaths, he heard a car door slam. He checked his weapon.

The sound of footsteps crunching on gravel made him look to his right. He saw a pair of legs advancing in his direction. Lying down on his stomach for a clear shot, he waited until the person rounded the trailer. He could see from the partial view it was a man and he was wielding a gun. Adrenalin surging, Kirby took careful aim and fire off two rounds. At once he heard screaming.

He bolted upright and ran over to the fallen man. He was lying on his side with his gun on the ground a couple of feet away. Kirby kicked the gun aside and rolled him over. *Jesus! Fitz!*

"What the fuck are you doing here, you stupid ass? You scared me to death! Forget that! I ought to shoot you again!" screamed Kirby.

"Boss, don't shoot, please!" Fitz pleaded, holding his thigh with both hands. "I was just trying to get you to stop so I could ask for your help."

"Why the hell didn't you ask before now? Now look what a mess you've got yourself into, you stupid fuck," he said. In a sudden rush of sympathy, Kirby added, "Let me take a look at that wound," and he bent down beside Fitz.

He ripped open his pants leg and saw that, in spite of all the blood, the bullet had missed the femoral artery. He stood up and told Fitz he would bandage it for him. "After that, I don't want to every see you again, got it?" Kirby warned.

"Boss, I don't know where to go! I don't have enough money to disappear like you—I need your help! I've been loyal to you, did what you asked me to do. Please!" Fitz panted and grimaced, grabbing his leg once more.

"First off," said Kirby, "stop crying, because I ain't your mama, and I'm not responsible for this mess you're in.

Secondly, you'll need to find someone you can trust to take care of that wound, and then, once more, I'm telling you to get the hell out of town. Look, Fitz, I'm sorry about shooting you, but you brought it on yourself by scaring the hell out of me. I'll help you as much as I can, but I don't have all that much money myself." Kirby turned to go back to his car.

"Boss, I'll need at least ten grand to be able to get by until I can find a way to make some money!"

Kirby came to a full stop. He slowly turned around and looked back at Fitz, who still looked at him pleadingly. Spinning around he quickened his pace to his car. He grabbed a bundle of cash from the duffle bag on the back seat, and then strutted back over to the pathetic man on the ground. He shoved the wad of cash in his former partner's face.

"Here's ten grand. That's all I can spare, and you better make it last!"

Fitz reached out, his eyes focused on the proffered bills, and a second later his brain matter was all over Kirby's shoes.

"Sorry about that," said Kirby as he stuck the gun behind his back once more, cramming it inside his belt. He scooped the blood-stained cash up and walked back to his car. Changing his plans once more, he headed straight for I-95 south.

CHAPTER FIFTY-ONE

It was sheer lust that propelled Tony to Lina's place, and he thanked heaven above when he nailed a parking place right in front of her door. In an experience nothing short of surreal he raced to her porch, knocked once, and was immediately yanked inside by a completely nude Lina, who smothered him with kisses. He wondered if this was what winning the lotto felt like.

"Am I going to have to undress you, or are you going to be able to do it yourself?"

Without answering her, Tony pulled off his clothes as fast as he could, not even stopping when he heard his shirt rip. Finally, after what seemed a painfully long interval, he found himself naked with Lina's arms wrapped around him. They managed to make it to the couch, feverishly kissing and touching one another.

Tony couldn't get over how soft her skin was—and how firm her nipples became—it was like he was touching her for the first time. It felt natural and right to be there, with her. He didn't feel his injured arm once.

With utter disregard for time, they satiated themselves. When they finally took a break to talk, Lina looked into his eyes with exaggerated concern.

"You're not going to be able to use *this*, if you keep getting hurt!" she admonished and grabbed his penis. "Do us both a favor and keep it—and you—safe!"

Tony burst out laughing. "I promise to do just that, if you'll get back to taking care of business!"

"Better get yourself some of those little blue pills, Mister, because when I'm through with you, you're gonna need them!"

The next morning, Tony was back at headquarters in the chief's office. The rest of the team was assembled there as well. After pastries and fresh coffee, they got down to the investigation.

"Good morning to everyone," the chief began. "I think we all know why we're here, so I'll get right to it. First, speaking for myself, I would appreciate someone giving me a complete rundown of the investigation, so that when the press asks what's going on, I'll have something to tell them and won't look like a fool."

Judge Gills stood and began to brief him. "We now know, Chief that the theft of narcotics from the Police Property Room has been going on for over a year, at least. As I understand it, all but two of the suspects involved in the case are in custody, and to be truthful, there are others in this room who can give you a better picture of the current state of the investigation." Pointing towards Assistant U.S. Attorney Sullivan, she added, "Sully, since the ball is in your court, so to speak, I'm sure you can reassure the chief about the steps your office has taken since the arrests of the suspects in this case."

Sullivan, who was seated off to the side, looking a lot more crisp, clean and empowered in his suit than he had in days, took over from there. "Chief, I know you're busy, so I'll make this brief. By the time you get back to your office, you should have a report on your desk from the U.S. Attorney, with a complete break-down of the case, including the names of all the sworn police personnel we now have in custody. I've also been in touch with the DEA, and they have agreed to assist with a joint investigation and audit, with your department, of the missing narcotics." He followed up with information about the BOLOs for Kirby and Anita, as well as their frozen assets.

"Can anyone explain to me how these people could have just disappeared without leaving some clue as to where they went?" asked the chief. "What the hell am I going to tell the press?" I can't go out there and say that the main suspects in the case have just disappeared, and we don't have a clue where they went!"

"Chief," interrupted Frank, "both of these suspects are smart, and know police procedure, and they've had time to think about this. I'm sure they both had a plan ready to go so this won't be easy or quick. I would suggest for right now you tell them that the investigation is continuing, and we are pursuing several leads at this time. That should buy us some time to work the case and hopefully catch these bums."

"Okay," answered the chief. "I'll set up a press conference for tomorrow, and I want all of you except for Judge Gills to be there to help answer questions. Check with my office later today to get the time. Does anyone have any other thoughts or questions?"

Everyone shook their heads no, and the meeting ended. Tony approached Sullivan as he was leaving and asked about Detective Sipe.

"He's proven worthy of his immunity deal, for sure. We're keeping him at a local military base—in isolation."

Tony answered with a smile and made a quick exit.

Detective Thomas was working the day shift at Morals Division when he heard about the arrests in IAD. Most of the detectives in his department rejoiced at the news, ready to go out and celebrate. Charlie didn't feel like celebrating anything. What he felt was an imaginary wire tightening around his throat, closing off his windpipe. His mind raced with thoughts of anyone connecting him to the narcotics rip-off scheme. Though he hadn't been directly involved in the removal of the drugs from the evidence room, he knew that if his association with Anita and Jo-Jo came to light, he was toast. Quickly getting up from his desk, he rode the elevator down to the first floor and made his way outside. He tried to enjoy the unseasonably warm weather as he dialed Anita's number on his cell. "This number is no longer in service. Please try your call again."

Now visibly shaking, Charlie decided to call Lieutenant Kirby, even though in the past he'd never dealt with him directly. He scrolled through his directory until he located the number. Again, a non-working number. Putting his phone back in his jacket pocket, he walked over and sat down on one of several stone benches nestled between the massive Federal Court building and the District Courthouse. Oblivious to passers-by, he racked his brain trying to think of anyone that might know of his involvement with Anita. Besides Jo-Jo and Anita herself, there was no one. If push came to shove, he would adamantly deny any connection whatsoever. If Anita ever alluded to their lunch meeting, he would say it was just a lunch date between two people who worked at Headquarters and nothing more. He headed back into the building.

Driving down I95, Kirby alternatedd between euphoria and rage. He had a good amount of money stashed away, but he cursed Anita for cheating him. Still, if he didn't get too crazy, he could buy himself a small boat and go fishing when he wanted. Even that thought didn't take away the sting of being royally screwed by a lowly clerk from Robbery Squad. *No sense of ethics,* Kirby thought to himself.

All at once a State Police cruiser pulled up alongside him. Kirby reflexively tapped his brakes and checked his speedometer. A few seconds later the cruiser picked up speed and drove out of sight. Kirby wiped sweat from his forehead with the back of his hand. He now knew how the people he had pursued all those years throughout his career felt. Not relishing the sensation one bit, he pulled onto and exit ramp and headed for a roadside diner. He needed a bathroom break and some coffee. It was going to be a long haul.

Anita sang along with the car radio. She had put some miles behind her and was starting to feel like she needed a break. She spotted an interstate sign for an ice cream shop and got off at the designated exit.

As she sat in the window of the ice cream parlor, never taking her eyes off her locked car, she ate her hot fudge sundae and thought about her future. She would get a hotel soon and stop for the night. *When I get to Brazil, then I'll find that plastic surgeon. Who knows? I may have my nose reduced. After that, I might go blonde for a change.* She got up from her chair, using the plastic spoon to scrape the last bit of fudge from the paper cup, tossed it in the trash and walked out. Back in her car, she accelerated onto the on ramp, set her cruise control at sixty-eight, put one finger on the wheel and sucked chocolate from her lips.

CHAPTER FIFTY-TWO

Tony was dreaming. He heard Lina's voice calling to him. She couldn't possibly want more sex—he was exhausted. His eyes snapped open. Lina stood over him, gently nudging his arm.

"Sweetie, it's Frank on the phone." She handed him the cordless. He sat up, blinking, and made a motion with his hand like he was drinking from a cup and Lina mouthed the words "on the way" and headed for the kitchen to make coffee.

"Tony! Wake up! They found Fitzpatrick and it ain't pretty. I'll be at your place in ten minutes—be ready!"

"Sure thing, Boss. You want cof—?" Frank was gone.

Tony jumped out of bed and started grabbing clothes. He ran into the bathroom, brushed his teeth and splashed some water on his face. Lina appeared in the doorway with a travel mug.

"I knew enough to make it to go," she said as she kissed him.

"Thanks, baby. They found Fitzpatrick and I gotta run. Frank'll be be here in five minutes." He took the coffee from her hand.

Tony walked outside into the cool, early morning air. It was overcast, a gray sky still looming overhead, sunshine to be announced. Frank's cruiser was already at the curb. He barely had his seat belt fastened before the car was in motion and Frank was talking a hundred miles an hour.

"Whoever shot him meant to kill him, and on top of that they found several thousand dollars stuffed into a duffle bag in his personal car."

"Was there anything else in the car that might help us?" Tony asked.

"No, not at first blush, but that's because the detectives on the scene were told to wait until we got there," answered his boss.

"I know he was a scumbag," said Tony, thinking, "but somehow I can't help but feel sorry for these poor bastards ending up like this. They were cops, for Christ sake!"

Frank didn't say anything and kept driving. After fighting his way through early rush hour traffic, Frank finally pulled into an industrial park. Tony saw parked scout cars and police tape strung across the roadway near several parked trailers that looked like they hadn't been moved in a long time. Pulling his cruiser in front of a loading dock, Frank shut off the engine and both he and Tony got out and started walking over to where a blanket covered the body in the roadway.

"You know what, Boss? I hate this part of the job. Every time a cop does something stupid we have to deal with the fall-out. It's starting to get old."

"I'll never understand how these assholes think they can get away with this shit," Frank replied, shaking his head.

A tall, olive-skinned man with the build of a runner approached them: Detective Holdsworth. Tony remembered him working with Robbery Squad a few years back. He had a thin mustache, and the look of a mafia hit-man, but Tony knew him to be a good investigator and an honest cop.

"Captain, Sergeant," he greeted them. "Would you like me to go over what I've got so far?"

"Yeah, let's hear it," Frank said, staring down at the blanket-covered mound.

"The call came in at approximately six A.M. Uniforms responded to the scene, and found an unidentified white male, suffering from a gunshot wound to the head, lying in the roadway. A preliminary search of the body revealed a police department I.D. card and badge belonging to one Raymond Fitzpatrick. We already knew that he was assigned to Homicide."

"Anything else?" asked Frank.

"No, Captain. Nothing but the car."

"Thank you, Detective," said Frank, bending down and lifting the blanket from the body.

Tony couldn't help but think of a balloon that had partially deflated. Fitzpatrick's head appeared to have sunk into itself around the point where the bullet entered the forehead. Looking more closely, he could see where most of the back of the skull had been shattered by the bullet, and portions of the skull, along with brain matter, had come to rest in a spray pattern on the pavement behind the victim's head.

Having seen enough, Frank turned to Detective Holdsworth and asked if they were finished with the scene. The detective nodded.

"We've got all we need; I'm going to release the body to the Medical Examiner—unless you have any objections, Captain?"

"No objections," answered Frank. "But do me a favor. Process the car and send me a copy of your report. By the way, I would like to offer my condolences to both you and your partner. I know you both worked with Detective Fitzpatrick, and this must be hard for you."

"Not necessary," said Holdsworth. "He made his choice, and it came back to bite him on the ass. He was never one of my favorite people anyway, and he's made us all look bad. Another thing about this guy, both he and his sleazy little partner, Sipe, were always out of service, and the rest of us had to pick up the slack."

Frank looked at the detective sympathetically. Tony shook Holdsworth's hand and thanked him then followed Frank back to the car.

On their way to Headquarters, Tony's phone rang.

"Spinella, who am I speaking with? …Thanks, we're on the way." He hit the "end call" button on his phone, looked over at Frank and grinned broadly.

"What's up?" asked Frank.

"It seems that Officer Stevens has had some time to reflect on his position, and is feeling like talking to us. Let's head over to the hospital, while he's in a talking mood," Tony said, chuckling.

Frank made a quick U-turn and headed for the hospital. Tony hoped that Stevens would give them information that could lead them to Anita or Jim Kirby. They arrived at the hospital, parked the cruiser and headed up to the Detention wing.

Stevens was sitting up in bed when they entered his room. The disgraced officer greeted them cheerily.

"Good morning, gentlemen!"

"'Morning," said Tony. "How you feeling today? Are they taking good care of you?"

"Yep," said Stevens. "They say that I may regain use of my ankle if I stick with my therapy regimen. Man, I sure wish you had shot me a little higher up," laughed Stevens.

"I'm not going there," Tony cautioned. "What do you have to tell us?"

"Well, I've been thinking." said the officer. "I know I fucked up, and I'm willing to take my lumps, but it would be nice if you could maybe talk to the U.S. Attorney and get me a little help with the charges against me."

"What do you have to trade?"asked Frank, speaking for the first time since they came into the room. "Because I'm not going to bat for you unless you come up with something that'll help us close this case."

"Well," said Stevens, "I bet you guys didn't know that your boy Kirby had just left the evidence room before you got there, with an attaché case loaded with drugs. It was so full, he had trouble carrying it. Now where do you think he took the stuff now that Lorenzo's no longer in the picture?"

"Enlighten us," Tony said, not appreciating Stevens' cavalier attitude.

"I think that I'll wait on that one until I talk the U.S. Attorney about my deal," he answered. "Here's another question for you guys. How do you think a police lieutenant from IAD was able to hook up with a guy like Lorenzo in the first place?"

"I'm sure you have the answer for us," Frank said dryly.

"You bet I do," Stevens replied. "And I would really appreciate it if you would talk to the U.S. Attorney and let him know that I have good information to trade."

"We'll look into it. You just sit tight, and we'll get back to you as soon as we talk to the U.S. Attorney's office," said Frank. With that, Tony and he walked out. Neither one said a word until they were back in the car.

"Do you think Sully will work out something for him if his information is good enough?" Tony asked.

"I think so," Frank replied. "It makes sense for him to deal with this guy if it helps us with the case. From what he just hinted at, I think Sully will be *very* interested in hearing what he has to say."

Frank pulled his phone from his jacket and called Sullivan. Tony could tell that Sullivan was more than enthusiastic about talking to Stevens.

"He's going to talk to him tomorrow," said Frank after he hung up. "He'll decide then if any of what he gives him is worth a deal. Do me a favor, will you? Call the office and see if anybody has heard anything about Kirby or Anita, and also tell them I won't be back in the office unitl tomorrow morning."

"Sure thing, Boss."

Tony called in to headquarters and after finding out there were no new developments and passing on Frank's message, he hung up.

"Mind if I take the rest of the day myself, you know, catch up on paperwork and bills at home?" he asked.

"Sure, Tony. I'll drop you at Lina's so you can get your car and then I'll see you bright and early tomorrow."

As soon as Frank left him at his car, Tony called Matt at his office. He asked him to fill him in on other major drug dealers in the area. Matt told him he would make some inquiries and get back to him as soon as possible.

As Tony drove home, he distracted himself with thoughts of the several days' worth of mail and newspapers that awaited him. He also remembered he'd forgotten to take the garbage out. He was just opening his front door when the pity party ended and his phone rang.

"I think we have a person of interest," said Matt when Tony answered.

"Who's the guy?" Tony asked as he stepped inside his house and shut the door.

"He goes by his street name, 'Jo-Jo,' but his real name is Alexander Williams. "From what I found out," Matt went on, "he runs a pretty good-sized operation, does quite a business. He's also known to be a vicious and sadistic thug. No rap sheet though—never been busted. Goes out of his way not to make too many waves."

"How come you guys haven't busted him before now?" Tony gently chided his friend.

"I asked the powers that be that same question," answered Matt, "but I was told that it's being handled, and to stay away from Jo-Jo, for now."

"That don't mean I have to stay away from him," snapped Tony. "I think that I need to talk to this mug, and try and get some answers."

"I understand," replied Matt, "but you know I won't be able to go with you on this unless I get some help from the judge."

"Well, I think I might be able to help you with that," replied Tony. "Just sit tight while I make a couple of calls."

Tony called Frank at home. Frank answered on the first ring with a strange lift in his voice.

"You expecting me, Boss?" Tony laughed.

"Nope, thought it was Virginia. You'll have to do for now. What's up?"

Tony related his conversation with Matt.

"Ok, I'll speak to Virginia in the next few minutes and let you know. I'm sure she'll be able to clear it with the DEA so Matt can assist us. Both of you just lay low until his boss gives him the 'ok.' The judge may be able to do this by end of day."

"Thanks, Frank. That's great news. I'll pass it on. See you in the morning."

After Tony called Matt back, he grabbed a cold beer and settled down with a large stack of mail.

CHAPTER FIFTY-THREE

The following morning found Tony in his boss's office drinking bad coffee and moaning about the lack of news about either Anita or Kirby. Frank inpatiently waved him off when his office phone rang.

"McCathran."

After listening a minute or two, grunting some brief one-word agreements, he hung up and grabbed his jacket. Motioning for Tony to follow him, they headed toward the elevators.

"What was that about?" Tony asked as Frank hit the "down" button.

"That was Sully. Stevens gave up a name of another detective involved in the scam."

"Who?" asked Tony, growing excited.

"Sully didn't say. That's why we're headed for the hospital."

While they were in the car, Frank's mood was somber.

"You know," he spoke up after several minutes of silence, "when all this is over, I think I might just put in my papers.

It's really starting to get old, and I don't feel like my heart's where it used to be. It's a young man's game, Tony. And I'm not young anymore."

Tony was stunned to hear his boss speak of retirement. He pondered for a moment before he replied.

"Frank, I know the shit with these cops has gotten to you. It's gotten to me as well, but you're not that old and you're still one helluva cop. After we wind this case up, we'll sit down over a couple of beers and talk about it."

"Ok, you got a deal, but I think I've made up my mind. Virginia is about ready to retire too, you know? Maybe we can both get the hell out while we still have some time left to live a little."

"Now that sounds a little better," said Tony, laughing. "Right now, let's go and kick a little ass."

Arriving at the Hospital Center, they once again made their way up to Stevens' room. Sullivan was there, with another man whom they didn't know talking to Stevens, who was now sitting in a chair by his bed. Sully immediately motioned for them both to go back into the hallway, where he joined them.

"Hi, guys. Here's what we have so far. He gave us the name of the detective who hooked Lorenzo up with Anita, to help facilitate the movement of the drugs. His name is Charles Thomas and he's assigned to Morals Division. He's got a clean record; I can't find any dirt on him at all. He might just be a bit player in all this. As to any other information, Stevens promised to give us the name of the guy that Kirby sold the drugs to. I was just about to question him when you two showed up. Let's go back in so we can all hear this together."

When Tony, Frank and Sullivan walked back into the room, Stevens waved hello like a prince greeting his public. *He loves being the center of attention,* Tony thought.

"Oh, good. You guys are here. You ready to listen to the rest of my story?"

"Yes, we're ready. Let's hear it," said Sullivan.

"I heard that the name of the guy who was supposed to buy the drugs from Kirby goes by the street name Jo-Jo, and I also heard he's a mean son of a bitch to deal with."

Tony's ears perked up and he reached out and touched Sully's arm, motioning for him to step outside the room once more. Once they were in the hallway, Tony related his earlier conversation with Matt about this dealer named Jo-Jo, and how they were planning to have a talk with him.

Once again, they stepped back into the room and continued to question Stevens about this Jo-Jo person. His knowledge of Jo-Jo was minimal, but he did give them his address in Northeast where he allegedly did business. Frank took Tony by the arm and pulled him aside.

"I want you to hook up with to your DEA buddy Matt, and both of you go pay a visit to this Jo-Jo character. Try not to bust his balls right off the bat. See if you can just convince him that we're not as much interested in him as we are in Anita and Kirby. I think that approach might pay off."

"Sounds good to me, Boss," said Tony. "I'll go and call Matt right now, and set it up for this afternoon. Did the judge talk with Matt's boss?"

"It's handled. Go ahead and give him a call."

After being dropped off at Headquarters, Tony drove over to the lodge where he wolfed down a quick cheeseburger and a soda before meeting Matt. He was still a few minutes late picking up Matt in front of his office.

"Man, I'm sorry for being late, but I had to get something to eat—I was starving!"

"No apologies needed, man," said Matt as he grabbed his seatbelt. "I had just walked out of the building when you drove up. I've been doing some thinking. We can't just walk into Jo-Jo's place and expect him to roll out the red carpet. We could use the old carrot-stick routine, but he's too sharp for that, I'm afraid. What might work is to let him know up front we're not so much interested in him as other people."

"Frank said the same thing," replied Tony as he pulled away. "*But*, if he gives us any shit, we need to let him know that we're the 'po-leece' and some bad juju is gonna rain down on his head unless he cooperates. You know something else? I'm tired of being shot, so it might be a good idea to check your weapon before we go in. I've heard this guy is a nasty piece of work. Another thing we've got to think about before we go in is how many guys he's got inside."

"You got a point, Tony," said Matt, checking his weapon. "All we got to remember when we get inside is to watch each other's backs and we should be alright."

It was a short drive over to Sixth and Maryland Avenue. Tony parked right across the street from where a very large black man was standing, giving them the eye. By the time they exited their vehicle, the man was waiting for them on Jo-Jo's front steps.

"What you want, Whitey?" he asked, arms folded and blocking their way to the house.

"Police," said Tony, showing his badge. "We're here to see Jo-Jo, and you'd be doing yourself a big favor by getting out of our way before you cause yourself a big problem."

"Look, my man," the giant said with a smirk on his face, "ain't nobody going into that house without my okay, and you ain't okay. So why don't you do yo'self a favor and get outta my face."

Tony was just about out of patience with this big piece of shit, and was about to take matters into his own hands, when Matt touched him on the arm.

"Let me take care of this," he whispered. You've already been shot, remember?"

Tony opened his mouth to argue but there was a sudden blur of motion and a loud *whack!* He instinctively reached for his weapon when he looked down and saw the big black guy sprawled unconscious on the sidewalk. Blood ran down the man's face as Matt bent down to check him.

"You know," Matt said with a flippant tone, "people should never run on a brick sidewalk wearing flip-flops." He pointed to the black man's feet. They both broke into laughter.

"You should maybe look for a job at the State Department. They could use someone with your skills," Tony quipped as he rang the doorbell. Before Matt could reply, the door opened and they were greeted by a white man in his forties dressed in an expensive suit.

"Good afternoon, gentlemen," he said, in a very soft voice. "I see you've met Tiny. Please allow me to apologize for his aggressive behavior. I've cautioned him about that before, but it seems the only way some people learn is through adversity. Please come in."

Tony looked at Matt, nodded, and they both followed the man into the living room, where they both took seats on a large leather sofa.

"I'm reasonably sure you gentlemen are here about Marko's murder, and I will be happy to tell you all I know about it, if you'll just give me a minute to have someone remove Tiny from in front of the house."

"Yeah, go ahead, but you should know that's not why we're here," said Tony, as the man walked to the hallway door and gave instructions for someone to go and help Tiny. He returned to the livingroom and sat down across from Tony and Matt.

"If you're not here about Marko, then what is the reason for your visit?"

"First," said Tony, "I'm Detective Sergeant Spinella, and this is Special Agent Hollis of the DEA, and we're here to ask you a couple of questions about an investigation we're working on."

"Gentlemen," said Jo-Jo, "let's not play games; you know who I am, and what I do for a living, so please tell me why I should help you with your investigation."

Matt jumped right in. "Because you don't want my agency to come down hard on both you and your operation, putting you out of business. I can do that, but I'd rather have a discreet conversation between us that might help put some bad people away for awhile."

"May I ask the names of the people that you're so interested in?" asked Jo-Jo, maintaining his cool demeanor.

"A man by the name of James Kirby, and a young woman named Anita," replied Matt.

Jo-Jo jumped to his feet. "That bitch killed one of my best men, and if I find her, you won't need to be concerned anymore!"

"Hey man, just take it easy. Tell us what you know," said Tony, motioning for Jo-Jo to take a seat.

"I'll tell you," said Jo-Jo, sitting back down, "but this conversation never happened. If you agree to that, we can talk."

Matt looked at Tony and nodded his head.

"You've got a deal, so tell us what you know about these people."

"I did a deal with Anita yesterday, and I paid her a quarter of a million dollars in cash for some high quality product. As far as the other person you mentioned, I don't know him, and I've never done any business with him. Anyway, when she left here, she was carrying the money in a large, tan attaché case, and I sent my best man, Marko, with her to make sure she got to where she going safely, and he never came back."

"Are you saying they ran off with the money together?" asked Matt.

"No," he said. "I found out later, through a police contact of mine, that his body was found lying in the street with two gunshots to the chest. The only one who could have done it was that bitch, Anita, and if I find her she's—"

"Don't say anything that might come back to haunt you," interjected Tony.

After giving Jo-Jo a moment to compose himself, Matt asked,

"It seems to me that it was awfully nice of you to send your man with Anita. Do you always send protection with your clients, or did you have something else in mind when you sent your man Marko to guard her and the money?"

"What are you implying?" asked Jo-Jo.

"Well, I'm thinking that maybe you might have decided that since you already had the product, what's to keep you from getting your money back too? I mean, she was only one woman, and your man should've been able to handle her and get your money back with no problem."

"Detective," said a smiling Jo-Jo, "I see that you have the heart of a businessman, and I also think that I have extended this visit a bit too long. Thank you for your company, and have a good day."

As soon as they left the house, Matt asked Tony, "Can you check to see if he's telling the truth about this Marko being shot?"

Tony pulled his cell from his jacket and called Homicide.

"Detective Holdsworth, please." He was asked to leave a message.

"This is Detective Sergeant Spinella from Robbery Squad, and I need to know if there have been any recent homicides involving a black male with gunshot wounds to the chest area."

Tony was put on hold for a minute. In the meantime he and Matt got into the car and drove away. The detective on the other end came back on and told him that there had been a black male found yesterday, over in Southeast, with fatal gunshot wounds to the upper chest.

"Can you tell me exactly where his body was found, and when?" asked Tony." A moment later, Tony put the phone back in his jacket pocket.

"I think our boy Jo-Jo might have steered us right. There was a shooting over in Southeast yesterday, and I'm not sure, but I think it was very close to where Anita lives. The victim was a black male who was shot twice in the chest, and left in front of some row houses in Southeast. I'm gonna have to check her home address, but I seem to remember some time ago, when she was on extended sick leave, that I mailed Anita's checks to that same Southeast address.

When arrived back at Headquarters, Tony confirmed that the body was found directly in front of Anita's place. Although he hated to call him on his day off, Tony had to call Frank.

"Sorry to bother you on your day off, Boss, but I thought you'd like to hear the latest on our girl Anita. I'm here with Matt and if it's ok with you, we'd like to come by your place…. Good! We'll see you shortly."

The two detectives drove to Frank's house where Frank greeted them at the door. He was wearing an old T-shirt, a pair of shorts and tennis shoes. Tony had to stifle a laugh. He didn't recall ever seeing Frank dressed so casually.

"Give it to me," Frank said, leading them inside.

"We talked to that drug dealer, Jo-Jo," said Tony, "and it looks like our girl may be involved in the shooting death of one of his thugs. Not only that, he said he paid her a quarter of a million dollars in cash yesterday for, as he put it, 'high quality stuff'."

"So now she's a wealthy killer," quipped Frank. "Do we have anything new pointing to where she might have gone?"

"No more than we had before," replied Tony, "which was almost nothing. I've added the new information to the BOLO, that she's also wanted for questioning in a homicide case."

"That's all we can do for now," Frank replied. "But do me another favor: call Sullivan and see if he's questioned that detective from the Morals Division yet."

"Will do," said Tony. "I'll call if anything new comes up. If not, see you tomorrow at the office." He and Matt said their goodbyes.

As they headed back to headquarters, Tony called Sullivan. He left him a message to call him.

"I'm sure he'll call as soon as he gets my message," he said, hanging up. Matt, do you get the feeling that this case has all of a sudden come to a screeching halt?"

"Tony, you know how this shit goes," his friend replied. "These types of cases have a rhythm all their own. Sometimes they slow down and you don't think anything is working, and then all of a sudden all hell breaks loose. That's what I think is going to happen with this one. They can't continue to hide, and they'll slip up sooner or later. We just have to be patient."

CHAPTER FIFTY-FOUR

Anita was tired. She had spent a sleepless night at a cheap motel patronized by rowdy truckers and then driven for several hours—she was only about an hour outside of Miami. She really wanted to stop and take a nap, but she knew that it wouldn't be much longer before they figured out the whole scheme and put out a BOLO on her. She needed to find someplace safe to stash the money, until she could make arrangements to get out of the country. It dawned on her that all she had to do was transfer the bulk of the money to her off-shore accounts.

When she arrived in Miami, she headed directly for Little Havana, a high-energy section of the city with a large Hispanic population, particularly Cubans but other Latinos as well. The area bustled with numerous small shops and restaurants, selling everything from hand-rolled cigars, to a delicious variety of Cuban dishes. After driving around for a while, she found a small, but nice, guest house, where she paid cash for a room for three nights. The sweet little old Hispanic lady manning the desk made a point of telling her that her room came with breakfast and dinner. After showing her to a small but very clean room, the lady took a few minutes to tell her that she must be very careful when going out after dark because of the criminals who preyed on women in this part of town. Anita thanked her, and after she closed the door, immediately lay down on the bed and slipped into a deep sleep.

Kirby was back on I95 after gorging on a dinner of meatloaf with mashed potatoes and lots of gravy. He would drive straight through to Miami, and then find some place to rest. After he got some sleep, he would look for a charter boat that took tourists over to the Bahamas, purchase a ticket, and after he got there, find a place to hide out for a few days until he could arrange for a private plane to fly him to one of the islands that doesn't have an extradition treaty with the United States.

When he arrived in Miami it was a little after midnight. He couldn't get a room in any of the finer hotels that dotted the landscape around Miami, so he decided to head over to Little Havana, where he thought the police might not be as careful checking the smaller hotels and numerous unlicensed guest houses that flourished in that area.

After driving around a bit, Kirby came upon a house in a run-down, less desirable part of the area that had a small sign in the front yard advertising rooms for rent. The house had an iron fence surrounding a small front yard, which he could see had no grass. After finding a parking place, he pulled his luggage along a narrow and uneven concrete sidewalk up to the house and rang the doorbell. The house was quiet and there were no lights on. He continued to push the doorbell while noticing that the wood around the door handle looked like it had been damaged and repaired recently. After several minutes, a light over the front door came on.

"What do you want?" came the voice on the other side of the door.

"I need a room," said Kirby.

"Stand directly in front of the door so I can see you under the light," said the voice. Kirby stepped under the light.

"Do you have a room available?" he asked. "I only need it for a couple of nights. I can pay cash." There was silence for a minute.

"Okay," said the voice. "I'll let you in, but you have to pay cash for the room."

"That will be fine," Kirby answered. Slowly the door opened to reveal a big, burly Hispanic male in his underwear, who motioned for him to quickly come inside.

"Fifty dollars a night. Two nights, one hundred dollars in cash, up front, okay?"

"That will be fine," said Kirby, reaching into his pocket and withdrawing some bills. After handing the man a hundred dollars, he followed him upstairs to a clean, nice-sized room facing the front of the house. Kirby locked the door and then looked out front. Everything was quiet.

He removed his shoes, put his gun on the small table by the bed, and lay back to catch a few winks. In the morning he would look for his charter boat.

Kirby awoke to the smell of bacon. He quickly dressed and made his way downstairs to a small kitchen. Walking into the room, he found the man who had rented him his room sitting at a small table, eating. He was still in his underwear. Kirby decided to skip breakfast. Instead, he asked him where the closest restaurant was. The man replied incoherently with a mouthful of food, so Kirby headed out to find a place on his own.

Anita woke up feeling refreshed and hungry. She checked her watch. She had slept for over eight hours. Remembering that the little old lady had mentioned something about breakfast being included with her room rental, she got up, made her way to the small bathroom, and quickly washed her face. Just before she left her room to go downstairs, she thought about the money and knew she had to do something about it before doing anything else. Deciding to forgo breakfast, she quickly went downstairs carrying the bag full of money, and before anyone could talk to her, left the guest house. She put the bag in the front passenger seat, got in the driver side, locked her seat belt and drove away, rolling down her window to enjoy the early morning breeze and the warm Florida sunshine.

Driving the crowded, narrow residential streets, Anita paid close attention to the traffic while looking for a local bank. She passed several small restaurants which, because she was really hungry, nearly diverted her from her main objective of finding a bank that might not pay too much attention to a woman with a large sum of cash. After driving around for almost half an hour, she was becoming a little frustrated when she spotted a small sign advertising "Casa Banco," on the side of a dirty-looking, two-story gray stucco building, located near the corner of a busy intersection.

At one time it might have been a respectable professional building, but it clearly hadn't received much maintenance in recent times.

A car pulled away from the curb across the street and she grabbed the space. She went around to the passenger side, retrieved her carry-on bag, and walked over to the bank entrance. Inside, she was pleasantly surprised to see that the interior of the small bank was not only clean, but had modern furniture and several beautiful paintings on the walls. She was approached momentarily by a pretty, young Hispanic woman who greeted her in Spanish.

"I don't speak Spanish," said Anita to the young woman. The woman paused, seemingly embarrassed.

"Please forgive me. Most of our customers are from this area and are Hispanic, so I assumed that you were Hispanic too."

"That's all right," said Anita. "I'm here hoping you'll be able to help me with a transfer of funds. And I also hope that you'll be able to accomplish this in a discreet manner, if possible."

"Please be assured that we'll be able to accommodate your needs here at Casa Banco," said the young woman. "Please, if you'll follow me, I will take you over to Mr. Thomas, who will assist you."

Anita followed the young lady over to where a nice looking man, roughly in his late fifties, was sitting behind a large, mahogany desk talking on the phone. Showing her to a seat in front of the desk, the young lady excused herself.

The man abruptly hung up the phone and introduced himself as Luis Thomas, vice president of the Casa Banco. Anita, without introducing herself, began to explain that she had lost her husband several months ago, and had recently sold their home. Since she converted most of her assets into cash, she wished to transfer some of that cash into her offshore accounts.

"Will that be a problem for Casa Banco?" she asked looking her most demure with legs crossed and hands clasped around her knee.

"How much money will you be transferring today?" Mr. Thomas asked curtly.

"Approximately two hundred fifty thousand dollars," she said. "Will that be a problem?"

"I assure you, madam," he said, "that it will pose no problem for Casa Banco. We assist our clients with large sums of money almost every day. All I will need from you are a few details to get started."

"Before we proceed," said Anita, "this is all new to me, and being a new widow I'm somewhat nervous. I will need your complete discretion in this matter."

"That absolutely goes without saying, madam," he responded. "I will see to it personally. Here are some required forms you will need to fill out so that we can start the process. They also spell out the bank's fees very clearly, so there won't be any misunderstanding."

She pulled the forms in front of her and began to fill them out, using the information from the fake driver's license and other identification she had acquired. Twenty minutes later, Anita walked out the front door of the bank with an empty carry-on bag and a smug look on her face. *Now, I can go get that breakfast that I missed earlier.*

She drove four or five blocks before she spotted what looked like a brand new diner, situated next to a car dealership. She parked in the adjacent lot and went inside where she was shown to a table in the corner of a room. The diner was filled with mostly Hispanic people who were engaged in both eating and talking loudly to one another. She loved it.

Looking at the menu, she quickly decided on the breakfast special: two eggs, a slice of fresh ham, home fries, toast and coffee. All of this came for the amazing price of four dollars. It didn't take long before her food arrived.

As she enjoyed her meal, she began to relax for the first time since she had shot that thug Marko. All she needed now was to arrange a safe way out of the country without being recognized, and she could start her new life. Her thoughts returned to her hair color. She chewed on savory ham as she fantasized over how she would look as a blonde.

"Hello Anita. Long time no see."

Anita looked up and nearly fell backward in her chair. There was Jim Kirby standing over her, with a "gotcha" grin spread across his weary face.

"Well?" He looked at her with a sardonic expression. "Are you going to invite me to join you or not?"

CHAPTER FIFTY-FIVE

Anita gathered her wits and removing the napkin from her lap, wiped her mouth and told Kirby to sit down. She took a long drink of water as he took a seat.

"How did you find me?"

"Let's just say lucky for us we have the same tastes in cuisine. It doesn't really matter how I found you now, does it? Let's just talk a little bit about the money you screwed me out of, and how you're going to give it back to me today."

"Jim, I know you're angry, and you have a right to be, but I had a very good reason for not meeting you after I got the money from Jo-Jo, and you need to listen to me before you go off half-cocked."

He tried to interrupt but she held up her hand.

"After I got the money, Jo-Jo insisted that his man, Marko, accompany me to where I was going, for 'added protection.' I objected, but he insisted, and this thug Marko followed me back to my house because I didn't want him to see me meet with you. Once we got to my house, this Marko guy tried to rob me at knife point, and I ended up having to shoot the bastard.

"After that, I panicked, thinking that my neighbors had seen everything, and would report me to the police. So I got out of town as fast as I could. I really feel bad about the way this went down, Jim, but I didn't plan it this way, and I had no other choice but to leave as fast as I could."

"Did you kill that piece of shit?"

"I think so," she replied.

"Okay, let's say I believe you. The question remains how I'm going to get my money. We both need to get out of the country, and the more money I have, the better chance I have of getting away. So, tell me how you're gonna get me my money?"

Anita was relieved. Kirby wasn't going to kill her on the spot. She really didn't feel particularly unhappy about giving him the money—she had more than enough to get by.

"Let me explain what I've done so far," she said. "I've wired the money I got from Jo-Jo to my accounts off-shore, and I should have no problem getting your money to you today. The bank is just down the block, and I get the impression they're used to doing business in a much less formal way than your normal bank. Why don't you order some breakfast, and I'll have another cup of this delicious Cuban coffee, while we do some planning? This meeting might just turn out to be good for the both of us."

Kirby smiled, and waved for the waitress to come over and take his food order. After the waitress had left, he looked at Anita warily.

"I'll feel a lot better about all of this after I get my money. I understand the reason you ran, but once I get the money, we can start planning how we're going to get out of here. I have an idea, but I'll run it by you later on this afternoon."

"That sounds good," she said, "but I was just thinking—do you want your money in cash, because carrying that much cash is not a good idea. You could, while we're at the bank, open your own account and it would be accessible to you anytime you want it."

"I'll think about it," he replied. "It does make a lot of sense."

Just then, the waitress arrived with his breakfast, and the two of them spent the next thirty minutes talking like old friends while he ate. As soon as he was finished, Anita suggested that she ride with him to the bank where she would take care of returning his money.

When they were riding along in Kirby's car, Anita asked him if he remembered how much money she owed him.

"I'm not sure," he replied, "because you didn't know how much you were going to get when you went to meet Jo-Jo."

She gave him a mischievous look. "Fifty thousand dollars," she said.

"Woo-hoo!" Kirby exclaimed. "That'll help me a lot, and maybe buy me a few mojitos too."

"Ok," Anita replied, looking down the street. "Turn left here and park in that small lot on the left, next to that building on the corner. When we go in, let me do the talking, because they already know me, and the transaction will seem more normal."

"That's fine with me," Kirby answered.

Once inside, it only took a few minutes for the bank to make the transfer, but Kirby had been required to open an account so he could receive the funds being wired from Anita's account. Mr. Thomas was very helpful with the process, no doubt hoping to get additional business in the future.

"I really don't know much about banking," Kirby said to Mr. Thomas as they were leaving, "but I would appreciate it if you could set up an off-shore account for me where I would be able to deposit additional funds in the future."

"Sir, I can assure you that we can accommodate your wishes. If it's agreeable to you, why don't we set an appointment for tomorrow afternoon around one o'clock, which will give us plenty of time to take care of all of your business requirements?" Kirby quickly agreed.

"Do you think it was a good idea to ask him about an off-shore account so soon after meeting him?" Anita asked Kirby as they walked out of the bank.

"Why not? By this time tomorrow, I hope to be on my way to one of the islands, and I can't be caught carrying a lot of cash with me."

"So, you have more cash with you?" asked Anita.

"Not a lot," he replied. "But more than I want to be caught with in my possession in case some nosey Immigration person decides to go through my things."

"That makes sense," she replied. "You can access your money from anywhere you end up. Have you decided where you're going?"

Kirby was silent for a moment or two before he answered. "Let's just leave that question unanswered if you don't mind. You and I both know you can't tell anything if you don't know anything."

"I hear that," Anita answered affirmatively as they headed back to the diner to get her car. When Kirby dropped her off, Anita asked him if he felt secure enough with Mr. Thomas to handle his business without her being there the following day.

"I don't foresee any problem. He told us that it was a simple matter to set it up, and I hope to catch a boat out of here by late afternoon. I'd like to say that I'm sorry about the unpleasantness earlier, but you can understand how I felt when you didn't show up with my money. But, you've been true to your word, Anita, and I wish you good luck with your new life, because I think we're both going to need it."

After saying goodbye to Kirby, Anita got into her car and drove away from the diner looking for a store where she could buy some hair coloring. She located a small drug store close to the guest house where she was staying, purchased the hair color she needed, along with a six-pack of soda and a bag of chips, and headed back to her room.

She made sure the door was securely locked, and went into the tiny bathroom where she dyed her hair to match her new identification. After she finished, she looked into the mirror and saw that it would work just fine. Later, after drying her hair, she styled it, and then put on the new glasses she had purchased. She looked into the mirror to judge the overall effect, and was amazed at the transformation. After her surgery, no one would be able to identify her as Anita ever again, and she could begin her new life without having to look over her shoulder.

She glanced at her watch and was surprised to see how much time had passed. It was already late afternoon. She hadn't had anything to eat since her breakfast with Kirby earlier that morning. She opened her suitcase, retrieved a pair of PJs and got comfortable. Opening the bag of chips and a can of soda, she kicked back on the bed and relaxed. Suddenly she envisioned Kirby's leer at the diner. She shook it off and shoved a handful of salty chips in her mouth.

CHAPTER FIFTY-SIX

Tony had just walked into his house when his cell phone went off. Matt Hollis was on the other end, and he couldn't talk fast enough. Telling him to slow down, Tony heard him say that Dade County had a hit on Kirby's plates.

"Where?" asked Tony, his own excitement mounting.

"His car was spotted parked in a residential area in what's known as Little Havana, in Miami," Matt replied. "I told them, for right now, just observe until we get down there to take him down."

"Whoa, just a minute," said Tony. "I can't just take off for Florida without first getting permission from Frank. I know you're excited, but give me a minute to call my boss and see if he can get the okay for me to go down there with you. I'll call you back in a couple of minutes and let you know what's up, okay?"

"Yeah, that'll work. Talk to you in a couple," said Matt.

Tony hit the speed dial on his cell.

"Frank, are you sitting down? I just heard from Matt." There was some static noise for a second or two before the captain replied.

"Yeah, I'm sitting down, and Inspector Billings is here with me in the office. You're on speaker so I won't have to repeat myself."

"Good idea. Well, I just got a call from Matt Hollis and he informed me they just got a hit from their agents in Florida to the BOLO we put out on Kirby's vehicle." Tony related everything Matt had told him.

"I get the distinct impression that you'd like to go down there with Hollis, am I right?" Frank asked.

"I *would* like to be in on the arrest when it goes down," replied Tony. "You know, we've invested an awful lot of work on this case, and I feel like we should be there when he's picked up,"

"Well," said his boss, "I think I can get the authorization for your trip, but you know you don't have any jurisdiction down there, so don't be getting into any shit where I'll have to clean up behind you, okay? In case I can't get the okay for you to go, you can always take some leave. You know I'll authorize it. For that matter, you should be on sick leave anyway, after being shot in the line of duty. Well, enough of this bullshit, just go, stay in touch, and keep me informed."

"Thanks boss," said Tony. "I'll call you the moment it goes down."

He phoned Matt back and told him what Frank said. Matt told him not to concern himself with jurisdiction, because being federal, he had that covered. They arranged to meet at Tony's place in forty minutes.

The next morning, Anita reviewed her options for getting out of Florida and decided that it might be a better idea to try and arrange for a private plane to take her to one of the nearby islands, where she could make a connection to Brazil without attracting undue attention. She had to get out of the states as quickly as possible. She also needed to find a pilot who would agree to take her to one of the islands where she could make a connection to Brazil, and also forget ever having seen her. She would pay another visit to Mr. Thomas at the bank and ask for his help. Knowing that it would cost her a bundle of cash, she nonetheless made up her mind that it was the best move for her right now. She was prepared to pay whatever it took. Quickly packing all her personal things, she headed over to Casa Banco to see Mr. Thomas.

Arriving at the bank just before eleven, she broke out in a sweat from the hot Florida sunshine the moment she left her air-conditioned car to walk the short distance to the bank. The pungent smell of Cuban food coming from several nearby restaurants filled her nostrils. Entering the bank, she was met by Mr. Thomas who was getting ready to leave.

"Well, hello again, Mrs. Pratt," he said, with a small bow. "What brings you back to Casa Banco? Is there something else that I can do for you?"

"As a matter of fact, I would appreciate a moment of your time," said Anita. "I know it's almost lunch time for you, but I would really appreciate a few moments of your time. I promise to be brief."

"Of course," he said. "Please come to my office and let's see if I can be of some assistance to you."

Once she was seated in his office, she explained that she needed to find a way over to the Bahamas as soon as possible, and she was hoping that he might know someone with a private plane who would be willing to fly her over without a bunch of paperwork being involved.

Mr. Thomas, without missing a beat, smoothly explained that it could be arranged, but would be expensive.

"Let's talk numbers," Anita replied smiling. After a brief bit of haggling over price, the deal was made, and he immediately made a call to someone named Dennis, who, from what she could hear of the conversation, demanded more money. Interrupting the conversation, Anita instructed Mr. Thomas to give the man what he asked for, and she would make up the difference with him.

Mr. Thomas concluded the business and hung up the phone. "Will a one o'clock departure this afternoon be okay with you? Dennis would like to get started as quickly as possible, so that he can make it back here before dark."

"That will be fine with me. Where do I go to meet this Dennis person?"

"Not a problem," he replied. "I'll take you to the airport myself, and introduce you to Dennis. He's an excellent pilot, and his plane is nearly brand new, so you won't have to worry about a thing. Oh, by the way, I have arranged for him to take you where you will not have to worry about those bothersome custom people."

"After we land, will I be able to arrange for a hotel room for tonight?"

"Don't worry about a thing. I will see to it while you're on your way. Do you need to go back to your hotel, or are you prepared to leave right away?"

"I think that I have everything I'll need for my short stay, so I'm ready to go if you are," she replied.

When they walked out of the bank, Anita was pleasantly surprised to see him walk over to a brand new luxury car, open the passenger door and motion for her to get in. The route from the airport changed from the congested streets of Little Havana to more open areas with luxurious gated communities, complete with guards posted at the entrances. The beautiful day, along with her surroundings, elevated her mood. Paying for such service as she was getting at the moment was worth the premium. She reminded Mr. Thomas she would be doing more business with him.

"Thank you," he said. "I'll be very happy to assist you with anything you may require."

They pulled into a small airport and right up to small plane. A man with a slight build, maybe mid-thirties, approached them as they got out of the car. He extended his hand.

"Hello, I'm Dennis, and I'll be your pilot for this afternoon. Do you have any luggage?"

"Just what I'm carrying," said Anita.

"That's wonderful," said the pilot, "because the more weight we carry, the more fuel we use. Are you ready to depart?"

"I'm ready when you are," she replied.

"Okay, let's get this show on the road," he said, holding out his hand to help her up into the plane.

Anita, assisted by the pilot, was quickly strapped in her seat. She waved goodbye to Mr. Thomas as he watched them from the tarmac. Before she could absorb the idea that she was leaving her country for good, they were airborne. Flying above the crystal blue water put Anita at ease. She sat back in her seat and looked toward the horizon. *As of right now, I am no longer Anita.*

CHAPTER FIFTY-SEVEN

Matt and Tony sat side by side in the cramped economy section of a Boeing 737, flying at thirty two thousand feet, sipping sodas from plastic cups while they discussed their strategy for capturing Kirby, if circumstances all worked out.

"Matt, you know you're gonna have to take the lead on this when we get there, don't you? I have no jurisdiction, and you're the one with all the juice, so it's your party."

"Hey, man," said Matt, "we're in this together, so just do what you usually do, and let me handle the fall-out we get, if any, from the locals."

"Works for me," replied Tony, raising his glass to signal the flight attendant for more soda.

When they landed in Miami they were met by one of the agents from the Miami field office. He had a military-style haircut and wore a dark blue suit, white shirt and a blue tie. Dark sunglasses topped off the look: he could have been on a recruiting poster for federal agents.

The young man brought them up to speed as to Kirby's location, and how the surveillance was set up. Matt asked the agent to take them directly to the location. The young agent paused, and seemingly embarrassed, told them that he had been instructed to take them to his office, where his boss would be waiting for them to give additional background on the case. Matt's eyes met Tony's for a second. He turned back to the agent.

"What's your name?"

"Murphy," he replied.

"Well, Murph, you're gonna take us to the site, and we'll deal with your boss later. Don't worry, I'll tell him that I ordered you to take us, so you'll be off the hook. Anyway, once we get there, I'll contact him and bring him up to speed about the on-scene situation, okay?"

The young agent sighed. "Follow me. The car's just outside," he said.

As they only had carry-on luggage they followed the agent directly outside where they were met by another agent, a virtual clone of Murphy, who identified himself as Ron Lutz. He opened the car door and Tony and Matt jumped in.

"If the rest of it goes this smoothly," said Matt as they were settled into the backseat, "we'll be home by tomorrow evening having a cold one."

"Hey, man," said Tony, "don't forget Murphy's law, no pun intended."

Matt laughed.

"We're not gonna do anything crazy, Tony. Just follow my lead and we'll be okay."

After a short ride, they pulled up next to another car with two men sitting inside who Murphy identified as agents from the local field office. Quickly exiting their vehicle, the two agents, who were casually dressed and appeared to be slightly older than Murphy and Lutz, approached their car and introduced themselves as agents McGrath and Fleri. They began to brief them about the status of the surveillance on the suspect's vehicle.

"For the short time we've had the vehicle under surveillance," said Fleri, "no one has been near it."

"Okay," said Matt, pointing at McGrath and Fleri, "here's what we're gonna do. You two find a new location where you can see his vehicle, and be prepared to block him if he makes it to his car and tries to leave. We'll take this position here, and block him from this angle if he makes a break for it. Remember, he's probably armed, and has nothing to lose at this point, so make sure you're very careful with this guy. He's dangerous."

Both agents nodded their heads in agreement, and left for their new position. Looking across the street, Matt noticed that Kirby's car was parked in front of a small grocery, which was part of a small house.

"Hey Tony, what do you think about us slipping into that bodega across the street and using it to watch for our boy? It will give us the advantage of being right on top of him when he shows up, and maybe we can grab him before he can pull a weapon."

"Good idea," Tony replied. "But how you gonna get that bodega owner to agree to us hanging out in his store?"

Matt laughed. "With my good looks and winning personality."

He started walking down the street away from where the suspect's car sat parked. Tony quickly caught up with him and they made their way to the corner, crossed over to the opposite side of the street, made their way back to the bodega, and went inside.

Matt surprised Tony when he started talking with the man behind the small counter in fluent Spanish. After a flurry of back-and-forth discussion, all in Spanish, Matt introduced him to the owner of the small store.

"Tony, this is Juan. He's agreed to assist us, and is willing to do anything he can to help."

Tony extended his hand over the counter to Juan, who enthusiastically grabbed it, and in broken English said,

"I help police, I good citizen."

"Muchas gracias, senior," Tony responded.

Later that afternoon the radiant Florida sun poured through the windows of the bodega and Matt, who was seated in an old lounge chair behind the front counter, was nodding off. Tony was back behind the meat counter, on his fourth soda, thinking he should hit the bathroom before Matt dozed off. The squawk of Matt's radio took his mind off his bladder. Matt snapped to attention and grabbed the radio. Tony was ready with questions as soon as he finished talking.

"What's happening? Is he moving?"

"Yeah," said Matt. "He just came out of a house down the block, on the opposite side of the street and he's walking this way. I told the guys to wait and observe until I tell them to move."

"Good idea," said Tony, sharp and alert with all the caffeine he had consumed. "I think we should tail him and see if he takes us to Anita. It won't hurt anything to wait and see what he's up to—we can take him anytime."

"I agree," said Matt. He spoke into his radio, giving instructions to the two teams of agents to begin a loose, leap-frog surveillance of the suspect until further notice. He also alerted the two teams that he and Tony would be following closely behind them, and for them to stay in contact with him at all times.

"Here we go," said Tony. "It's show time."

Matt winked. "But this time it's *our* show, old pal." He handed Tony a Glock 9mm. "Let's roll."

Kirby slept the entire night and most of the morning. When he awoke, he enjoyed a nice, hot shower, even though the small shower stall in his room could have used a thorough cleaning. It was a beautiful day, so he walked the four blocks to the bank to finish his business with Mr. Thomas. After that, he could leave the country that afternoon.

He sauntered through Little Havana, breathing in the aroma of Cuban food and admiring the beautiful women who passed him on the street. The exotic atmosphere had an intoxicationg effect on him, making him more relaxed and less paranoid than he had been in days. He was going to be early for his appointment with Luis Thomas, but no matter. He would have time to grab some robust Cuban cuisine for lunch, then return to his room and pack up. Not long after that, he should be on a tourist boat on his way to the Bahamas.

He rounded a corner and crossed the street, headed for the entrance to Casa Banco. He was glad to see the beautiful young Latina from the other day.

"Is Mr. Thomas available?" he asked, looking her up and down.

"Yes sir, he is," she replied. "One moment please."

Kirby ended up waiting for some time. He was growing impatient when Mr. Thomas finally appeared.

"Good afternoon, sir." Thomas shook Kirby's hand and led him toward his office. "It seems you have arrived a bit early for your appointment, but it so happens I just had a client call and cancel their appointment, so I will be available to assist you. Do you wish to set up the offshore account we discussed yesterday?"

"Yes, that's why I'm here. After we get that business taken care of, I'd like you to recommend a charter boat that goes over to the Bahamas, if you would."

"I would be happy to do that for you," replied the banker.

Kirby was content to sip some excellent Cuban coffee served by the attractive Latina while he waited for Mr. Thomas to complete the arrangements for his offshore account.

"I think we've taken care of all of the details," said Mr. Thomas after he got off the phone. "Now all you have to do is sign the papers, and you're good to go."

Thomas pushed the papers across the desk and Kirby gathered them up, gave them a cursory once-over, and began signing. Suddenly he heard the Latina shouting for Mr. Thomas in Spanish from the lobby. She appeared in the doorway, her face one of alarm, rattling away in her native tongue. Mr. Thomas began to shout back at her authoritatively in Spanish. Kirby reached over the desk and gripped Thomas by the arm.

"What's happening? Is there a robbery or something?"

"Nothing serious," Mr. Thomas said, reverting back to English. "She becomes scared sometimes because we are in a high crime area; she worries all the time about being held up."

Kirby wasn't satisfied. He was on high alert now. "What scared her?" he demanded, giving Mr. Thomas a brief shake.

"She says there are men outside the bank acting suspiciously—but that happens a lot here, so don't give it a second thought. I had her call my nephew, who sometimes works for us as security on Friday and Saturday, and tell him to come right over, so please, *no te preocupes, señor*—do not concern yourself. He only lives a few blocks away, and should be here any minute. So, have you signed all the forms?"

"They're all done," replied Kirby, releasing Thomas's arm as he calmed himself, "and I would like to thank you for being so helpful. If you don't mind, I'd like to ask another favor of you."

"I'd be happy to help, if I can," replied the banker, massaging his arm and smoothing the sleeve of his linen jacket. "What can I help you with?"

"I would appreciate being able to leave by a rear exit if possible," said Kirby. "I know it's a little unorthodox, but after hearing about those men outside, I would feel a lot better about using another door."

"Unfortunately," answered Mr. Thomas, "the back exit has an alarm, and we cannot use it unless it is an extreme emergency, because it will send an alarm to the local police, and the FBI. Why don't you take a seat, have some more of our excellent coffee, and wait for my nephew to arrive? He'll see you to your car with no problems. *Elena! Mas café para el senor, por favor!*"

"I'm not driving," said Kirby. "I walked the four blocks here, and if it would be possible, perhaps your nephew could accompany me back to where I'm staying. I'll be happy to pay for his services."

"Totally unnecessary," replied the banker. "This will be my thanks to you for your business."

Elena brought Kirby another cup of coffee while he sat and listened to Mr. Thomas's proposal for a private boat charter to the Bahamas. There would of course be a small fee. Kirby assured him he was quite interested and was about to start negotiating price when they were interrupted by a muscular young man wearing a light tan jacket.

"Tio Luis! Has llamado para mi?"

"Ah, Roberto! You've arrived! Yes, I did call for you," Mr. Thomas responded as he got up from his desk. He approached his nephew and took him by the arm, leading him over to where Kirby was seated.

"Señor, this is my nephew, Roberto," Mr. Thomas said proudly. Kirby stood to shake his hand.

"Roberto is a very serious man, Señor, and he will take good care of you until you leave for the islands—will you not, Roberto?" Thomas said, looking directly at his nephew for the expected agreeable nod, which he readily got. At that point he took Kirby by the arm and pulled him aside.

"My nephew will stay with you and protect you completely while you are here. He will also see you safely to the boat, and if I may offer a suggestion, it would be proper to offer him a gratuity for his services."

"I'll be happy to show my appreciation to your nephew," Kirby said, impatiently waving Thomas off, "but I also need to know how much I owe you for setting up the boat over to the island."

"You must understand that these things are expensive to arrange," Thomas said, rubbing his chin. He was going in for the kill and Kirby braced himself. "Because of the short notice, I was forced to pay a premium to have you transported over to the island and dropped off in an area where you would not be bothered by Bahamian customs; therefore, my fee must be seven hundred dollars, but remember, included in this service is my promise that none of my people will remember anything of this transaction.

It was highway robbery, but Kirby didn't have much of a choice. He paid the banker in cash and then gave his new, temporary bodyguard a nod and said "Let's go, Roberto."

As they exited through the lobby, Kirby stopped short of the front door.

"Roberto, earlier when you first got here, did you see anything or anyone unusual outside the bank?"

"No, Señor," he replied, "I saw nothing out of the ordinary."

"No one at all? Anyone who didn't look like they were from the neighborhood?"

"No, Señor."

Kirby was somewhat reassured. After all, all he had to go on was Elena's paranoia, and from what he could see she was all for show in the operation. *Not a lot going on upstairs there*, Kirby thought cynically. Still, it didn't hurt to be a little extra careful.

"Roberto," said Kirby, "I want you to stay close to me all the way back to my room. It's only about four blocks, and you should be finished with me shortly."

"Yes, Señor," he said. "Are we ready to go?"

"Let's get rolling," Kirby replied.

CHAPTER FIFTY-EIGHT

As they exited the bodega, Matt received another update on his radio.

"Copy that. Make sure we have teams covering both the front and rear and wait for us to arrive at the location…over."

"What's happening?" Tony asked urgently.

"Our boy just went into a bank around the corner. I've got both the front and the rear covered, and I think that maybe we can grab him when he comes out without anyone getting hurt."

"Matt, don't forget he might be armed," warned Tony. "We got to get him before he can get to his weapon."

"Tony, I appreciate the input," Matt said as they rounded the corner, "but this is gonna have to be our show; all I want you to do is watch our backs in case the shit hits the fan, okay? Anyway, you've already filled your quota for being shot, and I don't want to have to explain you getting shot again."

Tony and Matt positioned themselves in an alley at the side of a building across the street. Matt peered around the corner of the structure, then looked back at Tony.

"Here's what I want you to do: hold this position, and if he gets past my guys, you stop him."

Tony nodded. "I can handle that."

Matt patted him on the shoulder and bolted across the street to take a position around the side of the bank building. Tony was relieved not to have to be the one to confront the disgraced officer, and he really wasn't up to taking another bullet, either. He leaned against the pink stucco wall of the building, a travel agency, and scanned the street in front of him. He saw that two of the federal agents had taken positions behind two huge palm trees situated across from the bank's entrance. Matt had taken his position, weapon drawn, and was intermittently talking on his radio. All at once everyone snapped to attention. Tony peeked around the pink stucco wall.

A young Latino, with slicked back hair and wearing a tan jacket and dark sunglasses, came walking down the street from the opposite direction, whistling as he strutted along. Tony got a strange feeling in his gut—the kind he had that time a few days back when he saw the raised window blind in his neighbor's window. He saw Matt give instructions on his radio as the young man stepped into the bank.

More people appeared on the street, many coming back from lunch or headed out for a late break. More pedestrians or bystanders meant more people in harm's way. *This isn't good*, thought Tony. He stepped back and put his weapon behind him. A young, dark-haired girl, maybe in her early twenties, walked past carrying a bag from a fast food place and sipping from her to go cup. He thought of Lina. He couldn't wait to wrap up this mess and get back home to her. As soon as the girl had moved on, he looked out into the street. One of the agents behind a palm tree had braced himself, pressing his back hard against the tree trunk.

The young man, along with Jim Kirby, had exited the bank and were weaving through traffic, crossing the street directly in front of Tony. *Shit!* While Kirby and his accomplice were trying not to get run over, Tony stepped out onto the sidewalk and started walking hurriedly. He ducked into the next building, a shoe repair shop. The smell of leather and shoe polish filled the small store.

A middle-aged man behind the counter spotted Tony's weapon and raised his hands in protest.

"*Policia*, police!" whispered Tony and he put his finger to his lips. He joined the man behind the counter and motioned for him to crouch down alongside him. Tony craned his neck over the edge of the counter until he saw Kirby and his friend pass the repair shop. Tony slowly got up and walked to the shop's entrance and stuck his head out the door. The men were walking away from him at casual pace. He stepped out onto the sidewalk and began following them.

He was within a few yards of the suspects when he suddenly became wary and ducked down behind a parked car. Scanning the perimeter for any of his comrades, he jumped when he heard Matt's voice behind him.

"Where the hell have you been?" Matt said quietly. He got down on one knee next to him.

"Hiding," said Tony, with a big smile on his face, "inside a shoe store. They were coming right at me, so I took off."

"Good thinking, pal. Here's the plan: Team One is heading towards them right now, and Team Two should be approaching them from the rear, so we're gonna take them down right now." At that moment, Matt's radio received a message from Team Two.

"Where are you? I can't see you?" Matt replied, his head swiveling in all directions.

Tony tapped him on the shoulder and pointed down the street where he could see one man walking on either side of the street, rapidly closing in on the two suspects who were proceeding down the sidewalk.

"Take them down, but be careful of civilians," ordered Matt into the radio. Grabbing Tony by the arm, he said,

"Let's go. It might be a good idea to have your weapon ready, just in case."

Tony stood up to see what was known politely in his profession as a "tactical error." The two greenhorn agents approaching from the front had stayed together, walking straight toward Kirby and his man. Kirby stopped in his tracks and the young Latino pulled out a gun.

Matt, who had immediately assessed the situation, uttered a curse word and hollered out loudly "Federal Agents! Drop your weapons!"

The Latino shoved Kirby into the wall of a nearby building and started firing. Agents Murphy and Lutz pulled their weapons and returned fire. McGrath and Fleri came up from the rear and, ducking behind a parked car, began firing as well. It was over as soon as it had begun.

The young Latino lay on the sidewalk, waving his arm and shouting.

"Cease fire!" Matt shouted and ran towards the fallen suspect. The man was screaming something about being wounded and not to kill him.

Tony kept his head down as he ducked and ran behind the cars parked along the street. As everyone dove for cover when the shooting ensued, Kirby had managed to give the agents the slip—all except one. Tony saw him run inside an adjacent apartment building.

"Oh no you don't!" said Tony under his breath as he dashed toward the apartments.

Knowing that Kirby wasn't about to try to escape out the front of the building, with all of the action on the street, Tony headed for the rear of the structure. He ran down a narrow alley, avoiding trash cans and other debris, and emerged onto another, wider alley behind. Spotting the apartment building's rear exit, an old, red steel door decorated with graffiti, he took his position behind an ancient, abandoned hulk that had once been a limousine.

"I'm getting to old for this shit," he reminded himself once more, panting and crouching down, his gun aimed through the windowless limo.

In a minute, the door crashed open, and Kirby came running out with a gun in his hand.

"Stop, Kirby!"

Kirby fired at him, hitting the car door frame, causing the bullet to ricochet through the window and come out the other side, narrowly missing Tony's head.

Now angry, Tony shouted "Kirby, stop! Don't do this!" only to be answered by two more bullets thudding into the old limo's body. Taking an abrupt step away from the car, Tony took aim and fired two shots in rapid succession. Kirby went down.

Tony hesitated, keeping his eye on the disgraced police officer, watching to make sure he didn't jump back up. He approached Kirby where he lay in the alley, in slow, measured paces. He was shocked to see that Kirby was still alive, though his chest was covered with blood, and frothy red bubbles were forming all over the front of his shirt. He was having trouble breathing, and every time he exhaled he would spray blood down his chin and onto his shirt. His face had turned a dull gray color. He clutched his weapon, and when Tony came near he made a futile attempt to raise it, his hand shaking violently.

Tony kept his gun trained on Kirby, walked slowly around him and spoke gently. "Drop your weapon, Jim. It's all over. Drop it, and let me get you some help, okay?"

Kirby weakly lifted his head to look into Tony's eyes.

"It's over for me. I should've known you'd be the one to get me. Spinella, you're a damn good cop, and I was a good cop too, but now it's too fucked up for me, and I ain't going to no prison." With that, he stuck the gun in his mouth and pulled the trigger, spraying bone, blood and brain matter all over the pavement.

Tony jumped back, pieces of Kirby spraying his shoes. His mouth open, he quickly looked away from the bloody aftermath. *Damn!*

"What the h—!"

It was Matt's voice. He, along with two other agents, came running up to Tony. Matt observed what was left of Kirby.

"*Fuck!* Tony, what happened?" He palmed the back of his head in disbelief.

"He ate his gun," Tony replied in a near whisper, slowling holstering his weapon.

"I'm sorry, brother." Matt looked down at Kirby. "At least nobody got hurt. There's only Anita left to deal with. I'll notify our Miami office and get a supervisor out here. Once the paperwork is done, we can head back to D.C."

"Matt, is my use of force going to cause any problems for you?" Tony was looking off into space as he spoke.

"Nope," he replied, "I think I can handle that; he did fire at you, so all you were doing was protecting yourself. Don't worry about it, I got it covered." Matt put his hand on Tony's back.

Several hours later, after calling D.C. for some help with an overzealous supervisor in the Miami DEA office, they were able to head over to the airport where, thanks to a civilian friend of Matt's in the travel office, they were soon on another Boeing 737, headed back to D.C. Seated in the cramped economy section of the aircraft, both men ordered a drink and settled back to discuss the operation.

"Why the hell would a man who had a good job, some rank and decent pay decide to get involved with this shit?" Matt mused.

"From what I could gather, he started going south after his wife died. I've talked to people who knew him and worked with him, and they say he changed after she died. Got into the booze pretty heavy." Tony picked up an extra plastic cup of ice and dumped some into his drink.

"That's no excuse for doing what he did," answered Matt, raising his hand to get the attention of the flight attendant. "You want another one?" he asked.

"Sure, why not?" Tony replied.

As soon as they landed at National Airport, Tony called Frank from baggage claim with some final updates, then told his boss that he was going home to try and get some sleep.

"Is everything okay at your office?" Matt asked when he was off the phone. "I mean, was your boss okay with everything that went down?"

"Everything is cool, Matt," said Tony. "Let's get outta here so I can call my girl and get some sleep."

The following morning, after a good night's sleep at his place, Tony was once again drinking bad coffee in his boss's office while they tidied up some loose ends with the case. One loose end had to remain hanging, much to everyone's disappointment: Anita.

"Tony, I think that Sully is going to recommend that we put this case to bed for now, and let the Feds worry about finding Anita," said Frank, resting his feet on his desk. "I agree with him. So for now, I want you to take a few days off, use sick leave and heal up, before coming back to work."

"So," said Tony, "we just forget about her, and what she did to this squad and our department?"

"For now, yes. Get outta here, go home and rest. Spend some time with Lina; we'll get her, sooner or later. Oh, by the way, is anybody over at DEA following up on Casa Banco?"

"Yeah," Tony replied. "Matt told me the Miami office is going to tear that place apart."

"Good. Now, get outta here," said Frank, reaching for his ever-present cup of coffee.

Tony left the office thinking that no matter what the department did, he would never stop looking for Anita. Too many people were dead because of her, regardless of their guilt or innocence. More importantly, she had caused him far too much pain and trouble to get a free pass. He rubbed his healing arm as he headed for his car.

Once on the road he phoned Lina. He had phoned her briefly the night before, just to let her know he was back. After more reassurances that he was all in one piece, he asked what her plans for the day were. She told him she had cleared her calendar for a certain hard-working police officer who needed a little TLC.

"Well," Tony replied, "this police officer is on sick leave. Why don't you meet me at my place in a little while, and assess my condition. I'll give you fair warning, though, that I plan to show you just how absolutely fine I am."

It had been well over two years since Anita had disappeared, and almost every day of that time, especially now when winter's end gave way to spring's renewal, she occupied Tony's thoughts. He would check constantly for new information or any clues to her whereabouts. After the Miami incident he settled back into the routine of supervising his team of six detectives. There was one significant change in his routine, however: he had recently made Lina an honest woman. He had hoped for a simple, small ceremony, but her Italian family had other ideas. The wedding was a huge affair, with numerous relatives from Italy flying over to add their exuberance and seemingly endless energy to the festivities. Tony loved it, and they loved him. The family stayed for over two weeks after the wedding but finally departed with much kissing and crying.

Tony and Lina resumed life together as a married couple. She moved into Tony's place and began the daunting task of changing the interior decor from that of a bachelor to one reflecting a woman's touch. She continued to work for her congressman, the job requiring her to travel only occasionally.

It was the Tuesday morning after all the relatives had left. Tony had just finished roll call and was catching up on some paper work when the phone on his desk rang.

"Sergeant Spinella, Robbery. How can I help you?"

"Hey buddy, it's me," said Matt Hollis.

"Hey, man, how you doing?" Tony hadn't seen Matt since the wedding. ."

"I'm great. I'm actually on my way up to see you and I hope you've got time because I've got some big news to share with you."

"Come on up! I'll be waiting," said Tony. A couple of minutes later Tony embraced Matt and told him to take a seat in a chair next to his desk.

"I just received a call from one of my friends at Interpol, and they told me that someone by the name of Patricia Pratt applied for a work visa from the Italian Embassy."

"So, what has that got to do with the price of apples?" asked Tony.

"Just wait for it, okay,"laughed Matt. "In Italy, they regularly print anyone making a request for a work visa, and our Miss Pratt's fingerprints raised a red flag at Interpol. What makes this significant is she made the request for the work permit at the Immigration office in Venice.

"I'm still waiting for you to tell me how this amounts to 'big news,'" said Tony.

"Well, my friend, it would seem the prints from Miss Pratt are a perfect match to our Anita's prints, and this person is currently in Venice."

Tony leaped out of his chair. "Yes! Matt, sit tight for a minute while I go tell my captain the news. I'll be right back."

"I know what you're thinking," said Frank once Tony told him the news, "and if you want my opinion, I don't think I can help you. If you're thinking about me getting the brass to okay you going over there to be in on the arrest, I can hear them now, asking me if I'm crazy, and telling me to let Interpol handle it."

"I know, Boss," pleaded Tony, "but how about me going over on my own, using my own personal time? Lina and I could take a short vacation to visit her family."

"Look, what you do on your own time is up to you, but, if you do this, you better make sure you don't mess up, or interfere with Interpol doing their job. If you fuck up," warned Frank, "I won't be able to do a damn thing to help you, and it could cost you your job."

"I hear you, Boss. I won't embarrass you, or our department," Tony assured him. "I'll talk everything over with Matt before I do anything."

"Just let me know what's up, so I don't get caught in the trick box," Frank called to him as he walked out the door.

Tony returned to his desk and an expectant look on Matt's face.

"Ok," Tony said. "Give me what you got."

"She made the application—we already know this—and at the time she applied, they told her it would be at least two weeks before they contacted her with the results. What that does is give us time to make the arrangements to be there when the bust goes down. Of course, that all depends on whether you want to be there when it all happens."

"Are you shitting me?" exclaimed Tony. "Of course I'm gonna be there!"

"Is your shop going to approve your involvement in this?"

"I don't think so," Tony replied. "I think this trip is gonna be on my dime, and you know what? I don't care, because this has bothered me for a long time now, and I need for this to be over."

"Way to go!" Matt said excitedly. "Now, all we gotta do is decide when we're going. I'm available almost immediately, but I know you have to iron out a few things. If you can arrange it, it would be great if we could leave by the end of the week, or sooner."

"Whoa," said Tony. "You gotta give me some time to talk to Lina, and get back with you. Maybe I can get her to come along. She can stay with her family while I'm working."

"Just let me know how you work it out."

"I'll get back to you this afternoon after I talk with my girl," said Tony as he stood up and walked Matt to the elevators. They said their goodbyes and then Tony went back to his desk.

Tony called Lina at work. When he told her about Matt's news, she was excited for him and worried at the same time. Tony consoled her.

"Come with me, baby. You can get time off, right? After I take care of this Anita business we can spend time with your family. They'll really be surprised to see us so soon after they left us."

"I can't, Tony," Lina replied. "The congressman has a fundraiser back in his home state and I have to coordinate the entire event. Just do what you have to do, sweetheart. I'll see you tonight."

Disappointed and excited at the same time, Tony called Matt's cell phone.

"It'll be just you and me, partner," he said.

Twenty-four hours later, Matt and Tony were on a Boeing 767 bound for DaVinci Airport in Rome.

After sharing a couple of cocktails with Matt, Tony slept on and off throughout the overnight flight. He was awakened by the pilot's voice announcing in both English and Italian that they had just begun the decent into Rome's Leonardo Da Vinci Airport, and for everyone to fasten their seat belts. Minutes later they were taxiing toward their gate.

They emerged from the jet way into the gate area and were promptly approached by two well-dressed men who identified themselves as Interpol agents. Matt, who seemed to know the taller of the two men, took the lead and addressed him first.

"Gabriel, it's been a long time." Gabriel shook Matt's extended hand. The agent was impeccably dressed in a gray sharkskin suit, a dark blue shirt open at the neck, and grey suede loafers. All of this attire set off his dark, curly hair, light green eyes and tan skin.

"Si, it's been too long, Matt. Let me introduce my associate, Bernard Westgate."

"Just call me Bernie," said the other agent, taking Tony's hand first. Everyone else does. Why don't we continue the introductions while we head to customs and gather up your luggage, and then we can be out of here."

"Sounds like a plan," said Matt, and they made their way into the mass of travelers stampeding through the congested, popular airport.

When they arrived at customs the bright, near-blinding morning sunshine came through the skylights overlooking the baggage claim area. While Tony and Matt gathered their luggage, Gabriel approached a uniformed customs agent and showed his identification. Speaking rapidly in Italian, the customs agent motioned for them to follow him, and moments later they found themselves outside the airport, bathed in the warm Italian sunshine, and being ushered into a large black Suburban. They wasted no time and sped away as soon as all were inside.

"Where we going, Matt?" Tony inquired.

"Well, it seems our friends here happen to have a nice Learjet nearby, and we're gonna ride in style up to Marco Polo Airport in Venice."

"On the short flight to Venice," interjected Gabriel, "I would like to inform you both on what we have on our suspect. For example, where she is stayng, where she goes to eat, et cetera." Tony and Matt nodded their heads as the Suburban pulled up right next to a gleaming white jet.

In no time they had boarded and were off the ground, cruising at thirty thousand feet. Once airborne, both Gabriel and Bernie took turns sharing the copious amount of information they had compiled on the person known to them as Patricia Pratt. The rest of the flight was spent enjoying some fine scotch and making plans for the arrest they hoped to make the following day.

"She has been dining at the same restaurant in Venice for the last two weeks," said Gabriel. "We hope to meet her there tomorrow afternoon *per pranzo*, or 'for lunch' as you say."

Tony could just imagine the look on Anita's face when she met up with her unannounced lunch dates. "How long have you guys been watching her?" he asked eagerly.

"I believe it is almost two weeks now since we received the alert from our home office, and we've had someone on her since then. She has been very easy to follow, and we believe she has no idea she is being watched," answered Gabriel.

"Are you absolutely sure it's the same person we're interested in?" Tony had to be sure.

"I do believe, and you should too, that fingerprints do not lie. In a few hours, you will have the opportunity to convince yourself when you identify this person to us," said the slightly irritated Interpol agent.

"No disrespect intended," said Tony, quickly adding, "I'm at your disposal and all you need to do is tell me what you want me to do. I'll do anything I can to help you."

Once they landed and taxied to a private aviation terminal at Venice's Marco Polo Airport, they were whisked away in another Suburban and after a short ride pulled up to the waterfront, where a water taxi awaited them. They carried their luggage on board the beautifully maintained wooden boat and the boat driver cast off. They threaded their way amidst a flotilla of both large and small boats carrying people and cargo towards the Grand Canal, which suddenly appeared in front of them. Tony and Matt were awestruck by the sheer size of the Canal, and the large number of beautiful, pastel-colored buildings that seemed to float on its surface. Mesmerized, Tony thought it was like a scene from a movie. *Lina would love this.* He promised himself they would come here together sometime soon to experience this fantastic place. The boat stopped suddenly and ended his reverie.

After they disembarked, Gabriel walked over to them and pointed to a beautiful old salmon-colored stucco building with a large balcony overlooking the Canal.

"This is where you will be staying. The hotel has been owned by the same family since 1856. I think you will enjoy the accommodations, and everything has already been arranged. You should get some food and rest, and we will meet in the hotel restaurant tomorrow morning at nine." Gabriel and Bernie took their leave.

Tony stood looking up at the big sign across the front of the hotel. "Hotel Gabrielli,"he said aloud.

Matt grabbed his arm. "Let's get checked in, go grab some food, and then hit the rack. What do ya say?"

"I'm ready," Tony replied.

Once inside the hotel they walked up to an ornately carved wooden front desk, manned by gentleman wearing a dark suit and tie. The brass name plate above his pocket indicated he was the manager. He acted as if their arrival was no surprise and went about getting them their room keys.Tony glanced around the lobby and was amazed at the interior: it must have looked the same hundreds of years ago, with its high, sculptured ceilings covered with scenes from biblical times, and walls dotted with niches containing statues of various mythic and historic figures.

The manager escorted them personally to their separate suites. Once he had checked out his luxurious room, he walked down the hall and saw that Matt had a room just as nice, and after some chit-chat, told Matt he was too tired to go out to eat, and instead, would like to try and get some sleep.

"You sleep. I'm gonna take a look around before I crash," said Matt. "See you in the lobby at nine."

"Ok," Tony replied and he returned to his room.

Refreshed after a good night's sleep, Tony made his way downstairs to the restaurant, which was located adjacent to the front lobby. The first person he spotted was Gabriel, carrying a cup of cappuccino over to a table occupied by his partner Bernie and Matt. The table was nicely situated next to a large window looking out onto the Canal. He spotted a waiter and politely told him that he would also like to have a cappuccino. He took a seat next to Matt.

"We might have a problem," Matt said immediately.

"What problem kind of problem? Tony asked pointedly.

"It seems," Gabriel piped up, "that the description of your suspect doesn't match the one given to us by Matt. Frankly, this puts a crimp in our plan to grab her. We can approach her nicely and ask for her cooperation, but based only on the fingerprint information we received, we are going have to try and get her fingerprints all over again, or have one of you positively identify her before we can arrest her."

"Bullshit!" exclaimed Tony, his anger flaring. "Finger-prints don't lie, and even over here, that should be enough for an arrest."

"I'm sorry, my friend," said Gabriel, "but my superiors insist that I play it this way. Is there anything about her that you can think of that would absolutely identify her? Think hard, Tony—a birth mark, some particular mannerism, anything you can remember?"

Tony was about to launch into a tirade about Interpol and its stupid procedures when his cappuccino arrived. He took a sip of the hot coffee and collected himself. He recalled a conversation he had with Anita years ago at the office, when he had noticed a scar on the top of her hand. She had explained that her dad had spilled hot coffee on her when she was about ten years old, and it had left a scar. He related the incident to the others at the table.

"Yes!" blurted Matt. "*That's* what we need, right Gabe?"

"That should certainly work," said Gabriel. "Do you recall which hand it was, Tony?"

"Not really, but if she has a scar on top of either hand, I think that should be enough."

"I agree," Gabriel replied. "Now that we have that established, we should go and check out this place where she dines.

"By the way, where is she now?" asked Tony.

"She is still inside the small hotel on the island of Burano, where she's staying, which is just a short water taxi ride from here. My agent will call as soon as she leaves, to let us know if there is any deviation to her routine," said Bernie, who had hardly spoken during their conversation.

It only took about ten minutes of walking through a maze of dark, narrow cobblestone walkways nestled between homes built hundreds of years earlier, for them to arrive at a beautiful, open courtyard containing a small outdoor restaurant called Al Colombo. Several small, bistro-style tables were situated under a large, colorful awning.

Bernie pointed to a table in the back of the dining area, near an entrance to another courtyard. "That's her usual spot. She sits there almost every time she comes, and most of the staff seems to know her."

"How you gonna work this? Will all the exits be covered, and what if she runs?" Tony questioned the agents. Bernie started to answer, but Gabriel held up his hand.

"We will have all the exits covered, Tony. What I would like for you to do, if you will, is approach this person and see if you can identify her, or maybe see the scar on her hand. If so, just raise your hand and we will close in and make the arrest."

Tony gave them an exaggerated bow. "Gentlemen, it will be my pleasure!" They turned and quickly left the courtyard to walk back to their hotel and wait.

Impatient for the time to pass, Tony looked at his watch as he closed the door to his suite. Lina would still be in bed, but she wouldn't mind being awakened by his call. She would want to know he arrived safely. After several rings, he heard her soft, groggy voice.

"This better be you, Tony, or whoever is on the line is going to be on my shit list forever," she teased.

"It's me baby. I really miss you. I'm sorry I woke you, but I only have a few minutes, and I wanted to tell you what's going on here."

"Did you get her?" Lina asked, her voice sounding more awake.

"No, but we will in about an hour. It'll be over soon. Lina, this place is the most beautiful city I've ever seen. We have to come here together, and soon." He went on telling her about the sights he had seen in his short time there when there was a sudden knock on his door.

"Baby, I have to go. I love you," he said hurriedly.

"I love you too! Be careful, Tony!" Lina said as he hung up.

He opened the door to find Matt standing there.

"It's on. We need to meet Gabriel downstairs."

"She's on her way," Gabriel said as soon as they met him outside. "We received a call from the agent who has been watching her, and she just walked down to catch a water taxi. We have about ten minutes to get there and get ready."

Wasting no time, the three men quickly made their way back through the maze of narrow walkways to the small restaurant. After checking to see that the men were in position, they entered a small doorway near the restaurant, where one of Gabriel's agents took them to an empty upstairs room with a window that overlooked the courtyard. Gabriel asked Tony if he could clearly see the table where the suspect usually sat.

"This is a good spot, Gabriel," he answered, "but if she's wearing a disguise, then I'm gonna have to go down and get close."

While they were talking, the small restaurant started to fill up. They began to worry that one of the waiters might put someone else at Anita's table, when a blonde woman wearing a beautiful yellow sun dress suddenly walked up to the host, who greeted her with familiarity, and was promptly guided to the vacant rear table.,

Tony's eyes narrowed as he studied the woman. She was the right build and height, but her face was not familiar to him.

"I need to go down there and get closer. If it's her, I'll raise my hand; if not I'll just apologize and walk away, okay?"

"Let's go," said Gabriel, and they walked down the stairs and out the door into the courtyard.

Tony made his way across the now crowded courtyard towards the corner of the restaurant. The woman sat flipping through a magazine and the closer Tony got, the more his doubts were raised. This person didn't look anything like Anita. He was all at once fearful of making an ass of himself.

Approaching the table from the left, he tried to get a look at her hands. Moving slowly and cautiously, he was able to get close enough to see her left hand, which was holding the edge of the magazine. There was no visible scar. He moved to the other side. The woman, suddenly aware of his presence, looked up from her magazine and put her right hand up to shade her face from the sun. Instantly Tony saw it. He raised his hand as he leaned over Anita like a hawk over its prey.

"Hello Anita. It's been a long time. May I sit down?"

ACKNOWLEDGMENTS

Writing an acknowledgment is sort of like writing a confession. In this case, yours truly is confessing that without the help and constructive input by numerous persons, this book would have been significantly harder to write.

My gratitude and thanks go out to retired police officers Frank McCathran, Clay Clark, Denny Martin, and Danny Fitzpatrick. Thanks for helping me get it right.

I hope that family and friends enjoyed the antics of their characters throughout the book. I had a lot of fun trying to figure out just where to use them. A very special thanks goes out to my loving wife, Sandy, who convinced me that I needed to go to Venice, Italy, to research the ending for my book. She was, of course, right!

Any errors in terminology or venue are, of course, the sole responsibility of the author. Any resemblances in this story to persons living or dead are purely coincidental, and except for friend- and family-based characters, were not intentional.

ABOUT THE AUTHOR

Lou Martin studied at American University and Pacific Western University, where he earned a bachelor of science degree in The Administration of Justice. He is a retired law enforcement official, former staff investigator for the United States Congress, singer, song writer and poet. This is his second published work. The father of three children, and six grandchildren, he lives with his wife Sandra on the shores of the Chesapeake Bay.

Printed in the United States
By Bookmasters